We hope you enjoy this book. Please return or renew it by the due date.

You can renew it at www.norfolk.gov.uk/libraries or by using our free library app.

Otherwise you can phone 0344 800 8020 - please have your library card and PIN ready.

You can sign up

D0589612

thriller guaranteed to freeze your soul'
Metro

Also by Donato Carrisi

The Whisperer
The Lost Girls of Rome
The Vanished Ones
The Hunter of the Dark

THE
GIRL IN THE FOG

DONATO CARRISI

TRANSLATED BY HOWARD CURTIS

ABACUS

First published in Italy in 2017 as *La Ragazza nella Nebbia* by Longanesi & C.
First published in Great Britain in 2017 by Abacus
This paperback edition published in 2018 by Abacus

1 3 5 7 9 10 8 6 4 2

Copyright © Donato Carrisi 2017
Translation © Howard Curtis 2017

A CIP catalogue record for this book
is available from the British Library.

ISBN 978-0-349-14260-9

Typeset in Horley by M Rules
Printed and bound in Great Britain by
Clays Ltd, Elcograf S.p.A.

Papers used by Abacus are from well-managed forests
and other responsible sources.

Abacus
An imprint of
Little, Brown Book Group
Carmelite House
50 Victoria Embankment
London EC4Y 0DZ

An Hachette UK Company
www.hachette.co.uk

www.littlebrown.co.uk

THE
GIRL IN THE FOG

23 February

Sixty-two days after the disappearance

The night everything changed for ever began with a phone call.

It came at 10.20 on a Monday evening. Outside, it was minus eight Celsius, and the countryside was shrouded in an icy fog. At that hour, Flores was snug and warm in bed beside his wife, enjoying an old black-and-white gangster film on TV. Actually, Sophia had dozed off a while earlier, and the ringing of the telephone didn't disturb her sleep. She even appeared oblivious of her husband getting out of bed and dressing.

Flores put on a pair of baggy trousers, a polo neck sweater and his heavy winter jacket to face that damned fog, which seemed to have wiped out all of creation, and got ready to go to Avechot's little hospital, where he had worked as a psychiatrist for more than forty of his sixty-two years. In all that time, he had seldom been dragged out of bed for an emergency, let alone by the police. In this Alpine village, where he had been born and had always lived, almost nothing happened after sunset. It was as if in such a place even criminals chose to lead a sober existence, regularly spending their evenings at home. That was why Flores wondered what could necessitate his presence at such an unusual hour.

All the police had told him over the phone was that a man had been arrested following a road accident. Nothing else.

The snow had stopped falling in the afternoon, but it had got colder during the evening. Flores left the house to be greeted by an unearthly silence. Everything was still, motionless, as if time had stopped. He felt a shudder that had nothing to do with the outside temperature – it came from inside. He started his old Citroën, and had to wait a few seconds for the diesel engine to warm up properly before he set off. He needed that sound to wipe out the monotony of the menacing quiet.

The road surface was icy, but it was the snow more than anything that forced him to keep his speed below twenty kilometres an hour, both his hands firmly gripping the wheel, his back stooped forward and his face a few centimetres from the windscreen so that he could make out the sides of the road. Luckily, he knew the route so well, his mind told him where to go before his eyes could.

Coming to a crossroads, he chose the direction that led towards the centre of the village, and at last saw something through the milky blanket. As he advanced, he had the sensation that everything had slowed down, as if in a dream. From the depths of the white mantle, intermittent flashes of light appeared. They seemed to be coming towards him, even though it was he who was approaching them. A figure emerged out of the fog, making strange, broad arm movements. As he drew nearer, Flores realised it was a police officer warning passing motorists to be careful. Flores passed him and they exchanged a fleeting wave. Behind the officer, the intermittent flashes resolved themselves into the flashing lights of a patrol car and the rear lights of a dark saloon car that had ended up in a ditch.

Before long, Flores reached the centre of the village. It was deserted.

The faded yellow street lamps looked like mirages amid the fog. He drove through the whole of the built-up area and out the other side before he reached his destination.

Avechot's little hospital was unusually animated. As soon as Flores walked in through the front door, a local police lieutenant came up to him, accompanied by Rebecca Mayer, a young prosecutor who had been making a name for herself lately. She looked worried. As Flores took off his heavy jacket, she updated him on the identity of tonight's unexpected guest. 'Vogel,' was all she said.

Hearing the name, Flores understood the reason for all this concern. It was the night everything changed forever, but he didn't know that yet. That was why he hadn't yet quite grasped his own role in this business. 'What exactly do you want me to do?' he asked.

'The doctors in Emergency say he's fine. But he seems in a confused state, maybe due to the shock of the accident.'

'But you're not sure, right?' Flores's question had hit the target, and Mayer didn't need to reply. 'Is he catatonic?'

'No, he reacts when stimulated. But he has mood swings.'

'And he doesn't remember any of what happened,' Flores said, completing the case history for himself.

'He remembers the accident. But we're interested in what

happened before. We need to know what happened this evening.'

'You think he's pretending.'

'I'm very much afraid he is. And that's where you come in, Doctor.'

'What are you expecting of me?'

'We have enough to charge him, and he knows it. That's why you have to tell me if he's fully aware of his actions.'

'And if he is, what'll happen to him?'

'I'll be able to charge him and proceed with a formal interrogation, without fearing that some lawyer will later contest it in court on a stupid technicality.'

'But it's my understanding that nobody died or was injured in the accident, is that right? So what would you charge him with?'

Mayer was silent for a moment. 'You'll understand when you see him.'

They had left him waiting in Flores's office. When Flores opened the door, he immediately saw Vogel sitting in one of the two small armchairs positioned in front of the cluttered desk. He was wearing a dark cashmere coat. His head was bowed, and he gave no sign of noticing that someone had come in.

Flores hung his jacket on the coat rack and massaged his hands, which were still numb with cold. 'Good evening,' he said, going to the heater to make sure it was on. In reality, this was only a pretext to take up a position facing the man, to get an idea of his condition but, above all, to understand what Mayer had meant.

Beneath the coat, Vogel was elegantly dressed. A dark blue suit, a powder-blue silk tie with a floral design, a yellow

4

handkerchief in the breast pocket of his jacket, a white shirt and oval cufflinks of rose gold. Everything looked creased, though, as if he had been wearing these clothes for weeks.

Without replying to the greeting, Vogel raised his eyes to him for a moment. Then he looked back down at his hands lying in his lap.

Flores wondered what bizarre trick of fate had brought them together. 'Have you been here long?' he began.

'What about you?'

Flores laughed at the joke, but Vogel remained grim-faced. 'More or less forty years,' Flores replied. During that time, the office had filled with objects and furniture until it was cluttered. To an outside observer, he knew, the whole effect must seem chaotic. 'You see that old couch? I inherited it from my predecessor. The desk I chose myself.' On the desk were framed photographs of his family.

Vogel took one and studied it. There was Flores surrounded by his numerous progeny, having a barbecue in the garden on a summer's day. 'Nice family,' he commented with vague interest.

'Three children and eleven grandchildren.' Flores was very fond of that picture.

Vogel put the photograph back where he had found it and looked around. On the walls, along with his degree, the various testimonials he had received and the drawings given to him by his grandchildren were the trophies Flores was proudest of.

He was an enthusiastic angler, and the walls displayed a large number of stuffed fish.

'Whenever I can, I drop everything and set off for a lake or a mountain stream,' Flores said. 'It's my way of getting back in touch with nature.' In a corner was a cupboard with fishing rods and a drawer containing hooks, baits, lines and other equipment. Over time, the room had ended up looking nothing like a psychiatrist's office. It had become his den, a place of his own, and he was dreading his retirement, due in a matter of months, when he would have to clear everything out.

Among the many stories those walls could have told, there was now a new one: the story of an unexpected consultation late one winter evening.

'I still can't believe you're here,' Flores admitted, with a hint of embarrassment. 'My wife and I have seen you so many times on TV. You're a celebrity.'

Vogel merely nodded. He certainly seemed to be in a confused state – unless he was a consummate actor.

'Are you sure you feel all right?'

'I'm fine,' Vogel replied in a thin voice.

Flores moved away from the heater and went and sat down behind the desk, in the armchair that over the years had taken on his shape. 'You were lucky, you know. On my way here, I passed the scene of the accident. You ended up on the right side of the road. True, there's quite a deep ditch, but on the other side there's a ravine.'

'The fog,' Vogel said.

'Yes, a freezing fog. You don't see them often. It took me twenty minutes to get here, usually it's less than ten by car from my house.' Then he put both his elbows on the arms of his chair and sank back. 'We haven't yet introduced ourselves: I'm Dr Auguste Flores. Tell me, what should I call you? Special Agent Vogel, or just Signor Vogel?'

Vogel seemed to give this a moment's thought. 'You choose.'

'I don't think a police officer ever loses his rank, even when he stops practising his profession. So for me, you're still Special Agent Vogel.'

'If you prefer it that way.'

Dozens of questions were crowding into Flores's mind, but he knew he had to choose the right ones to start. 'Frankly, I wasn't expecting to see you around here any more. I thought you went back to the city some time ago, after what happened. Why have you come back?'

Special Agent Vogel slowly passed his hands over his trousers, as if trying to remove non-existent dust. 'I don't know.'

That was all he said. Flores nodded. 'I understand. Did you come alone?'

'Yes,' Vogel replied, and it was clear from his expression that he hadn't understood the meaning of the question. 'I'm alone.'

'Does your presence here have anything to do with the missing girl?' Flores ventured. 'Because I seem to remember you were removed from the case.'

These words evidently awakened something in Vogel, who seemed to Flores to get on his high horse, as if his pride were wounded. 'Why are you detaining me? What do the police want with me? Why can't I leave?'

Flores tried to summon up all his reserves of patience. 'You had an accident this evening, Special Agent Vogel.'

'I know that,' Vogel replied angrily.

'And you were alone when it happened, is that right?'

'I already told you that.'

Flores opened a drawer in his desk, took out a little mirror and placed it in front of Vogel, who didn't seem to take any notice. 'And you emerged unscathed. No injuries whatsoever.'

'I'm fine, how many times are you going to ask me that?'

7

Flores leaned towards him. 'Then explain something to me. If you're unscathed, whose blood is that on your clothes?'

Suddenly, Vogel didn't know what to say. The anger evaporated, and his eyes came to rest on the mirror that Flores had put in front of him.

Now he had to see them.

Little red stains on the cuffs of his white shirt. A couple of bigger ones over the stomach. A few darker ones, less visible because of the colour of the suit and the coat, but noticeable from the thicker texture. It was as if Vogel was seeing them for the first time. But part of him knew they were there, Flores was sure of that. Because Vogel wasn't unduly surprised and didn't immediately deny their presence.

There was a different light in his eyes now, and his confused state started to fade as if it were fog. But the real fog was still there, outside the window of the office, hanging over the world.

The night everything changed for ever had only just begun. Vogel looked Flores straight in the eyes, suddenly lucid.

'You're right,' he said. 'I think I owe you an explanation.'

25 December

Two days after the disappearance

The fir woods clung to the mountain slopes like the serried ranks of an army preparing to invade the valley. The valley was as long and narrow as an old scar, and through it ran a river. The river was an intense green, sometimes placid, at other times treacherous.

That was where Avechot was, bang in the middle of this landscape.

An Alpine village a few kilometres from the border. Houses with protruding roofs, a church with a steeple, a town hall, a police station, a small hospital, a school, a couple of bars and a sports stadium.

The woods, the valley, the river, the village. And a huge mine like a monstrous futuristic scar on the past and on nature.

There was a restaurant just outside the built-up area, by the side of the main road.

From the window, you could see the road and the petrol

pump. Over it was a neon sign wishing passing motorists HAPPY HOLIDAYS. Inside, though, the letters were the other way round, which resulted in a kind of incomprehensible hieroglyphic.

In the restaurant, thirty-odd blue Formica tables, some hidden inside booths. They were all laid, but only one was occupied. The one in the middle.

Special Agent Vogel was alone, eating a breakfast of eggs and smoked pancetta. He was wearing a lead-grey suit with an olive-green waistcoat and a dark blue tie, and hadn't taken off his cashmere coat to eat. He sat bolt upright, his gaze fixed on a black notebook in which he was writing with an elegant silver fountain pen that he put down on the table every now and again in order to take a forkful of food. He alternated the gestures at precise intervals, diligently respecting a kind of inner rhythm.

The elderly proprietor wore a grease-stained apron over a red and black checked shirt with the sleeves rolled up to the elbows. He left the counter and approached with a newly made pot of coffee. 'To think I didn't even want to open today. I said to myself: Do you really want to come here on Christmas morning? This place used to be full of tourists, families with children ... But ever since they found that fluorescent crap, things have changed.' He uttered these words as if regretting a distant, happy era that would never return.

Until just a few years earlier, life in Avechot had been quiet and uneventful. People lived off tourism and selling craftwork. But one day, someone from outside had come in and speculated that beneath those mountains lay a fair-sized deposit of fluorite.

The old man was right, Vogel thought: ever since then,

things had changed. A multinational had arrived and purchased the lands above the deposit, paying the various owners
handsomely. Many had become rich overnight. And those
who hadn't been lucky enough to own one of the lots had
found themselves suddenly impoverished because the tourists
had disappeared.

'Maybe I should make up my mind to sell this place and
retire,' the man continued. Then, shaking his head irritably,
he topped up Vogel's coffee, even though he hadn't been asked
to. 'When I saw you coming, I thought you were one of those
salesmen who come in every now and again to try and flog me
their cheap rubbish. Then I realised . . . You're here because of
the girl, aren't you?' With an almost imperceptible movement
of his head, he indicated the flyer on the wall next to the front
entrance.

On it was a photograph of a smiling teenage girl with red
hair and freckles. Then a name, Anna Lou. And a question:
Have you seen me? followed by a telephone number and some
lines of text.

Vogel saw that the old man was trying to peer at his black
notebook, so he closed it. Then he put the fork down on the
plate. 'Do you know her?'

'I know the family. They're good people.' The man pulled
one of the chairs out from under the table and sat down opposite Vogel. 'What do you think happened to her?'

Vogel put his hands together under his chin. How many
times had he been asked that question? It was always the same
story. They seemed genuinely apprehensive, or made an effort
to appear so, but in the end there was only curiosity. Morbid,
pitiless curiosity. 'Twenty-four hours,' he said. The old man
didn't seem to understand the meaning of this reply, but before

he could ask for clarification, Vogel went on, 'On average, teenagers who run away from home can only stand keeping their mobile phones switched off for twenty-four hours. Then, inevitably, they have to call a friend or check if people are talking about them on the internet, and that's how they're located. Most come home after forty-eight hours anyway ... So, for two days after their disappearance, unless they run into someone nasty or have an accident, there's a strong possibility that things will end happily.'

The man seemed thrown by this. 'And what happens then?'

'Then they call me in.'

Vogel stood up, put his hand in his pocket and dropped a twenty-euro note on the table to pay for his breakfast. Then he headed for the exit, but before walking out the door he turned once again towards the proprietor of the restaurant. 'Listen to me: don't sell this place. In a little while, it'll be full of people again.'

Outside, the day was cold but the sky was clear and everything was lit by a bright winter sun. Every now and then, a heavy goods lorry passed along the road and the displacement of air lifted the flaps of Vogel's coat. He stood motionless, both hands plunged in his pockets, on the restaurant forecourt, next to the petrol pump. He was looking up.

A young man of about thirty came up behind him. He, too, was wearing a suit, a tie and a dark coat, although not a cashmere one. He had fair hair with a parting on one side and deep blue eyes. He looked earnest and good-natured. 'Hello,' he said. There was no reply. 'I'm Officer Borghi,' he persisted. 'I was told to come and get you.'

Vogel still didn't deign to respond, but continued to stare up at the sky.

'The briefing starts in half an hour. They're all there, as you requested.'

At this point, Borghi leaned forward and realised that Vogel was actually looking at something on the roof over the petrol pump.

A security camera pointing at the road.

Vogel finally turned towards him. 'This road is the only access to the valley, am I right?'

Borghi didn't even need to think about it. 'Yes, sir. There's no other way to get in or out. It runs straight through it.'

'Good,' Vogel said. 'Take me to the other end.'

Vogel walked quickly towards the anonymous dark saloon car in which Borghi had come to fetch him. Borghi hesitated for a moment, then followed him.

A few minutes later, they were on the bridge that crossed the river and led into the next valley. The young officer parked the car on the side of the road and waited outside it while Vogel, some metres from him, repeated the same action as earlier, this time staring at a speed camera perched on a post beside the carriageway, while vehicles passed close to him and drivers sounded their horns in protest. But Vogel was unfazed and continued to do what he was doing. Whatever it was, Borghi found the situation both incomprehensible and paradoxical.

When he'd had enough, Vogel walked back to the car. 'Let's go and see the girl's parents,' he said and got in without waiting for Borghi's reply. The young officer looked at his watch and patiently climbed in behind the wheel.

*

'Anna Lou has never given me any trouble,' Maria Kastner stated confidently. The girl's mother was a tiny woman, but you nevertheless sensed an unusual strength in her. She was sitting on the sofa next to her husband, a solid but apparently inoffensive man, in the living room of the little two-storeyed house where they lived. Both were still in their pyjamas and dressing gowns, and they were holding hands.

There was a sickly-sweet smell in the air, a mixture of cooked food and air freshener. Vogel couldn't stand it. He was sitting in an armchair, Borghi on another chair a bit further back. Between them and the Kastners was a low table with cups of coffee that would soon get cold since nobody seemed interested in drinking it.

Elsewhere in the room was a decorated Christmas tree, beneath which seven-year-old twin brothers were playing with presents they had just unwrapped.

One package was still untouched, with a nice red ribbon around it.

The woman saw where Vogel was looking. 'We wanted the boys to celebrate the birth of Jesus anyway. It was also a way to distract them from the situation.'

The 'situation' was that their eldest child, who was sixteen and the only girl, had disappeared almost two days earlier. She had left home that winter afternoon at about five to go to a meeting in the local church, which was a few hundred metres from the house.

She had never arrived.

Anna Lou had taken a short walk in a residential area of identical houses – small houses with gardens – where every-body had always known everybody else.

But nobody had seen or heard anything.

The alarm had been raised at about seven, when her mother realised she hadn't come home and had called her in vain on her mobile phone, which had been switched off. Two long hours in which anything might have happened to her. The search had gone on all evening, but then they had yielded to common sense and decided to resume it in the morning. In any case, the local police didn't have the resources for a thorough search of the area.

As of now, there were no theories as to why she might have disappeared.

Vogel again observed the parents in silence. They were hollow-eyed from lack of sleep. In the weeks to come, this sleeplessness would cause them to age rapidly, but for now it had only just started to leave its mark on them.

'Our daughter has always been a responsible girl, ever since she was little,' the woman continued. 'I don't know how to put this . . . But we've never had to worry about her: she grew up without any prompting from us. She helps out around the house, she looks after her brothers. At school, her teachers are pleased with her. She recently became a catechist in our brotherhood.'

The living room was modestly furnished. On entering, Vogel had immediately noticed that the place was full of objects bearing witness to a deep religious faith. The walls were covered with sacred images and Biblical scenes. Jesus was everywhere, in the form of plastic or plaster statuettes, but the Virgin Mary, too, was well represented. And there was a vast array of saints. A wooden crucifix hung over the TV set.

Also in the room were framed family photographs. A girl with red hair and freckles appeared in many of them.

Anna Lou was a female version of her father.

And she was always smiling. On the day of her first communion. In the mountains with her brothers. With skates over her shoulder at the ice rink, proudly displaying a medal after a competition.

Vogel knew that this room, these walls, this house would no longer be the same. They were full of memories that would soon start to hurt.

'We won't take down the Christmas tree until our daughter comes home,' Maria Kastner announced, almost proudly. 'We'll keep it lit so that it can be seen through the window.'

Vogel pondered the absurdity of this, especially in the months to come. A Christmas tree used as a beacon, pointing the way home for someone who might never return. Because that was the risk, although Anna Lou's parents didn't yet realise it. Those festive lights would signal to everyone outside that within these walls a drama was being played out. They would become a burdensome presence. The neighbours wouldn't be able to ignore the tree and its significance. On the contrary, as time went on they would be upset by it. Passing the house, they would cross the street to avoid seeing it. That symbol would alienate everyone from the Kastners, making their solitude even worse. The price you had to pay to keep going with your own life, as Vogel well knew, was indifference.

'They say it's normal for children to be rebellious when they get to the age of sixteen,' Maria said, then shook her head resolutely. 'Not my daughter.'

Vogel nodded. Although at this stage he had no evidence for it, he was sure she was right. He wasn't simply humouring a mother who was trying to absolve herself and her own role as a parent by vouching for her child's incorruptibility. Vogel was convinced she was telling the truth. What gave him this conviction was Anna Lou's face smiling at him from every corner of the room. That simple, almost childlike air told him that something must have happened to her. And whatever it was had happened against her will.

'We have a very strong bond. She's very much like me. She made this for me, she gave it to me a week ago . . . ' The woman showed Vogel a bracelet of coloured beads she was wearing on her wrist. 'They've been her passion lately. She makes them and gives them to the people she loves.'

Vogel noticed that as she told him these details, which were of no significance for the investigation, her voice and eyes betrayed no emotion. But it wasn't coldness. He knew what it was. The woman was convinced that this was some kind of *test*. They were all being subjected to a test so that they could demonstrate how firm and intact their faith was. That was why, deep down, she accepted what was happening. She might think it was unfair, but she nevertheless hoped that someone up there, maybe God himself, would soon put things right.

'Anna Lou confided in me, but a mother is aware that she doesn't know everything about her children. Yesterday, while I was tidying her room, I found this . . . ' The woman let go of her husband's hand and held out to Vogel the brightly coloured diary she had been keeping close to her chest.

Vogel reached out across the low table to take it. On the cover was a picture of two sweet kittens with ruffled fur. He started leafing through it absently.

'You won't find anything suspicious in it,' the woman said.

But Vogel closed the diary and took his fountain pen and his black notebook from the inside pocket of his coat. 'I assume you're familiar with all the people your daughter mixed with . . . '

'Of course,' Maria Kastner said with a touch of indignation.

'Has Anna Lou met anyone new recently? Made a new friend, for example?'

'No.'

'Are you absolutely sure?'

'Yes,' she said emphatically. 'She would have told me.'

She had only just admitted a mother couldn't know everything about her own children, but now she was making a great show of certainty. It was typical of parents in missing persons cases, Vogel recalled. They want to help but they're aware that they're partly to blame, at the very least for not paying enough attention to their children. When you try to point that out, though, the instinct for self-defence kicks in, even if it means denying the evidence. But Vogel needed more information. 'Have you noticed any unusual behaviour lately?'

'What do you mean by unusual?'

'You know how young people are. A lot of things can be figured out from small signals. Has she been sleeping well? Eating regularly? Has her mood changed? Has she been sullen?'

'She was the usual Anna Lou. I know my daughter, Special Agent Vogel, I always know when something's wrong.'

The girl owned a mobile phone. From what Vogel could tell, it was an old model, not a smart phone. 'Did your daughter surf the internet?'

The two parents looked at each other.

'Our brotherhood frowns on the use of certain technologies,' Maria said. 'The internet is full of snares, Agent Vogel. Misleading notions that can compromise the upbringing of a good Christian. But we've never forbidden our daughter anything, it's always been her choice.'

Yes, of course, Vogel thought. About one thing, though, the woman was right. The danger did usually come from the internet. Sensitive teenagers like Anna Lou were particularly susceptible. There were hunters out there, clever at manipulating vulnerable young people and insinuating themselves into their lives. Lowering their defences little by little and inverting relationships of trust, they managed to replace the teenagers' closest relatives and remotely control them until they could make them do whatever they wanted. In this sense, Anna Lou Kastner was the perfect prey. Maybe the girl had only apparently supported her parents' wishes while going on the internet elsewhere, at school or in the library. They would have to check. For the moment, though, there were other aspects he had to go into. 'You're among the fortunate few in the village who sold land to the mining company, is that right?'

The question was addressed to Bruno Kastner, but it was once again his wife who spoke up. 'My father left us a plot of land up in the north. Who would ever have imagined it was worth so much? We gave part of the money to the brotherhood and paid off the mortgage on this house. The rest is intended for our children.'

It must be a tidy sum, Vogel thought. Probably enough to guarantee a more than decent existence for several generations of Kastners. They could have allowed themselves all sorts of luxuries, or chosen to buy a larger and more impressive house. Instead, they had decided not to modify their lifestyle. Vogel couldn't understand how you could ignore such a windfall so easily. For the moment, he simply registered it. Head still bent over his notebook, he said, 'You haven't received a ransom demand, so I'd rule out a kidnapping. But have you received any threats in the past? Is there anyone – a relative, an acquaintance – who has reason to envy you, or bear you a grudge?'

The Kastners seemed taken aback by these questions.

'No, nobody,' Maria said immediately. 'The only people we see regularly are the members of the brotherhood.'

Vogel reflected on the implication of these last words: the Kastners were naïvely convinced that conflict was impossible within the brotherhood. In fact, he'd never doubted that this would be the response. Before setting foot in their house, he had looked into their lives, trying to find out everything there was to know about them.

Public opinion, as usual, went entirely on appearances. That was why, when something unusual happened, like a simple, well-brought-up girl going missing, and when it happened within the context of a respectable family, everyone tended to assume that the evil had come from outside. But an experienced police officer like Vogel was always reluctant to look outside, because in all too many cases the explanation was more simply – and horribly – hidden within the walls of the family home. He had dealt with fathers who abused their daughters and mothers who, instead of protecting them, had treated their own daughters as dangerous rivals. Then, for the sake of a quiet life, the parents reached the conclusion that the best way to save their marriage was to get rid of their own offspring. He had once investigated the case of a wife who, on discovering the abuse, had chosen to cover for her husband, and to avoid her own shame, had killed her daughter herself. In short, the range of savagery within the family was ever more varied and fantastic.

The Kastners seemed respectable.

He was a lorry driver, and hadn't given up work on becoming unexpectedly rich. She was a modest housewife, completely devoted to her family and her children. In addition, both were fervent in their religious faith.

But you never could tell.

Vogel pretended to be satisfied. 'It seems to me we've covered everything we can, for the time being.' He got up from his armchair, immediately imitated by Borghi, who had remained silent throughout. 'Thank you for the coffee. And for this,' he added, waving Anna Lou's diary. 'I'm sure it'll be of great help to us.'

The Kastners walked the two policemen to the door. Vogel glanced again at the children playing imperturbably by the Christmas tree. God alone knew what would remain of all this in their adult memories, he thought. Maybe they were young enough to escape the horror. But the package waiting for Anna Lou, its red ribbon still uncut, told him that there would always be something to remind them of the tragedy that had struck their family. Because there was nothing worse than a gift that doesn't reach the person it is intended for. The happiness it contains slowly decays, poisoning everything around it.

At that moment, Vogel realised that the silence between them had lasted too long, so he turned to Borghi. 'Could you wait for me in the car, please?'

'Yes, sir,' Borghi said deferentially.

Alone now with the Kastners, Vogel spoke in a new, thoughtful tone, as if he had taken 'the situation' to heart. 'I want to be frank with you,' he said. 'The media have got wind of the story, they'll soon be arriving in their droves . . . Sometimes, reporters are better than the police at digging up news, and what ends up on television isn't always relevant to the case. Not knowing where to look, they'll look at you. So if you have anything to say, *anything* . . . now's the time to say it.'

A silence followed, a silence Vogel drew out longer than necessary. It was like sealing a pact. His advice had contained a warning: I know you have secrets, everybody has them. But now your secrets belong to me.

'Good,' he said at last, breaking the silence to release them from further embarrassment. 'I see you've had flyers printed with a photograph of your daughter. That was a good idea, but it's not enough. So far, it's been the local media who've dealt with the matter, but now we'll need to do more. For example, it'd be helpful to make a public appeal. How do you feel about that?'

Husband and wife looked at each other questioningly. Then Anna Lou's mother took a step forward, slipped off the bead bracelet her daughter had made for her, took Vogel's left hand and put the bracelet around his wrist, as if in a solemn investiture. 'We'll do everything that's necessary to help you, Agent Vogel. But you'll bring her home, won't you?'

As he waited in the car, Borghi was busy speaking into his mobile phone. 'I don't know how much longer he'll be, he asked to do it,' he was explaining to one of the officers who had been waiting for more than an hour for the scheduled briefing to start. 'I have family, too. Calm them down and assure them that nobody will miss their Christmas dinner.' Actually, he wasn't sure he should be making a promise like that, because he didn't know what Vogel had in mind. He knew only what he needed to know, and this morning all he knew was that he had to be Vogel's driver.

The previous evening, his immediate superior had told him he would have to go to Avechot in the morning to help Special Agent Vogel in investigating the disappearance of a minor. Then he had handed him the meagre file on the case and had concluded with some unusual instructions. He was to be at the roadside restaurant on the outskirts of the village at eight thirty on the dot, wearing a dark suit with a shirt and tie.

Obviously, Borghi had heard plenty of rumours about Vogel and his eccentricities. He and his cases were often featured on television, and he had been a guest on a number of crime-related programmes. He was in great demand for newspaper and TV interviews. He was at his ease in front of the cameras, always able to talk off the cuff, confident of success.

Then there were the stories that were told in the police, which described him as a meticulous character, a control freak, concerned only with looking good on screen and making sure that attention was focused on him, never on anyone around him.

Recently, though, things hadn't gone so well for Special Agent Vogel. One case in particular had called his methods into question. That had pleased some in the police, but it still seemed to Borghi, naïvely perhaps, that there was a lot to learn from an officer like Vogel. After all, he himself was just at the beginning of his career, and this experience certainly wouldn't do him any harm.

Except that Vogel had always dealt with unusual crimes, especially gruesome murders that had a strong emotional impact. And it was said that he always chose his cases carefully.

Which was why Borghi was now wondering what Vogel had seen that was so extraordinary in the disappearance of a young girl.

Even though he found the fears of Anna Lou's parents understandable, and suspected that something horrible might have happened to her, he couldn't see it as a media sensation. And usually those were the only kinds of cases that interested Vogel.

'We'll be there shortly,' he assured the officer at the other end, just to finish the call. As he did so, he spotted a black van parked at the end of the street.

In it were two men, observing the Kastner house without exchanging a word.

Borghi would have liked to get out of the car and check who the men were, but just then he saw Vogel come out of the house and walk along the drive in his direction. After a moment, though, Vogel slowed down and did something that made no sense.

He started clapping.

Softly at first, then increasingly loudly. As he did so, he looked around. The sound echoed, and faces started to appear at the windows of the neighbouring houses. An elderly woman, a married couple with their children, a fat man, a housewife with curlers in her hair. Gradually, others joined them. They all watched the scene uncomprehendingly.

Vogel stopped clapping.

He looked around one last time, still watched by the neighbours, then resumed walking as if nothing had happened and got in the car. Borghi would have liked to ask him the reasons for this strange behaviour, but once again it was Vogel who spoke first. 'What did you notice in that house today, Officer Borghi?'

The young man didn't need to think about it. 'The husband and the wife held hands the whole time, they seemed very united, yet she was the one who did all the talking.'

Vogel nodded, looking through the windscreen. 'The man's dying to tell us something.'

Borghi made no comment. He started the car, forgetting all about the clapping and the black van.

The village police station was too small and cramped for what Vogel had in mind, and he had asked for a place more suited to the investigation. So the school gym had been placed at his disposal as an operations room.

The mats and the gym equipment had been piled up along one of the walls. A big basket of volleyballs stood forgotten in a corner. Some desks had been brought in from the classrooms, and a few folding garden chairs had also been procured. There were two laptops and a desktop computer provided by the library, but only one telephone connected to an outside line. A blackboard had been placed under one of the baskets on the basketball area, and on it someone had written in chalk: *Case findings*. Underneath were stuck the only elements gathered so far: the photograph of Anna Lou that featured on the flyers printed by the family and a map of the valley.

At that moment, the room echoed with the chatter of a small group of plain-clothes officers from Avechot, gathered around a coffee machine and a tray of pastries. They were talking with their mouths full and kept impatiently checking the time. It was impossible to make out what they were talking about in that clamour, but from their expressions it could be inferred that they were all complaining about the same thing.

The dull thud produced by the fire door being thrown open made them all turn. Vogel entered the gym, followed by Borghi, and the chatter faded. The door closed with a bang behind Vogel. Now the only sound in the room was the distinct squeak of his leather shoes as he walked forward.

Without saying hello or deigning to look at anybody, Vogel

approached the blackboard beneath the basket. He looked for a moment at the 'case findings', as if studying them carefully. Then, with an abrupt gesture, he rubbed out the words with one hand and tore off the photograph and the map.

With the chalk, he wrote a date: *23 December.*

He turned to the small audience. 'Nearly two days have passed since the girl disappeared,' he said. 'In missing persons cases, time is our enemy, but it can also be an ally – it all depends on us. We have to take full advantage of it, which means we have to get moving.' He paused. 'I want roadblocks on the main road in and out of the valley. I don't want anybody stopped, but we have to send a signal.'

Those present listened in silence. Borghi had taken up a position against the wall and stood there watching them.

'The security camera over the petrol pump and the speed camera on the main road,' Vogel said. 'Has anyone checked if they're working?'

After a few moments' hesitation, one of the officers, a paunchy man in a check shirt and blue tie, raised the cup of coffee that was in his hand. 'Yes, sir,' he said self-consciously. 'We've got hold of the videos for the time of the disappearance.'

Vogel seemed pleased. 'Good. Now trace all the male motorists who drove by at that time and check the reasons they entered or left the valley. Concentrate on those with a history of violence or a criminal record.'

From his privileged vantage point, Borghi sensed the men's displeasure.

A second officer spoke up, an older man confident that he could allow himself a criticism. 'Sir, there aren't many of us, we don't have many resources, plus there's no money for overtime.' There was a murmur of approval from the others.

Vogel was unfazed. He looked at the desks arrayed in front of him. The shortage of resources was obvious, and made them all look ridiculous. He couldn't blame these men for being sceptical and unmotivated. But nor could he allow there to be any excuses. So he continued in a calm tone: 'I know you'd all like to be at home celebrating Christmas with your families right now, and that you see Officer Borghi and myself as two strangers who've come here to order you about. But when this business is over, the two of us, Borghi and I, will be able to go back where we came from. Whereas you . . . ' He looked briefly from one to the other of them. 'You'll have to keep meeting that girl's parents on the street.'

There followed a brief silence. Then the older officer intervened again, humbly this time. 'Sir, forgive my question, but why are we looking for a man when it's a girl who disappeared? Shouldn't we be concentrating on her?'

'Because someone took her.'

As he'd intended, this statement had a powerful effect on the audience. For a moment, they didn't know what to say. Vogel looked around at those present. Any police officer with common sense would have dismissed the statement as a procedural heresy. There was no evidence to support the hypothesis, not so much as a single clue. It came out of nowhere. But all Vogel had to do was plant in their minds the idea that it was *possible*. He just needed that seed of a possibility, and soon the certainty would grow. He knew that if he could convince these men, he'd be able to convince anybody. That was the challenge. Not in a real operations room equipped for a crisis, but in a school gym. Not with professionals with five years' experience in the field, but with ill-equipped local officers who had no idea how to conduct a complex investigation. In these few minutes, the fate of the case would be decided, and so perhaps would that of a sixteen-year-old girl. That was why Vogel started bringing out all the tricks he had learned over time, with the aim of selling his merchandise.

'There's no point beating about the bush,' he continued. 'We have to call a spade a spade. Because, as I've said, anything else is a waste of time. And that time belongs to Anna Lou, not to us.' Then he took his black notebook from his coat pocket, opened it with a flick of the wrist and consulted his notes. 'It's about five o'clock on 23 December. Anna Lou Kastner leaves home to go to a church meeting, the church being about three hundred metres from her house.' Vogel turned and drew two dots on the blackboard, some distance from each other. 'As we know, she'll never get there. But she isn't the kind of girl who'd run away. That's what those who know her say, and it's confirmed by her lifestyle: no internet at home, no profile on social networks, and she only had five numbers in the memory on her mobile phone.' He counted on his fingers: 'Mummy, Daddy, home, grandparents' house and church.' He turned again to the blackboard and drew a line between the two points he had previously drawn. 'The answers are all in those three hundred metres. Eleven other families live there: forty-six people in all, thirty-three of whom were at home at that hour. But nobody saw or heard anything. The security cameras point towards the houses, not at the street, so they're useless. What is it they say? "Everyone cultivates his own garden."' He put the black notebook back in his pocket. 'The kidnapper studied the habits of the neighbourhood, he knew how to pass unobserved. The fact that we're only *hypothesising* his existence tells us that he prepared well before he went into action . . . and that he's winning.'

Vogel put down the chalk, clapped his hands to get the dust off them, then scrutinised the audience, trying to see if the concept he had just outlined had made any progress. Yes, he'd done it. He had instilled doubt in them. But he had done more than that: he had offered them a motivation. From that moment on, he would manoeuvre them easily and nobody would again question a single word of his orders.

'Good, now remember: the question is no longer where Anna Lou is now. The question is: *Who is she with?* Now let's get going.'

Borghi, who hadn't yet eaten anything, went back to the little hotel room he had reserved the previous afternoon, along with one for Special Agent Vogel. He'd been sure there wouldn't be any vacancies on Christmas Day. But although it was among the last hotels still active in the valley, the Fiori delle Alpe was practically empty. All the other hotels and guest houses had closed down after the arrival of the fluorite mine. Borghi had wondered at first how come they hadn't been converted to guest apartments for those working for the multinational that ran the mine, but the doorman had explained to him that the workers were almost all local, while the company's executives came and went in their helicopters and never stayed very long.

Barely three thousand people lived in Avechot, and half the male workforce was employed in the mine.

The first thing Officer Borghi did when he got into his room was take off his leather shoes and his tie. He had been shivering in those clothes all day. Usually, he only wore a suit when he had to go and make a statement in court. He wasn't used to having one on for such a long time. He waited for the temperature of his body to harmonise with that of the room, then took off his jacket and shirt. He would have to wash the shirt and hang it in the shower, hoping it would dry by the next day, because his wife had forgotten to put in a spare one when she had packed his suitcase. Caroline had been very distracted lately. They had been married for just over a year and she was seven months pregnant.

It's hard to explain to a young wife who's expecting a baby why you can't spend Christmas Day with her, even when the reason is something you can't get out of, like your work as a police officer.

Borghi called her as he was dropping his shirt in the bathroom sink. It was a fairly rapid call.

'So what's happening in Avechot?' she asked curtly.

'Actually, we don't know yet.'

'Then they might as well have given you the day off.'

It was obvious that Caroline was looking for a quarrel. It was exasperating having to deal with her when she acted that way.

'I told you, it's important for me to be here, for my career.' He was trying to be conciliatory, but it was difficult. Then he was distracted by the voices coming from the TV, which he had switched on. 'Sorry, I have to go now, someone just knocked at the door,' he lied. He hung up before Caroline could start her whining again and immediately focused on the news bulletin.

On the evening of Christmas Day, when people had finished celebrating and were getting ready to bring a long day to its end, Anna Lou's parents appeared on television.

They were sitting side by side behind a large rectangular table set up on a low platform. They were wearing thick jackets that looked too big for them, as if the anxiety of the last few hours had eaten away at them from within. They looked shy and modest, and still held each other by the hand.

The appeal had been filmed that afternoon by a local TV channel under Vogel's supervision. Borghi had been there, too, but seeing it all again on a small screen gave him a strange sensation he couldn't explain.

Kastner held a framed photograph of his daughter up to the camera. It had been taken at the end of a religious ceremony and showed Anna Lou in a snow-white tunic with a wooden crucifix. His wife Maria, with that same crucifix around her neck, read a press release. 'Anna Lou is one metre sixty-seven tall, and has long red hair which she usually wears in a ponytail. When she disappeared, Anna Lou had on a grey tracksuit, trainers and a white down jacket. She also had a brightly-coloured school satchel with her.' Then, after catching her breath, she looked straight at the camera, as if directly addressing all the parents watching, as well, perhaps, as whoever might know the truth. 'Our daughter Anna Lou is a kind girl, those who know her know that she has a good heart: she loves cats and she trusts people. That's why we're also appealing to those who've never known her in her first sixteen years of life: if you've seen her or have any idea where she is, help us to bring her home.' Finally she spoke to her daughter, as if she could really hear her in some remote, unknown place. 'Anna Lou . . . Mummy, Daddy and your brothers love you. Wherever you are, I hope that our voice and our love reach you. And when you come home, we'll let you have the kitten you want so much, Anna Lou, I promise you . . . May the Lord protect you, my child.'

She had repeated the name of her daughter several times, even though it wasn't necessary, Borghi thought. Perhaps because she feared losing the last thing she still had of Anna Lou's.

Now, not only a simple, nondescript girl, who would never have imagined she might appear on television one day, but also a little village in the Alps named Avechot were both on their way to becoming sadly famous. Borghi understood the sensation he had felt a while earlier, when he had found himself watching an event he had already seen as if he didn't know it.

It was the effect of being on television. It was as if words and gestures took on a new consistency on the small screen.

Once upon a time, television had limited itself to reproducing reality, now it instigated the process. It made reality tangible, something with texture and solidity.

It created reality.

Without knowing why, Borghi thought again of the words Vogel had used about Anna Lou's father once he had got back in the car after that strange interval of clapping outside the Kastners' house.

'The man's dying to tell us something.'

He himself was about to become the father of a baby girl. For more than forty-eight hours now, the man over whom Vogel had cast a sinister shadow had been in the dark as to what had happened to his own daughter. Borghi was struck by a sudden anxiety. He was forced to wonder if the world awaiting his daughter was indeed that cruel.

It was nearly midnight, and the Kastners' house was silent. But there was nothing peaceful about that silence, because it merely emphasised the emptiness that had grown in the house over the past forty-eight hours. Anna Lou's absence was now palpable. Her father could no longer ignore it as he had done all day long, avoiding looking at the places usually occupied by his daughter, like her chair at the table, the armchair in which she loved to huddle in the evening to read a book or watch television, the door of her room. And he had filled the absence of her voice with other sounds. For example, when the pain of not hearing her speak, laugh or hum to herself became unbearable to him, Bruno Kastner would move an object, so that the noise would fill the emptiness left by Anna Lou and distract him from that terrible silence.

Dr Flores had prescribed tranquillisers for Maria, to help her sleep. Bruno had made sure she took them and then had gone to tuck in the twins and had lingered in the doorway of their room, watching over their restless sleep. They were holding out, but it was clear that they, too, were disturbed. All day long, they had continued to ask questions in an almost casual way and had seemed content with the brief, evasive answers they were given. But their apparent indifference concealed a fear of knowing the truth. A truth you're not prepared for at the age of seven.

Bruno Kastner didn't know what the truth was either, all he knew was that he was terrified.

He sat down at the dining room table. He was once again wearing slippers and pyjamas. After the visit of the two police officers, he had dressed to go out, without knowing exactly where to go. He had found comfort in the routine of his work, and so had spent the succeeding hours in his lorry, driving aimlessly along the mountain roads. He was looking for a sign of Anna Lou, anything at all. In reality, he was also escaping his own anxieties, his own sense of powerlessness – the kind of powerlessness that only a father who knows he hasn't looked after his nearest and dearest as he should have done can possibly feel.

33

Now, at the end of that interminable day, even though he was very tired, he wasn't sure he would be able to sleep. He was afraid of the dreams that awaited him. He couldn't take a sleeping pill because somebody had to keep protecting the house, the family. Although that was probably pointless, given that evil had found a way of getting in regardless. And then there was the unhoped-for eventuality that Anna Lou might come back or that the telephone might ring and free them from that evil spell.

So he went into the living room and from the drawer of a cabinet took the albums of family photographs that Maria had collected lovingly over the years. He carried them into the dining room and sat down at the table but didn't switch the light on. All he needed was the light from the street lamp outside filtering in through the window. He started to take the photographs out of their pockets and place them on the table, one by one, according to an order that only he knew, like a fortune teller trying to predict the future from the cards in front of him.

The photographs showed his girl from when she was very little.

Anna Lou started to grow in front of his eyes. The day she crawled, the day she learned to walk, the day he taught her to ride a bicycle. There was a series of firsts: her first day at school, her first birthday, her first Christmas. And then so many other moments, scattered through time. Other Christmases, trips to the mountains, ice skating competitions. An array of happy memories. Because – it seemed foolish even to think this – people don't take photographs of bad days. And if they do, they certainly don't keep them.

There were the images of the last holiday they had taken

together, the year before, when they had gone to the seaside. Anna Lou looked funny and a little awkward in her bathing costume, and she knew it. Maybe that was why she always stood somewhat apart in those snaps. Unlike so many of her contemporaries, she had not yet fully blossomed. She was like a child, with her red ponytail and her freckles. Bruno Kastner would have liked Maria to talk to her, to explain to her that she was normal and that one day, all of a sudden, her body would change, and for the better. But for his wife, religious as she was, subjects like sex and puberty were taboo. And he certainly couldn't do it. It would be his turn to talk to the twins one day. But that kind of conversation wasn't something a father could have with his only daughter. It would have embarrassed her. She would have blushed and, aware that her cheeks were on fire and there was nothing she could do about it, would have felt even more exposed and vulnerable.

His daughter was like him, shy and a little self-conscious when it came to interacting with the rest of the world. And that included her family.

Bruno wished he had given her more. For example, he wished he could have spent part of the money from the sale of land to the mining company on sending her to a better school, outside the valley, maybe a nice private school. But the land was his wife's, and consequently so was the money. And Maria, as always, had decided for all of them. He hadn't been opposed to the idea of making a big donation to the brotherhood, but he would have liked their children to have their share now and not in some hypothetical future.

Because Bruno Kastner didn't even know if Anna Lou would have a future.

Irritably, he dismissed that thought. He felt like punching the table. He was strong enough to break it in two. But he held back. He'd been holding back his whole life.

He rubbed his eyes and when he opened them again he lingered over one photograph in particular. It was quite a recent snap, and showed his daughter, smiling as usual, with another girl. The contrast between the two girls underlined all too plainly the fact that Anna Lou, with her tracksuit and her trainers and her red hair gathered in the usual ponytail, looked like a child. Her friend, on the other hand, was made-up, fashionably dressed, and looked every inch a grown woman. Studying the two of them, Bruno Kastner would have liked to cry, but he couldn't.

What had happened was his fault, and his alone.

He was a believer, although his faith wasn't quite as firm as Maria's, and that made his guilt all the keener. If he'd been strong enough to impose his views over his wife's, Anna Lou would be safe in her room in a boarding school somewhere right now. If he'd had the courage to tell Maria what he really thought, to express his own opinions, his daughter wouldn't have disappeared.

Instead, he had kept silent. Because that's what sinners do: they keep silent and, in keeping silent, they lie.

That was Bruno Kastner's verdict on himself. He put almost all the photographs back in place, closed the albums and prepared to face his third sleepless night.

There was only one photograph on the table now. The one of Anna Lou with her friend.

He put it in his pocket.

26 December

Three days after the disappearance

The weather had changed. The temperature had dipped and the bright Christmas sun had been replaced by a thick blanket of grey clouds.

Avechot was still slumbering lazily after the excesses of the festive season. Vogel and Borghi, though, had woken early to take full advantage of the day. They drove around the streets of the village in the dark saloon car. Vogel seemed in good spirits and was dressed as if on his way to an official meeting. Highly polished shoes, Prince of Wales suit, white shirt, pink woollen tie. Borghi was wearing the same clothes as the day before and hadn't had a chance to iron the shirt he had washed in the hotel. He felt awkward next to his superior. While he concentrated on driving, Vogel looked around.

The walls of the houses bore religious slogans in white paint. I'M WITH JESUS! CHRIST IS LIFE. HE WHO WALKS WITH

ME WILL BE SAVED. From the look of them, it was clear they weren't the work of some anonymous fanatic. The owners of the houses had put them there themselves, as an overt testimony to their faith. In addition, there were crosses everywhere: on the facades of the public buildings, in the middle of flower beds, even on the shop windows.

It was as if the village had been swept by a wave of religious fanaticism.

'Tell me about the brotherhood the Kastners belong to.'

Vogel's request didn't catch Borghi unprepared: he had done some research into the subject. 'Apparently, there was a scandal in Avechot about twenty years ago: the local priest ran away with one of his female parishioners, a devout wife and mother of three.'

'I'm not interested in gossip,' Vogel said acidly.

'Well, sir, that's when everything started. Anywhere else, a thing like that would have given rise to – yes, gossip and idle chatter, but in Avechot they took it very seriously. The priest was young and charismatic, it seems. He'd won everyone over with his sermons and was much loved.'

In a narrow community, hemmed in by the mountains, it would certainly take charisma to win people's hearts . . . or to take advantage of their credulity, Vogel thought.

'The fact remains, he was able to build a large following. The community has always been quite observant, which is why, after what happened, they must have felt somehow betrayed by their spiritual guide. At that point, the local people became more suspicious than ever, and the congregation started reject-ing all the replacements sent by the Curia. So, after a couple of years, some members took on the role of deacons, and since then the community has been self-governing.'

'Like a religious sect?' Vogel asked, his curiosity suddenly aroused.

'Sort of. They used to live on tourism in these parts, but strangers have never been really welcome. They disturbed things, they had customs that didn't match – let's put it this way – the "local culture". When the fluorite deposit was discovered, these people were finally able to get rid of them and almost completely cut themselves off from the rest of the world.'

'Maria and Bruno Kastner must have been among the most fervent of them, seeing how much money they've given to the cause.'

'Have you noticed that they talk about their brotherhood as if it was an exclusive club? It's like "us and them" ... I'm not sure how best to express the idea.'

'You express it well.'

'The members of the community were the first people to organise a search for Anna Lou. I get the impression they've been quite close to the family. This morning, some of them even moved in to the Kastners' house to look after them and make sure they're not left alone.'

They came to the church. There was a more modern building next to the priest's house.

'That's the meeting hall. They use it much more than the church itself, especially for prayer meetings. Apparently, the community is very influential in the valley. It even has a say in the decisions of the mining company. The mayor, the councillors and all the public officials are elected by the brotherhood. As a result, they've imposed a series of prohibitions, like no smoking in public, no serving alcohol on Sundays and feast days or after six in the evening. They're also against abortion and homosexuality, and they aren't too keen on unmarried couples cohabiting either.'

Fucking fanatics, Vogel thought. But part of him was extremely pleased.

The context surrounding Anna Lou's disappearance was perfect. The mysterious disappearance of a young girl, evil striking a community strictly devoted to God and His precepts, a whole village forced to question itself about what was happening.

Or had already happened.

Vogel had asked to meet the mayor and one of the forest rangers. Borghi had immediately proceeded to set it up, although he had been somewhat surprised by Vogel's request to hold the meeting on the banks of the river that flowed through the valley.

When they arrived, Borghi parked the car in a broad, gravelled open space on which stood a disused wooden kiosk that had once, according to an old sign, been used for selling live bait and renting fishing rods. The mayor and the forest ranger were already there, standing by a four-by-four with municipal registration plates.

The mayor was a sturdy man with an exaggerated paunch barely held in check by his trouser belt. He was wearing a thick mountain jacket open at the front, a blue cotton shirt and a tie with hideous red diamonds. His tie pin was of gold and ended in a little amethyst crucifix. Vogel didn't betray the contempt he felt for this outfit, or for the ridiculous comb-over on the mayor's pear-shaped head, or the moustache above his thick lips. The mayor, he thought, was one of those individuals who are always hot, even in winter. His perennially red cheeks were evidence of that. When he approached Vogel with his most cordial smile, the special agent accepted his energetic hand-shake but didn't return the enthusiasm.

'I've known the Kastners my whole life, Special Agent,' the mayor said, his smile turning to an expression of distress. 'You have no idea how pained I am by what's happening right now. We're happy that you're here dealing with our Anna Lou. Given your fame, I know she's in excellent hands.'

Anna Lou had suddenly become everyone's daughter, Vogel thought. When it came down to it, that's how it always was, or at least it was what people paid lip service to. But when they closed the doors of their houses behind them, they'd all be grateful that this had happened to someone else's child.

'Your girl will be our top priority,' Vogel replied, and the mayor didn't catch the hint of sarcasm in his voice. 'Now can we see the river?'

Vogel walked round him and headed for the river bank. The mayor was taken aback for a moment, then hurried after him, followed by the forest ranger and Borghi. Borghi wondered how close to the river Vogel wanted to go. To his great sur-prise, he saw him walk past the edge of the gravel, dip his feet in the mud and keep going, unworried about soiling his fine suit and expensive shoes.

At that point, the others were forced to do the same.

The forest ranger was the only one wearing boots. The others were soon up to their knees in mud. It struck Borghi that he would have to do another wash at the hotel this evening, although it might not be enough to save the only suit he owned.

'The river has an average width of eight to ten metres and a fairly strong current,' the forest ranger said. 'This is the point where it slows down the most.'

Vogel had already questioned him on a series of details. The forest ranger didn't understand why they interested him so much. 'What depth does it reach?' Vogel asked.

'A metre and a half on average, two and a half at some points. Deep enough to let a lot of rubbish accumulate there that the current can't clear away.'

'So you have to do it?'

'Once every two or three years. In autumn, before it starts raining, we set up an artificial dyke and the dredges get the work done in a week.'

Borghi turned towards the bridge that spanned the river. It was some eight hundred metres away. And on it stood the black van he had spotted before outside the Kastners' house. He assumed the two men he had seen then were still on board. He thought of pointing it out to Vogel.

'Ever since the mine slowed down the river to drain part of the water,' the forest ranger went on, 'all kinds of stuff has been piling up on the bottom, including animal carcasses. God alone knows what's down there. The river is sick.'

These final words provoked the mayor to correct his subordinate. 'The council has convinced the company to finance a programme of environmental safeguards. Large sums are being spent on drainage.'

Vogel ignored the comment and turned to Borghi, distracting him from the van. 'We'll have to talk to the company and ask for lists of their outside suppliers and the names of the workers who commute.'

The mayor appeared visibly worried. 'Come on, now, why bother them over what might turn out to be just a bit of childish mischief?'

Vogel turned and looked at him. 'A bit of childish mischief?' he asked gravely.

The mayor tried to amend what he had said. 'Don't misunderstand me, I'm a father, too, and I know how the Kastners must be feeling ... But doesn't this alarmism seem a little hasty? The company gives work to a lot of people in the valley. They won't appreciate this kind of publicity.'

The mayor was using sincerity to win over Vogel, Borghi noted. But political pragmatism wouldn't work with him.

'Let me tell you something,' Vogel said, going right up to the mayor and lowering his voice as if imparting a confidence. 'I've learned that there are two periods of time in which to do things. Now and later. Putting things off may seem wise, sometimes we need to think deeply about situations and their possible consequences. But unfortunately, in some circumstances, thinking too much may be taken for hesitation or, worse still, for weakness. Delaying never makes things better. And there's no worse publicity than failure, believe me.'

When he had finished his little lecture, Vogel turned to the area of open ground from which they had come. He had been alerted by a voice trying to overcome the noise of the river. The others immediately turned in the same direction.

There on the bank, before the muddy section started, stood a blonde woman in a blue tailored suit and a short dark coat, waving her arms in their direction.

When they came level with her, Borghi guessed from her dirty shoes that the woman had tried to walk in the mud but had been prevented by her heels.

She introduced herself. 'I'm Prosecutor Mayer.' She was young, about thirty, not very tall and quite pretty. She wore no make-up and had a sober appearance. She immediately asked to take the two officers aside and speak to them. She seemed upset. 'I just heard there was a briefing yesterday. Why wasn't I informed?'

'I didn't want to take you away from your family on Christmas Day,' Vogel replied slyly. 'And besides, I didn't think prosecutors participated in the preliminary stages of an investigation.'

Mayer wasn't about to be brushed off so easily. 'Did you by any chance mention a kidnapper yesterday, Special Agent Vogel?'

'For now, we can't rule out any hypothesis.'

'I understand that, but is there any evidence pointing in that direction, a rumour, a witness, a clue?'

'As a matter of fact, no.' Vogel was annoyed, but wouldn't let her see it.

'So I can only deduce that this is pure intuition,' Mayer said with a touch of sarcasm.

'If you want to put it that way,' Vogel said, pretending to humour her.

Borghi was listening in silence to this heated exchange.

'There are various leads to choose from,' Vogel went on. 'From experience, I know that it's best to begin immediately with the worst-case scenario, that's why I mentioned a possible kidnapper.'

'I took the trouble to gather information about Anna Lou Kastner before you got here. She was a quiet girl who led a simple life. Bracelets, kittens, church. Rather too much of a child compared with other girls her age, I admit. But that certainly doesn't mark her out as a likely victim.'

Vogel was amused by the prosecutor's profile. 'What conclusions have you come to?'

'A strict upbringing, a mother who was always interfering. For instance, Anna Lou wasn't allowed to mix with any kids her own age who didn't belong to the brotherhood, even at school. She wasn't allowed to go out with friends or to pursue any activities outside those considered "legitimate" according to a very strict set of religious beliefs. In other words, she wasn't allowed to decide anything for herself, not even to make her own mistakes. And when you're sixteen, it's almost your right to make mistakes. That's why it sometimes happens that kids rebel against the rules.'

Vogel nodded pensively. 'So you think she ran away?'

'It's not unusual, is it? You know as well as I do that statistically it's the likeliest thing. Especially as Anna Lou left home with a school bag and none of her relatives can tell us what was in it.'

While Vogel was pretending to ponder these conclusions, Borghi remembered the diary that Anna Lou's mother had given Vogel the previous day when they had gone to see her. In it, there was nothing that suggested any desire to escape.

'Your hypothesis is persuasive,' Vogel agreed.

Mayer, though, wasn't the kind of person to let herself be bought off with sweet talk. 'I know your methods, Vogel,' she said. 'I know you like the limelight. But you won't find any monster for your sideshow here in Avechot.'

Vogel tried to change the subject. 'The operations room is a school gym, my office is in a changing room. The men I have at my disposal have no expertise in this kind of case and are ill-equipped. I'd like a forensics team to go over every inch of the street where the girl disappeared. Maybe we'll confirm your hypothesis and be able to rule out anything else.'

Mayer let out an amused little laugh, then turned serious

again. 'Do you have any idea what would happen if news got out that the police suspect it was a kidnapping?'

'There won't be any leaks,' Vogel assured her.

'How can you have the nerve to ask me for a forensics team when you don't have a single lead?'

'There won't be any leaks,' Vogel repeated in a firmer voice.

Borghi saw a darker vein appear on Vogel's forehead. Up until now, he hadn't seen him lose his composure.

Mayer seemed to get off her high horse. Before walking away, she looked both of them in the eye. 'This is still a missing persons case, don't forget that.'

As they drove back to the gym, there was absolute silence in the car. Borghi would have liked to say something, but he was afraid that if he spoke he would unleash the anger that Vogel had been holding in from the start.

At that moment, Borghi glanced in the rear-view mirror and again saw the black van. It was following them.

This didn't escape Vogel, who lowered the sunshade and used the little vanity mirror to check the road behind them. Then he closed it again with an abrupt gesture.

'They've been tailing us since yesterday,' Borghi said. 'Do you want me to stop them?'

'They're vultures,' Vogel said. 'They're scavenging for news.'

Borghi didn't understand at first. 'You mean they're reporters?'

'No,' Vogel replied immediately without looking at him. 'They're freelance cameramen. As soon as they sniff the possibility of a juicy story, they rush to the scene with their cameras, hoping to get some footage they can sell to the networks. Reporters don't waste time on missing girls unless there's the likelihood of foul play.'

Borghi felt stupid, only now realising that Vogel had already noticed the van that morning, and even the day before, outside the Kastners' house. 'What are these vultures looking for, then?'

'They're waiting for a monster to emerge.'

Borghi was starting to understand. 'That's why we went to the river this morning . . . You wanted them to think we're going to start searching for a body.'

Vogel said nothing.

Borghi didn't like this silence. 'But you just told the prosecutor there wouldn't be any leaks.'

'Nobody likes to look bad when the public are watching, Officer Borghi,' Vogel said curtly. 'Not even our Signorina Mayer, believe me.' He turned to look at him. 'To find Anna Lou, I need resources. By itself, an appeal from the parents isn't enough.'

With these words, Vogel put an end to the discussion. They didn't touch on the subject again until they reached the operations room. But during the ride, Borghi had got a clear idea of Vogel's intentions. At first, the special agent's behaviour had struck him as cynical, but now he could understand its logic. If the media didn't take an interest in the case, if the public didn't decide to 'adopt' Anna Lou, their superiors wouldn't grant them the necessary resources to conduct the most through investigation possible.

As Vogel withdrew to his own office in the changing room, Borghi went out again. His destination was a nearby hardware shop. When he got back to the gym, he distributed cellophane packages containing house painter's overalls.

'What do we have to paint?' one of the men asked in a jokey tone.

Borghi ignored him. 'Just put them on and go to the river.'

'To do what?' the other man asked, surprised.

'We'll talk about it when you're there,' was Borghi's evasive reply.

That evening, it had started to snow. Not an abundant fall, just a light dusting that vanished upon contact with surfaces, like a mirage.

The temperature had gone down several degrees, but inside the roadside restaurant it was pleasantly warm. As usual, there weren't many customers. A couple of lorry drivers sat at two different tables, eating in silence. The only sounds were the voice of the elderly proprietor giving orders in the kitchen, the clicking of the billiard balls and the muffled sounds of the TV set above the counter, broadcasting a football match that nobody was watching.

The third customer in the restaurant was Borghi, who was sitting in one of the booths over a bowl of vegetable soup, tearing small pieces off a slice of bread, dropping them in the bowl and then collecting them with his spoon. As he did this, he kept checking the time on his mobile phone.

'Everything all right?' the waitress asked in the tone of someone who is obliged to be polite. She was wearing a red scarf and a little amethyst crucifix over her uniform. Borghi had noticed a similar crucifix on the mayor's tie pin. He assumed it was the emblem of the brotherhood.

'The soup's very good,' Borghi replied, attempting a smile.

'Would you like me to bring you anything else?'

'I'm fine for now.'

'Then would you like me to get you the bill?'

'I'll wait a while longer, thank you.' He didn't have long to wait now until his appointment.

The waitress walked away without insisting, returning sadly to the counter. Another evening with not many tips. Borghi felt sorry for her. She was almost certainly a wife and mother. Her face bore evident signs of weariness. Maybe this wasn't her only job. But there was something else. The woman kept adjusting the red scarf she wore round her neck. God alone knew what those in the brotherhood thought of husbands who beat their wives, Borghi thought.

He should have called Caroline. That day, they had exchanged only texts. She was with her parents now and Borghi wasn't worried, but she kept asking him when he would be coming home. The truth was, he didn't know. And he didn't think he even wanted to very much. There were too many things to do, everything had to be reorganised in preparation for the child's arrival. In the last few months, Borghi had had to make a whole series of decisions, one after another. To rent a larger apartment, refurbish it, put in furniture. He had changed cars, choosing a second-hand model that could transport the new family comfortably. He'd had a lot of expenses to meet and occasionally felt a kind of panic, especially now that Caroline had given up her job and was entirely dependent on him. He hated to upset her, and whenever she complained that he worked too hard, he couldn't just reply that with a daughter on the way and only one salary coming in he had no alternative.

He took out his mobile phone but once again put off calling his wife. Yet again, he checked the time. He wanted to be sure that his idea had borne fruit.

It was exactly eight o'clock. His appointment.

After a while, the lazy atmosphere in the restaurant suddenly came alive. It happened when the owner changed channels on the TV and raised the volume. The billiard players interrupted their game and the two lorry drivers turned towards the screen. A small group formed beneath the TV set, including the kitchen staff.

It was an item on the national news. Borghi recognised the banks of the river that ran through the valley of Avechot. The footage had been shot from the bridge that spanned it. He saw his men, all in painter's overalls, moving around in the mud beside the river. They were looking down on the ground, pretending to collect finds and put them in plastic bags which they then sealed, respecting to the letter the instructions he himself had given them.

'The case of young Anna Lou has taken an unexpected turn,' said the voice of the newsreader. 'Officially, the police are still treating this as a missing persons case, but this afternoon some technicians from the forensics team carried out a search along the river.'

Even though nobody was looking in his direction, Borghi tried not to betray his satisfaction. The trick had worked.

'We have no idea what they were searching for,' the newsreader continued. 'What we do know is that they have removed a number of finds which Special Agent Vogel, famous for solving several major cases, has defined as "interesting" without any other comment.'

At this point, Borghi got up from the table, went to the cash desk and paid his bill. In spite of his wretched police salary, he would leave the waitress a large tip.

27 December

Four days after the disappearance

The van, which contained a fully equipped control room, was parked in the little square in front of the town hall. Outside it, a technician with a mass of dreadlocks gathered in a ponytail was laying cables. All around, crates of equipment. And a folding chair with the name *Stella Honer* on the back of it.

Blonde, elegant, aggressively beautiful, with a touch of make-up that emphasised her large dark eyes, Stella was sitting comfortably, gazing with absent-minded curiosity at the technician, her feet propped up on a camera with the logo of the network for which she worked, her splendid legs outstretched and calves crossed, set off by shoes with vertiginously high heels. And to think that at school in the village where she grew up she hadn't been a favourite with the boys! Strangely, they had shunned her, even though she was prettier than most of the girls. For years, she had wondered why. It wasn't until much later that she had realised men were actually a little scared of her. That was why she tried at times to seem like a bit of an airhead. Not to win them over, but to entice them so that she could then snap their heads off.

There was only one man she had never managed to trick that way.

She saw him walk slowly towards her through the morning mist, his hands deep in the pockets of his cashmere overcoat and a strange smile on his face.

'Here's the man who'll tell us what we're doing here!' she said in a triumphant tone to the technician. 'This place doesn't go with my shoes.'

'I'm sorry you've had to come such a long way, Stella,' Vogel said in greeting. His tone was sardonic. 'I'm sure you had something much more important to occupy your time. I seem to recall a report of yours about a man who killed his wife . . . Or was it his fiancée? I can't remember . . . All these murders are so alike.'

Stella smiled with the air of someone who can take sarcasm and give as good as she gets. She waited for Vogel to draw level with her, then threw a glance over her shoulder at the technician. 'You know, Frank, this man has already managed to convince everyone that there's a monster out there, even though he doesn't have a single shred of evidence.'

Vogel listened with an amused expression on his face, then also turned to the technician. 'You see, Frank? That's what journalists do: they manipulate the truth to make you appear worse than they are. But Stella Honer is the queen of correspondents. When it comes to location reports, nobody can touch her!' Then, again looking at Stella: 'Isn't it a bit chilly for you to be out in the open?'

'Precisely. A missing girl? Come on now! If I have to freeze my butt off, I want to do it for a real story. But I don't see any story here. I'm going home.'

The technician, who hadn't said a word and wasn't even interested in their conversation, went back inside the van, leaving them alone.

Stella dropped her caustic tone and went on the attack. 'Where is your kidnapper, Vogel? Because, frankly, I don't believe there is one.'

Vogel was unfazed. He knew it wouldn't be easy to convince Stella, but he was well prepared. 'A single road leading in and out of the valley. At one end, a speed camera, at the other the security camera over a petrol pump. We're checking all the vehicles that passed through and taking a look at their owners. But I already know it'll be completely useless.'

Stella seemed puzzled. 'Why go to all that effort, then?'

Vogel took the first rabbit out of his hat. 'To demonstrate my theory, which is that the girl never left here.'

Stella was silent for a moment too long, a sign that the case was starting to interest her. 'Go on . . .'

Vogel knew he should be grateful to Borghi for the fact that Stella had gone to the bother of coming all the way up here. It had been a brilliant idea of the young officer's to get all those overalls. The boy knew what he was doing. But now it was up to the master to play his role. He resumed speaking in an emphatic tone. 'A remote valley. But one day, they discover a miracle under these mountains, a miracle called fluorite. So normal people become suddenly rich. A place where everybody knows everybody else, where nothing ever happens. Or rather, things do happen, but nobody talks about them, nobody says anything. Because the custom here is to hide everything, even wealth. You know what they say, don't you? Small community, big secrets.' It was a perfect introduction, and now, to rein-force his story, Vogel put his hand in his coat pocket and took out the diary Anna Lou's mother had entrusted to him. He threw it at Stella, who caught it in mid-air. Stella first looked at it for a moment, then started leafing through it.

'*Twenty-third of March,*' she read aloud. '*Today I went with my friend Priscilla when she took her kitten to the vet. The vet gave it its annual vaccination and said it should go on a diet . . .*' She turned to another page. '*Thirteenth of June: along with the boys from the brotherhood, we're preparing a recital about the childhood of Jesus . . .*' She leafed through more pages. '*Sixth of November: I've learned how to make bead bracelets . . .*' Stella closed the little book abruptly and looked pensively at Vogel. 'Kittens and bracelets?'

'Were you expecting something different?' Vogel asked, amused.

'These are the things I would have written if my mother had been in the habit of sneaking a look at my diary . . .'

'Well?'

'Don't pull my leg. Where's the real diary?'

Vogel seemed pleased with himself. 'You see? I was right: a religious family and an upright girl . . . But when you dig, something always comes out.'

'You think Anna Lou Kastner had something to hide? A relationship with someone older, maybe even an adult?'

'You're going too fast, Stella,' Vogel said, laughing.

Stella looked at him suspiciously. 'But you wanted me to read this so that I should think . . . Aren't you afraid I might spread the rumour that there's something murky in the girl's life? The public would like that.'

'You'd never do it,' Vogel replied confidently. 'The first rule of our profession: sanctify the victim. Monsters aren't so monstrous if people start to think: "Hey, that one was asking for it!" Don't you agree?'

Stella pondered this for a moment. 'I thought you still had a grudge against me because of the Mutilator.'

Yes, it was true: he did have a grudge against her over the case that had lost him a good deal of his prestige and credibility. The 'Mutilator' had been a disaster in terms of strategy. Even though, when it came down to it, Vogel had had his reasons for acting as he had, they were too complicated to explain. And the public hadn't understood. 'I'm not the kind of person to bear a grudge,' he assured her. 'So – have we made peace?'

Stella, though, knew the true purpose of the armistice. 'You want me here because you know that then the other networks will follow suit.' She pretended to think about it a while longer, even though she had already made her mind up. 'But you will give me an exclusive on every development in the investigation, won't you?'

Vogel had known she would try to negotiate. First he shook his head, then he said, 'I'll give you a twenty-five-minute head start on the competition.' He said it in the tone of someone making a final offer.

Stella pretended to be indignant. 'Twenty-five minutes? That's nothing.'

'It's an eternity, and you know it.' Vogel looked at his watch. 'For example, you have twenty-five minutes with that' – indicating the diary – 'before I put it with the case evidence.'

Stella made to protest, but in her mind the countdown had already begun. She got out her mobile and started photographing the pages of Anna Lou Kastner's diary.

*

By 11 a.m., Stella Honer had put together her first report from Avechot for the morning bulletins. Not far from Anna Lou's house, a permanent location had been set up from which she would tell viewers all about the latest developments in the investigation. At midday, the network's main news magazine programme joined Stella to be updated in real time about the case.

That afternoon, Vogel gathered the officers on his team in the school gym for another briefing.

'From now on, things are going to be different,' he announced to a very attentive audience. 'What will happen next will be crucial in solving the mystery of Anna Lou Kastner's disappearance.'

Vogel certainly knew how to inspire his men, Borghi thought.

'This isn't just a local case any more. The whole country has its eyes on Avechot now, and on us. We can't disappoint them.' He repeated these last words, as if to emphasise that if they didn't find the culprit it would be their fault. 'Many among you must be wondering how the attention the case is getting in the media might benefit us. Well, the bait's been set, now let's hope that someone falls into the trap.'

From the way they were listening to him, Borghi realised that things really had changed. Three days ago, they had regarded him as an intruder who had come up here to tell them how to do their job and stick his nose in their business. A conceited big-city officer looking for fame on the back of their efforts. But now they saw him as a guide, a man able to bring the nightmare to an end and, above all, someone ready to share the glory with them.

Before explaining his plan, Vogel gave a short preamble.

'We all like being famous, even those who would never admit it. Something strange happens: at first you don't think you need it, you think you can do without it and just lead a quiet life. And you're right to think that way.' He paused. 'But as soon as the spotlight's on you, something else happens. Suddenly, you discover you like the fact you're no longer the anonymous individual you thought you were. You had no idea of it before, but now you actually start to like it. You feel different from the others, special, and you want this sensation never to end, you want it to last a long time, maybe for ever.' Vogel folded his arms and took a step towards the blackboard, on which the date *23 December* still stood out. He looked at it, then began walking back and forth. 'Right now, everyone's telling the story of Anna Lou, a young girl with red hair and freckles who vanished into thin air, but the kidnapper knows that what they're really talking about is him and what he's done. He's succeeded, in so far as we aren't yet able to identify him. He's done a good job, and he's proud of it. But it's only a "good" job, nothing more. What does he need to make it a *masterpiece*? A stage. So if you can be sure of one thing, it's that he won't stay in the shadows and let someone else steal the limelight. He'll want his share of fame: when it comes down to it, he's the real star of the show. We're here because he decided it, because he wanted it. Because he's run the risk of being captured, of losing everything. That's why he's now going to claim the tribute that's due to him.' Vogel stopped and looked at all of them. 'Somewhere out there, our man is savouring the sweet taste of celebrity. But it's not enough for him, he wants more. And that's how we'll flush him out.'

With this agenda, Borghi thought, the search for Anna Lou

was officially relegated to the background. Now there was another priority.

To flush out the monster.

At this point, Vogel gave a concrete example of what he had in mind. First, he sent a couple of his men off to buy candles and small lights and a dozen cuddly toy cats. Then he ordered a few plain-clothes officers to place these objects by a low wall in front of the Kastners' house.

Now it was just a matter of waiting.

By about 10 p.m., the main newspapers in the country all had their own correspondents outside Anna Lou's house. It was the Stella Honer effect, but not only that.

When, at dinner time, the TV news bulletins had broadcast that lots of anonymous, compassionate people had started leaving tokens of their solidarity with the Kastner family on the low wall in front of the house, many others had decided to follow their example. A spontaneous pilgrimage had begun, involving not only the townspeople of Avechot, but also people from the neighbouring valleys. Some had come all the way from the cities to take part in this demonstration of support.

In her heartbreaking appeal, Anna Lou's mother had promised her daughter that when she returned home she would finally get the cat she had so wanted. Vogel had homed in on those words, and now cats of all kinds – cuddly toys, rag dolls, ceramic figurines – surrounded the house, occupying the entire perimeter wall and much of the adjoining street. In the midst of them, candles and small lights produced a reddish glow, conveying a powerful sense of warmth in the sharp cold of the winter evening. Many of the gifts were accompanied by notes. Some were addressed to Anna Lou, some to her parents, and others were simply prayers.

There was an almost constant coming and going of people. To stop an invasion of cars, the mayor had been forced to order the closure of the surrounding streets. Despite that, the area was under siege. But everything was done in an orderly fashion. The pilgrims would arrive, stand for a few minutes in silence, as if collecting their thoughts, then leave.

Vogel had sent his own men to mix with the crowd. They were in plain clothes, wore well-hidden earphones and carried microphones concealed in the lapels of their jackets. Knowing that reporters were in the habit of listening in on police communications, Vogel had brought in sophisticated transmitters that were impossible to intercept.

'Don't forget that we're interested in male suspects,' Borghi said over the radio, 'especially any men who are here on their own.' Next to him, Vogel was keeping a close watch on the scene before him. They had deliberately positioned themselves on the edge of the crowd.

This had been going on for a couple of hours now.

They took it for granted that the kidnapper was a man because there were very few cases in the manuals of abductions of adolescents being carried out by adult women. This wasn't just a statistical fact, it was a matter of common sense.

They could even venture a profile of the perpetrator. Contrary to the popular conception, kidnappers were almost never either misfits or career criminals. They were usually normal individuals, averagely well educated, capable of interacting with others and, for that very reason, able to conceal their behaviour and pass unobserved. Their true nature was a secret they guarded jealously. They were clever and far-sighted. All this made them hard to identify.

'All quiet here, over,' one of the officers said into his radio. Each of them had been instructed to report every ten minutes.

Vogel felt the need to intervene with a little speech, to make sure the tension didn't drop. 'If the kidnapper really does come here this evening, he knows we'll be here, but doesn't care, he wants to feel the sensation of walking undisturbed in the middle of those who are hunting for him.' But there was an effective way to spot him. 'Don't forget that he's here because he wants to enjoy the spectacle. If we're lucky, that won't be enough for him: he'll want to take a souvenir away with him.'

His recommendation was to concentrate, not on those who brought a gift, but on those who surreptitiously tried to remove something.

Just then, Vogel and Borghi noticed a strange movement in the crowd. It was as if someone had given a silent command and all those present had turned in the same direction. The two officers now did so, too, and realised that what had drawn their attention was the sudden appearance of Anna Lou's parents in the doorway of the house.

Bruno had his arm around his wife's shoulders. They were flanked by members of the brotherhood, who were all wearing little amethyst crucifixes and had arranged themselves in a semicircle, as if to protect the Kastners. Immediately, the TV cameras turned to the front door of the house.

Although she was obviously exhausted, it was once again Maria Kastner who spoke, addressing the small crowd. 'My husband and I wanted to thank you all. This is a very difficult time in our lives, but your affection and our faith in the Lord are a great comfort.' Then she pointed to the array of kittens and candles. 'Anna Lou would be happy about all this.'

From the members of the brotherhood there rose a unison 'Amen'.

The crowd burst into applause.

They all seemed moved, but Vogel didn't believe in their compassion. On the contrary, he was convinced that many were there because of the media stir and were driven by curiosity, nothing more. Where were you all on Christmas Day, when this family really needed solace?

Borghi was thinking the same thing. While less cynical than Vogel, he couldn't help pondering on how things had changed in just a few days. The morning they had gone to see the Kastners, there had been nobody outside the house apart from the van with the 'vultures'. He recalled Vogel's applause and how it had echoed through the silent neighbourhood. Borghi still wasn't sure what that act meant, or why, on getting into the car immediately afterwards, Vogel had felt the need to say of Bruno Kastner, 'The man's dying to tell us something.'

While Anna Lou's parents, still guarded by the members of the brotherhood, were being greeted by some of those present, a voice came over the radio. 'To your right, sir, near the end of the street: the boy in the black hooded top has just stolen something.' Vogel and Borghi turned simultaneously in the direction indicated. It took them a while to spot him in the crowd.

The teenager was wearing a denim jacket over his top and his hood was pulled down over his head to conceal his face. He had probably taken advantage of that moment when everyone was distracted to appropriate something, which he was now hiding under his clothes as he hurried away.

'He took a cuddly kitten, I saw him,' the officer assured them over the radio.

Borghi signalled to another officer who was closer to the route taken by the boy.

'I have him,' he said over the radio. 'I have his face. I'll stop him.'

'No,' Vogel said peremptorily. 'I don't want him to suspect anything.'

In the meantime, the boy had got on a skateboard and was speeding away undisturbed.

Borghi was incredulous about Vogel's decision. 'Why don't we at least follow him?'

'Think what would happen if one of the reporters who are here saw that,' Vogel replied without losing sight of the suspect.

He was right, Borghi hadn't considered that.

Vogel turned to face him. 'He's a boy on a skateboard, how far can he go? We have his face, we'll find him again.'

30 December

Seven days after the disappearance

The roadside restaurant was packed.

On the window overlooking the petrol pump, the words *Happy Holidays* were still visible. The owner was going back and forth between the kitchen and the tables, making sure that everyone was served and satisfied. He'd had to hire more staff to deal with the sudden invasion of customers. There were reporters, TV technicians, news photographers, but also ordinary citizens who had come to Avechot to see for themselves the places mentioned in the story the whole country was talking about.

Vogel called them 'horror tourists'.

Many had faced a long journey with their families. There were quite a few children, and there was a euphoric atmosphere in the room, as if they were on an outing. At the end of the day, they would take souvenir photographs home with them as well as the feeling that they had taken part, however marginally, in a media event that fascinated millions of people. They seemed not to care that, a few hundred metres away, dog units and frogmen, as well as search teams and forensics, were at work looking for any trace, any clue as to the fate of a sixteen-year-old girl. Vogel had predicted it, and it had come to pass: the media uproar had convinced his superiors to ignore budget restrictions and grant him the resources he needed. They would do everything they could not to lose face in the public spotlight.

Vogel was sitting at the same table he had occupied on Christmas Day, when he was the restaurant's only customer. As usual, he was writing meticulously in his black notebook with his silver fountain pen as he ate.

This morning, he was wearing a grey-green tweed suit and a dark tie. His elegance was in marked contrast to the other customers. But that was how it should be. He needed to mark the difference between himself and the rowdy, coarse humanity around him. The more he observed them, the more he realised something important.

They had already forgotten Anna Lou.

The silent heroine of the story had been relegated to the background. And her silence was a pretext for other people's chatter, for their being able to say anything they wanted about her and her brief life. The media were doing it, but so were ordinary people – in the street, at the supermarket, in the bars. Without any shame. Vogel had predicted this, too. Whenever it happened, a strange mechanism was set off. Real events turned into a kind of serial.

A crime occurred every seven seconds.

But only an infinitesimal number of them had newspaper articles, TV news items, entire episodes of talk shows devoted to them. In this minority of cases, criminal and psychiatric experts were called in, psychologists, even philosophers. Rivers of ink were spilled, and hours and hours of the TV schedules given over to the case. This could all go on for weeks, sometimes for months. If you were lucky, for years.

What nobody said was that a crime could give rise to a genuine *industry*.

A crime well told generated excellent results in terms of audience share and could bring in millions in sponsorship and advertising to a network, all for the minimum outlay.

A correspondent, a camera and a cameraman.

If a striking crime – like a terrible homicide or an inexplicable disappearance – happened in a small community, during the months of media overexposure that community would see a growth in the presence of visitors and consequently its own wealth.

Nobody could explain why one crime suddenly became more popular than others. But everyone agreed that there was an imponderable element.

Vogel had a particular intuition about this, a kind of sixth sense, to which he owed his fame.

Except in the case of the Mutilator.

He mustn't forget the lesson he had learned then. But considering the impact that Anna Lou's disappearance was having, this was a great opportunity to redeem himself.

Obviously, he couldn't expect everything to happen according to the script he had in his head. In the days following the spontaneous pilgrimage to the Kastners' house, a number of unpleasant episodes had occurred.

The inhabitants of Avechot, who at first had been passionate in their participation, had suddenly started to keep their distance. It was a natural effect of overexposure. The media had begun to invade everyone's lives. And since there were still no answers, they had spread a sense in the public that the solution to the mystery was hidden somewhere in those houses, among those people.

It wasn't yet a specific accusation, but it was rather like one.

In Avechot, they had always been very suspicious of strangers, and becoming the object of a process of thinly veiled defamation had accentuated their suspicion. The brotherhood, in particular, had shown signs of not appreciating all this media attention.

At first, the inhabitants had avoided the cameras. Then they had started giving brusque, sometimes angry answers to the reporters' questions. In such an incandescent climate, one of rage ready to explode, it was inevitable that someone would pay the price.

That someone was a young outsider who had come to the town to look for work. His only fault, or carelessness, had been to approach a local girl to ask for information. Unfortunately for him, this had been seen by customers in a bar, who had first threatened him, then resorted to force and beaten him up.

After lunch, as he was taking advantage of another day of winter sun to walk back to the operations room, Vogel saw Prosecutor Mayer waiting for him in the forecourt in front of the gym.

From her expression, it was obvious he couldn't expect a pleasant conversation.

She came towards him resolutely, her heels echoing on the

asphalt. 'You can't come here, sow doubts in these people's minds, and then think nothing will happen,' she said in an accusatory tone.

'It was all their doing,' Vogel retorted. When he had set foot in the valley he had found himself up against a community that was even more confused than it was frightened. Huddled there in the mountains, they had assumed they were safe from the ugliness of the world. They weren't prepared to live in a state of uncertainty. And even now, they were convinced that the evil had come from outside. But deep in their hearts, they harboured the suspicion that it had always been among them, nurtured in silence, protected. And Vogel knew that this terrified them more than anything else.

'Exactly what I was afraid of has happened,' Mayer said. 'You've mounted a show.'

'Do you know a single case of a runaway teenager that hasn't been resolved within a matter of days?' The question sounded like a challenge. 'By now, we should be ruling that out as a possibility and concentrating on other things. We're no longer dealing with a girl who's run away from home, don't you understand?'

On Vogel's express orders, Mayer hadn't been informed about the boy on the skateboard whom they'd spotted three evenings earlier outside the Kastners' house.

'Even supposing we have a crime on our hands, that doesn't give you the right to get the people of Avechot riled up, or to bring in TV crews and photographers. Because you brought them here, don't deny it.'

Vogel had no desire to stay and listen to her complaints. It had been a good day so far, and the walk from the restaurant had given him renewed energy. So he turned his back on her, intending to go, then thought better of it and retraced his steps. 'No screams,' he said.

Mayer looked at him uncomprehendingly.

'Anna Lou didn't scream as she was being taken away. If she had, the neighbours would have heard. All I had to do to attract attention was clap my hands. I stood outside her house and clapped, and everybody looked out of their windows.'

'Are you insinuating that the girl followed someone of her own free will?'

Vogel fell silent, letting the idea germinate in the prosecutor's head.

'She trusted him, looked him in the face,' Mayer said. 'And if she looked him in the face . . .'

Vogel completed the sentence for her. 'If she looked him in the face, then Anna Lou's already dead.' He followed this statement with a long pause.

Mayer's expression had changed. The anger had been replaced by something else. Dismay.

'We can wait for things to take their course or we can prevent it happening again,' Vogel concluded. 'Which do you prefer?'

This time, he did walk away. The prosecutor stood there motionless for a few moments, until she heard a coughing fit that made her turn.

Stella Honer was lurking behind the corner of the building, surreptitiously smoking a cigarette. Obviously, she had seen and heard everything. 'If the public knew my little sins it'd be the end,' she said in an amused tone, throwing the cigarette on the ground and crushing it with the tip of her shoe. 'It's hard enough for a woman to make her way, don't you find?' Then she turned serious. 'He's an arsehole, but he knows his job.

And opportunities like this happen rarely in a prosecutor's career.'

Mayer watched her as she walked past, but didn't reply.

The gym being used as an operations room was in ferment. The number of police officers had increased fivefold. The school desks had been replaced by real desks, with computers and telephones that never stopped ringing. Instead of the old slate blackboard, there was now a large white screen and a video projector. The huge noticeboard had filled up with reports, photographs and forensics results. In the centre of the room was a scale model of the valley, updated every so often with indications of the areas being searched by the crime scene teams, who had been able to work twenty-four-seven thanks to special night-vision equipment.

'Sir, the people from Alpine Rescue have just finished checking the northern crevasses,' a policeman in shirtsleeves and tie reported to Borghi, who was supervising activities.

'Good, now they need to move to the eastern slope.' Borghi turned to another officer sitting at a desk, making an animated phone call. 'What happened to the helicopter we requested?'

The officer moved the receiver away from his mouth for a moment. 'They say it'll be here by midday.'

'They said that yesterday. Stay on that phone and don't hang up until they give you a specific time.'

'Yes, sir.'

The helicopter was important, Vogel had emphasised that several times. It made much more of an impression than a pack of dogs busily sniffing around. And it would be visible from every vantage point. The cameramen would be kept busy all day long staying with it. By now, Borghi had embraced Vogel's philosophy in full. But as he walked over to the scale model to update the positions of the units on the ground, he had to admit that this strategy and all the effort they were making were proving to be in vain. Apart from the boy on the skateboard, they didn't yet have a concrete lead. And there was still no trace of Anna Lou Kastner.

Borghi reached the scale model and paused. He had noticed something. He stopped a passing officer and pointed discreetly to the fire door. 'How long has he been there?'

The officer turned and also noticed Bruno Kastner standing by the wall with what looked like a letter in his hands. He was looking around with a humble, disoriented air, as if waiting for someone to notice him.

'I don't know,' the officer replied. 'Maybe an hour.'

Borghi dropped what he was about to do and went up to the man. 'Good day to you, Signor Kastner.'

Kastner nodded in return.

'What can I do for you?'

The man seemed lost. He couldn't find the words. Borghi decided to help him. He went closer to him and placed a reassuring hand on his shoulder. 'Has something happened?'

'It's just that ... I'd like to talk to Special Agent Vogel, please.'

Borghi sensed that this wasn't a simple request. It was an appeal for help. Vogel's prophecy that Kastner was dying to tell them something echoed in Borghi's head. 'Of course,' he said. 'Come with me.'

In the changing room that was serving as his office, Vogel was sitting with his feet up on the desk, busy reading documents with great attention, a hint of a smile hovering over his lips.

The documents weren't police reports, they were TV ratings data.

Every day he received viewing figures for the talk shows and news bulletins that featured the Kastner case, as well as a round-up of what was happening on the internet. They had gained two points in the total share. That meant the disappearance would still be in the headlines of the leading newspapers. In addition, the case remained at the top of the list of trending topics on social networks, and was being taken up and commented on by all the bloggers.

As far as the numbers went, the public hadn't yet tired of the case. But Vogel knew that if he didn't give the media something else soon, their interest would diminish and they would move on to juicier stories.

The public was a fearsome beast. And it was ravenous.

When he heard a knock at the door of the changing room, Vogel took his feet off the table and hid the documents away in a drawer. 'Come in,' he said.

Officer Borghi appeared in the doorway. 'The girl's father is here. Do you have a moment?'

Vogel motioned to bring him in. Bruno Kastner entered behind Borghi, still clutching the envelope in his hand.

'Please, Signor Kastner,' Vogel said, going to meet him. Then he motioned him to one of the benches in front of the lockers and sat down next to him. Borghi remained standing by the door, arms folded.

'I don't want to disturb you,' Kastner said.

'You're not disturbing me at all.'

'The afternoon she disappeared, I wasn't there. I was a long way away, with a customer. And I keep thinking that if I'd been at home, all this might have been avoided. When my wife called to tell me that Anna Lou hadn't come home, part of me already knew.'

'These are needless regrets,' Vogel said, encouragingly. He didn't tell him that they had checked his alibi and taken him off the list of suspects.

'We heard what they're saying on TV,' the man went on. 'Is it true that someone took my Anna Lou? Is that what happened?'

Vogel gave a slight smile, followed by a look of feigned compassion. But he couldn't help glancing down at the envelope. 'You shouldn't believe everything the reporters say.'

'But you are looking for someone, aren't you? Can you at least tell me that?'

Once again, Vogel was evasive. 'In my experience, it's best if the relatives don't know all the developments in an investigation. That's partly because we don't want to leave any stone unturned, so we're constantly following new leads. It can be confusing to an outsider.' It can also create false hopes, he would have liked to add.

Bruno Kastner didn't insist. He started fiddling with the envelope. It took him a while to open it and take out the contents. Vogel and Borghi exchanged questioning glances.

Inside the envelope was a photograph. It was the one showing Anna with her best friend.

Kastner held it out. Vogel took it and looked at it, uncomprehendingly.

'There are days when I can't get it out of my head,' Kastner said, putting his big hands together and wringing them until the skin over the knuckles turned white. 'Why her? I mean, Anna Lou isn't . . . beautiful.'

The statement had cost him an enormous effort, Borghi thought. What father could say something like that about his little princess? The man really must be in desperate search of an explanation.

Vogel studied the photograph. The difference between the two girls was obvious. One looked like a woman, the other like a child. That was precisely why he had chosen her, he would have liked to tell Kastner. An invisible girl, the kind you can watch from a distance without arousing suspicion. The kind you can spirit away on a winter evening, a stone's throw from her house, without anyone noticing a thing. But then Vogel realised that there was something else. Kastner's powerful shoulders slumped in a gesture of surrender.

'I did something I'm ashamed of,' Kastner said in a thin voice. It sounded like the beginning of a confession. 'The other girl in the photograph is called Priscilla. One day, I looked for her number on Anna Lou's mobile phone. I started to call her. As soon as she answered, I would hang up. I don't think she knew it was me. I don't know why I did it.'

Vogel and Borghi looked at each other again. A tiny tear appeared on Bruno Kastner's anxious, weary face and slid rapidly down to his chin. He sniffed and with an almost childish gesture rubbed his nose with the back of his hand.

Vogel took him by the arm and helped him to his feet. 'Why don't you go home now and forget all this? Believe me, it's better this way.' He motioned to Borghi to take hold of the man.

Borghi approached, but Kastner hadn't finished yet. 'My wife has faith, the brotherhood ... It's hard to be a perfect father and husband with such an example of rectitude by your side. Sometimes I envy her, you know? Maria never wavers, never has doubts, never. Not even now that this has happened to us. On the contrary, she believes it's part of a design, that

God has thought it would be better for us to be confronted with grief. But what kind of grief is this? Should we be in mourning? If someone told us that Anna Lou is dead, at least we could resign ourselves. But like this . . . And I've been an unworthy father, because I should have taken care of her, protected her. Instead . . . I've been weak. I've fallen into temptation.'

'I'm sure you're a good parent,' Vogel said reassuringly, but only to convince him to drop this aspect of the case. If the media got wind of it, they would crucify him. Even though what he'd done amounted to very little, in everyone's eyes Bruno Kastner would become the father who molested young girls. A monster. That would harm the image of perfection that Vogel had constructed around the family. And distract attention from the real culprit, whoever he was.

'There was a boy,' Kastner said as they were almost at the exit.

Vogel's interest was immediately aroused. 'What boy?'

Kastner kept his eyes down as he spoke. 'Her mother would never have let her see him anyway, he doesn't belong to the brotherhood. But it's possible Anna Lou liked him.'

'What boy?' Vogel insisted.

'I don't know who he is, but I used to see him hanging around outside our house. A black hooded top and a skateboard.'

Borghi was alarmed by the revelation. Vogel, though, was merely angry. 'Why are you only telling me this now?'

At last, Kastner looked up at him. 'Because it's hard to point the finger at someone else when you think it's God's will to punish you for your sins.'

31 December

Eight days after the disappearance

The name of the boy on the skateboard was Mattia.

The police had already identified him some days earlier, well before Bruno Kastner had gone to see Vogel to clear his conscience.

To be precise, it had happened at about midnight on the night of the pilgrimage to Anna Lou's house, when the boy had taken one of the cuddly toys that people had left spontaneously outside the house. A pink kitten.

But Vogel had put a blackout on that area of the investigation. The name of the teenager and what had happened that evening absolutely mustn't get through to the reporters, or it would irredeemably compromise what they had achieved.

Vogel, however, was conscious that the reporters were still trying to buy information. He feared that one of the local officers would be attracted by the prospect of a Christmas bonus to supplement his wretched salary. But he had been good at preventing anything like that, instilling in his men the terror of being discovered. He had simply had to tell them that any leak would be punished with dismissal.

Mattia was sixteen years old, like Anna Lou. He was something of a problem child.

'I spoke to the boy's psychiatrist,' Borghi said, bringing Vogel up to date on the latest developments. 'The doctor's name is Flores, and he's been treating him since Mattia and his mother moved to Avechot nine months ago. Apparently, the family have moved around a lot in the last few years. The reason is always the same: the boy's character disorders.'

'Tell me more,' Vogel said, apparently very interested.

Borghi had taken notes. 'Mattia is a solitary boy, incapable of integration and communication. In addition, he has sudden aggressive impulses. In the places where he's lived with his mother, he's always got into trouble. An attack on another teenager, or an uncontrollable fit of anger. He once smashed everything in a shop for no reason. Each time, the mother has felt obliged to abandon everything and move.'

She probably thought that was the best medicine for her son, Vogel told himself. She must have hoped a radical change of place and habits would sort things out. In reality, it had only made them worse. Perhaps because the mother was ashamed, or perhaps because she felt guilty towards her son, who had grown up without a father figure, running away and starting again was a constant in their lives.

'Mattia was treated at a clinic in the past,' Borghi went on. 'This Dr Flores told me that currently he's taking drugs to control his anger.'

Now that he knew of Mattia's tormented past, it immediately

struck Vogel that the mystery of Anna Lou's disappearance might be on the verge of being solved.

So far, they hadn't gathered much information about the boy. They knew only that the mother got by with humiliating and ill-paid jobs, that she had been hired by a cleaning firm, and in addition washed dishes in one of the few restaurants that had remained open in Avechot. Mother and son lived in a modest little house on the outskirts of the village. Vogel had already had it put under discreet surveillance.

Mattia, though, hadn't been seen again.

He had vanished into thin air, and all trace of him had vanished with him, just like Anna Lou Kastner. But the circumstances of his sudden disappearance were different.

The mother was carrying on with her life. She went to work and returned home every evening, as if nothing had happened. And she hadn't felt the need to report her son's disappearance – a sign that the boy was hiding and she was protecting him. That indicated that she knew Mattia had done something wrong. Not the usual fist fight with a classmate. Something more serious.

They knew the boy wasn't at home: the bugs they had placed around the building hadn't picked up any suspicious noises when the mother was out. Vogel hadn't yet ordered a search, because that would alert the woman. Instead, he was having her followed, hoping she would lead them to her son.

But so far that hadn't happened.

It looked as if any contact between the two had abruptly ceased. In addition, the boy's mobile phone was constantly off.

Wherever he was, Mattia couldn't hide much longer without food and with the police combing the area in search of Anna

Lou. Vogel knew that, which was why he preferred to wait for the boy himself to step out of the shadows.

The frogmen were inspecting a sewage well near the mine. According to the maps that Borghi had got from the town hall, there were at least thirty such wells, some operational, some now disused. Not to mention those not listed. In addition, the valley was criss-crossed by a host of underground tunnels, a real spider's web.

They were perfect for hiding a body. And it would take an eternity to search them all.

The sky was a single block of cast iron enclosed by the mountains. The effect was like a vice slowly squeezing everything. Borghi parked the car a few metres from the spot where the frogmen were hard at work. He watched them from behind the veil of condensation that covered the windscreen. The silence inside the car and the thin diaphragm of steam gave the scene an unreal quality, as if it were part of a fairy tale. An evil fairy tale, where the only possible ending is an unhappy one.

Borghi was conducting the search without much expectation of success: the frogmen would take turns going down into the muddy water and each would re-emerge after fifteen minutes, shaking his head. That same gesture, that same choreography, was being repeated incessantly.

The saloon was parked in the middle of a bare field. The cold of the morning was sharp. Borghi put his hands together in the shape of a shell and blew on them to warm them. The relief only lasted a moment. For the first time since the beginning of the investigation, he felt a sense of frustration. Part of him was thinking that they would never get to the bottom of it, that all that remained of Anna Lou Kastner would be a name on a list of people who had gone missing without a reason.

After a while, it was as if they had never existed.

But there was another reason he was troubled, something that really bothered him. He kept thinking about something that Vogel had mentioned during the first briefing, almost fleetingly. Which was that Anna Lou had only five numbers in the contacts list of her mobile phone.

Mummy, Daddy, home, grandparents' house and parish church.

Vogel had mentioned this to emphasise how far above suspicion the girl's usual behaviour was. That brief list of names and places was also the extent of her life, of her world. It was all simple and comprehensible, no subterfuges, no secrets. Everything exposed to the light of day.

Mummy, Daddy, home, grandparents' house and parish church.

Anna Lou's whole universe was concentrated in those places, among those people. There was also the school, obviously, and the skating rink. But the things that really counted were on that list. They were the numbers she usually called, and it was from them that she would look for help or comfort when in need.

But seeing Bruno Kastner the day before had aroused a doubt in him. A suspicion that had started when he had seen the photograph the man had brought with him.

Anna Lou with her best friend, Priscilla.

In all this time, their investigation had been concentrated elsewhere. They had devised tricks to involve the media and receive more funds. Then they had used those resources to intensify the search. They had managed to identify the boy with the skateboard and were now hunting him in secret. But it hadn't occurred to anybody, even the media, to talk to Priscilla and see if she knew anything that could help them. The reason was simple. It wasn't just carelessness.

Mummy, Daddy, home, grandparents' house and parish church.

If Priscilla, as Bruno Kastner claimed, was Anna Lou's best friend, why wasn't her number in the address book on the mobile phone?

Borghi lifted the sleeve of his coat to the windscreen and used it to wipe off the condensation. Then he started the engine. The time had come to discover the answer.

Avechot was preparing to greet the New Year in a sober manner. People would celebrate at home because the mayor had cancelled all the planned public events.

'There can be no joy if a member of the community is unable to celebrate with us,' he had declared to reporters, following his heartfelt words with an emotion-filled silence.

In the last few days, he had been very active in providing the media with a positive image of the valley's inhabitants. To silence any slander, he had even recruited local volunteers for the search parties. They were beating the woods inch by inch, alongside the police.

Late that morning, he had presided over a prayer meeting held in the brotherhood's assembly hall, dedicated once again to the return of Anna Lou. The Kastners had also been present.

Sitting in his car, Borghi saw them leave the hall and head for home, still escorted by a small group of brotherhood members who were shielding them from the reporters and photographers trying to steal a comment or an image of their pain. But Borghi was interested in something else.

Priscilla was one of the last to come out. She was wearing a green parka and combat boots, her hair was gathered in a bun and she had sunglasses on even though the sky was overcast. She wasn't flashily dressed, but she looked pretty all the same. She was in the company of an adult woman. The resemblance between the two was so striking, the woman could only have been her mother. The two set off, ignoring the cameras and microphones that were now being thrust at the members of the community. While the mother talked with the other members, Priscilla lingered behind her, as if she wanted to put a distance between them. At the same time, she looked around, assessing the situation. After a while, she took advantage of the crush to move away from the group and head off in another direction.

Borghi saw her turn the corner and get into a sports car that set off rapidly. There was a boy at the wheel.

He soon caught up with them in an open space behind the village's small cemetery. He parked some hundred metres from the other car. From that position, he could see the two of them as they stripped off their clothes, all the while kissing so passionately that they didn't even realise someone was watching them. When Borghi decided he'd had enough, he opened the window, placed the flashing light on the roof of his car and switched it on, setting off a brief siren.

The boy and girl stopped immediately, startled.

Borghi drove forward slowly, giving them time to get dressed. When he reached the other car, he brought his to a halt. Then he got out and walked towards them. He leaned in at the window on the driver's side. 'Hi, kids.' His smile was deliberately menacing.

'Good morning, officer, is there any problem?' The boy was trying to appear calm. In spite of his bluster, you could see that he was scared stiff.

'I assume you borrowed your father's car without permission, son. I don't think you're old enough to drive, or am I mistaken?' It was a typical police phrase. In reality, he wanted to underline the fact that while the boy might have a licence, his passenger was still a minor.

'Listen, we haven't done anything wrong,' the boy tried to reply, stupidly. But his voice was trembling.

'Are you trying to act tough with me, son?' Borghi's tone was now that of a police officer losing patience.

To stop that idiot from saying anything else that might make the situation worse, Priscilla leaned towards the window. 'I beg you, officer, don't say anything to my mother.'

Borghi looked at her and let a few seconds go by, as if he was thinking. 'All right, but I'll drive you home myself.'

As they drove through the streets of the village, Borghi managed to get a better look at her. She was quite short, but her boots made her look taller. There were coloured piercings in one ear and a small amount of eye pencil around her eyes. She had delicate features. Beneath the green parka she was wearing a black polo neck sweater that gave a sense of her small, firm breasts. She was also wearing a pair of flowered leggings, with a split at the height of one thigh. A deodorant with an excessively sweet strawberry smell mingled with a vague smell of sweat, cigarette smoke and mint chewing gum. All in all, she was a typical teenager.

Borghi wanted to get some information from her. He had deliberately scared her at first, and now she was vulnerable. He knew that Priscilla would be honest with him in order not to make her position worse. 'What can you tell me about Anna Lou?'

'What do you want to know?'

'You're her best friend, aren't you?'

'Well, she was a really good person, I think.' The girl was watching the road, all the while eating the pink varnish from the nails on her right hand.

'What do you mean?'

'I mean the kids in our school gossip a lot. Some of them are now saying she had secrets. But she was good to everybody and never got angry.'

'What type of secrets?'

'That she slept around, that she did it with older guys. All bullshit.'

'Did you go out together? What did she like to do?'

'I was the only person her mother would let her go out with. Not that there's much to do in Avechot in the evening. And anyway, she only had permission to see me in the afternoons, when she came to my house to do homework.'

'But you weren't in the same class.'

'No, that's right. But we saw each other because Anna Lou's very good at mathematics and gives me a hand.'

'As far as you know, did she have a boyfriend?'

Priscilla gave a little laugh. 'A boyfriend? Oh, no.'

'Did she like anyone?'

'Yes, my cat.' She laughed again. But her humour wasn't appreciated, so she turned serious. 'Anna Lou was different. She wasn't interested in things like pleasing the boys or getting up to mischief with her friends.'

'So you were the only one she saw, apart obviously from her classmates.'

'That's right.'

Priscilla was determined to be thought of as the person Anna Lou was friendliest with. Maybe to divert suspicion from herself, Borghi thought. 'What do you think happened to her?'

Priscilla paused. 'I don't know. They're saying all kinds of things, like that she ran away. I don't believe that.'

'Maybe something happened and she didn't tell you.'

'Impossible: if there'd been anything, she would have said.'

She was lying, Borghi was sure of it. 'Even after you quarrelled?'

This hit home, and Priscilla turned and looked at him. 'How did you know that?'

Borghi didn't tell her it was because Anna Lou had erased her number from the contacts list on her mobile phone. He slowed down and parked at the kerb. Then he switched off the engine because he wanted to look her full in the face. 'It'll stay here, but I want the truth.'

Priscilla resumed chewing the polish from her nails. 'I didn't tell anyone because I already have enough trouble with my mother,' she said defensively. 'Ever since my last stepfather left, she's been obsessed with the brotherhood. He was the sixth or seventh bastard who dumped her. Usually they're losers who've landed themselves in the shit. She picks them up, the way some people pick up stray dogs. She puts them back on their feet and then they leave without saying so much as a thank you. Now she's telling everyone that the brotherhood saved her, and she wants to save me, too. She says Jesus loves her, but as far as I can see he's just another man on her list. I go with her to meetings to keep her happy, but I'm not interested in religion.'

'Anna Lou was your cover, am I right? As long as you kept

seeing her, your mother had no reason to go on at you about your friends. So you never told her anything about the quarrel, or she would have made things difficult for you.'

Priscilla got on her high horse. 'I'm not a bitch, I really did like Anna Lou. But it's true, we hadn't spoken for at least two weeks when she disappeared.'

Borghi looked at her. 'Why?'

'Don't get any ideas,' she said resolutely. 'It's not a big deal. I just opened her eyes about something that was happening.'

'What?'

'The nerd who was following her.'

Mattia, Borghi immediately thought. 'Do you know who he is?'

'Of course, he's in my class, his name's Mattia. He doesn't talk to anybody, and nobody wants anything to do with him.'

'Why was he following Anna Lou?'

'I don't know. Maybe because he liked her or maybe because she was the only one who talked to him. But when she did that she encouraged him, and I told her she was making a mistake. Anna Lou would never have become his girlfriend, but in my opinion he was deceiving himself that she would, because he was always hanging around her.'

Borghi was beginning to understand, but once again Priscilla wasn't telling him everything. 'So you warned her but she didn't listen to you. That doesn't strike me as a good reason to break off a friendship.'

His scepticism convinced her to tell him the rest of the story. 'All right: something else happened. One day, he was following her around as usual, trying to make her notice him. I couldn't stand it any more: I went up to him and told him what I thought. I was expecting him to react, start arguing. Instead, he looks at me like a scared puppy and doesn't say a word. And then he pisses himself.'

'He pisses himself?'

'That's right. I see the dark stains start to form on his trousers, through his pants. And then the pee forms a kind of puddle under his gym shoes. Can you believe it?'

Borghi sighed and shook his head. Teenagers, he thought. What a mess. 'So Anna Lou blamed you.'

'What could I do? She'd even made one of her bracelets for him, she wanted to give it to him as a present. So then she got angry with me, said I'd humiliated him and she didn't want to speak to me again.'

Borghi realised he had underestimated Anna Lou. He had thought she was a weak, submissive character. But she had a mind of her own and, when necessary, she could be fair. She had punished Priscilla for her needless cruelty. He couldn't ask the girl if she thought Mattia had anything to do with the disappearance. It was obvious that Priscilla didn't suspect him, partly because she couldn't know that the boy who had pissed in his trousers in front of her had had problems with controlling his anger in the past. So he asked, 'Why do you think Mattia was some kind of danger to Anna Lou? All right, he followed her, but I don't understand—'

'He followed her with a camcorder.'

The various eight o'clock TV news bulletins ran items on the New Year celebrations in various cities around the country. But when the time came to talk about the Kastner case, the correspondents showed a dark house in a residential neighbourhood of a mountain village, where two parents were still worrying about the fate of their eldest child.

Mixing the bitter with the sweet was a well-tried formula of the media.

The TV set in the hotel room was on but unwatched. The sound, though, reached Vogel in the bathroom. He was in his dressing gown, standing at the mirror and slowly, delicately putting dark dye on his eyebrows with a small brush. As he did so, he kept his mouth open. It was an involuntary gesture, which made him look ridiculous but which he didn't notice in the mirror.

The wardrobe next to the bed was wide open. In it hung the row of elegant suits that Vogel had brought with him, as if he would be spending months in Avechot. Each was on its own wooden hanger with a little canvas bag of dried lavender next to it to deter moths and keep the material fresh. Fixed to one of the doors was a crossbar on which his ties were lined up: silk, wool, cashmere. They had different patterns, but Vogel had carefully arranged them in a particular scale of colours. Last but not least, the shoes were at the bottom – at least five pairs. All tightly laced, English and Italian, hand-finished and polished. One beside the other, like the soldiers in a firing squad.

The wardrobe's contents were only a fraction of what Vogel kept at home. They were the result of years of passionate research. Each suit was matched to a specific eau de cologne, meticulously sprayed on the pocket handkerchief. Vogel was fanatical about this. His collection of shirts and cufflinks reeked of obsession.

He despised those colleagues of his who went around looking scruffy. It wasn't just a question of appearance or mere vanity. For him, these clothes were like a knight's armour. They expressed strength, discipline and self-confidence.

But that evening, the suits would remain in the wardrobe.

87

He had no intention of going out. Outside, a storm was gathering and he would stay here and wait for the New Year on his own, as he always did. He had ordered a light dinner and would open a bottle of Cabernet from his own cellar, which he had slipped into his suitcase before leaving.

While he stood at the bathroom mirror, already savouring the thought of the evening ahead, he went over what had so far emerged in the case.

Anna Lou knew her kidnapper. That was why she had followed him without putting up any resistance.

She's almost certainly dead. Dealing with a hostage was quite complicated, especially for a solitary kidnapper. He had probably killed her after abducting her. She might only have survived a few hours.

The girl felt the need to keep a fake diary for her mother. But what had happened to the real one? And what shameful secrets did it contain?

His mobile phone started ringing. Vogel snorted irritably, but given that the device didn't want to stop, he broke off dyeing his eyebrows and went to answer.

'Mattia was making videos of Anna Lou,' Borghi said without even saying hello.

'What?' Vogel asked, surprised.

'He followed her everywhere and filmed her.'

'How did you find that out?'

'Her best friend told me, but this afternoon I looked for confirmation. Apparently a police patrol caught him a while back filming the couples who go off into a corner behind the cemetery.'

It was excellent news, Vogel thought. It seemed he wasn't the only one to have obsessions. But Mattia's obsession was a lot more disturbing than his own innocuous passion for dressing well. In the light of this new scenario, he came to a decision. 'Are our people still keeping an eye on the boy's house?'

'A couple of agents at a time, on four-hour shifts. But they haven't seen anything unusual yet.'

'Tell the men to stand down.'

At the other end, Borghi was silent for a moment. 'Are you sure, sir? I thought, since tonight is New Year's Eve, Mattia might decide to take advantage of the bustle there'll be to go back home and stock up with supplies.'

'He won't do that, he's not so stupid,' Vogel said immediately. 'I'm convinced he'll try and get in touch with his mother. She's washing dishes this evening.'

Borghi, though, didn't seem convinced. 'I'm sorry, sir, but I don't understand: what's the plan?'

But Vogel had no intention of sharing his strategy with him. 'Do as I say, officer,' he replied calmly. Then he added: 'Trust me.'

Borghi asked no further questions. 'All right,' was all he said, but there wasn't much conviction in his voice.

Why the hell do you want to know my plan? Vogel thought irritably as he hung up.

1 January

Nine days after the disappearance

It was just after midnight when Vogel drove through the village in a service car.

There were only a few night owls hurrying to private parties. Vogel could see them through the lighted windows of the houses as they celebrated, embracing one another and smiling over the end of the old year and the beginning of the new one. Ridiculous superstitions. He had no need of them. Getting rid of the past was only a way of not admitting your own failure. And in twelve months, the future they would soon be greeting with such joy would be a pointless thing they would be trying to forget.

Vogel, though, thought like the media. The only thing that mattered was the present. Some made it, others merely endured it. He felt part of the first category, because he knew how to achieve success in every situation. The second category was composed of those who, like Anna Lou, were predestined for the role of victim and paid the price for other people's fame.

That was why, right now, Vogel wasn't interested in the New Year. He had more important things to deal with. And as he drove straight to his goal, he picked up his mobile phone and dialled a number he knew by heart.

It took less than two rings for Stella Honer to answer. 'I'm here,' was all she said.

'Twenty-five minutes before the others, remember?'

Stella knew what that meant: something was going to happen tonight.

Vogel parked a hundred metres from the house where Mattia and his mother lived, a small chalet at the top of a low hill, surrounded by a bare, untended lawn and a fence that needed urgent maintenance. It was dark, apart from a reddish glow behind one of the windows.

Vogel was aware that calling off his men wasn't sufficient, because the perimeter around the house was strewn with bugs ready to capture any sound inside. That was why he had to act with extreme caution: nobody must know that he was there. But he had a solution for that, too.

He looked at his watch. He only had to wait a few minutes. Then, as predicted in the weather forecast, it started to rain. The rain beat down on the ground and the houses, drowning out every other sound.

Vogel got out of the car and walked quickly towards the house along the dirt path. Reaching the shelter of the porch, he shook the water from his coat and cautiously climbed a couple of steps. Outside the front door, he took a pair of rubber gloves from his pocket to avoid prints, as well as a screwdriver which he used to break the lock. It wasn't difficult. The door opened and, after making sure there was nobody around, he slipped into the house.

The first impression was one of respectable poverty. A smell of cabbage and damp. Old furniture and dust. Clothes hung up to dry between two chairs. Dirty plates. Cold. In that disorder, though, was also a woman's love for her wayward son. Vogel could sense her fear, her terror at not making it, at failing, seeing everything collapse overnight. Because she knew that the boy she had brought into the world was a danger to himself and others. And she also knew that the drugs and the psychiatrists would never be able to do anything about it.

The old wooden floorboards squeaked beneath the weight of Vogel's steps, but the rain beating on the roof drowned the noise. So he started to walk through the few rooms.

In a corner of the kitchen that also functioned as a living room stood an oven from which came the reddish glow he had glimpsed through the window. But it gave out only a weak heat that didn't even warm the room. He passed a collapsed sofa and continued towards another room. There was a double bed with a small wooden crucifix above it and some shelves that took the place of a wardrobe, but apart from them the walls were bare. A few towels were heaped on a chair and there was a pair of worn slippers by the bedside table.

The third room was a bathroom. Chipped tiles, newspapers stacked up. The toilet flush made a kind of muted sob, and obviously needed repair. The bathtub was small and encrusted with limescale.

Given that this was the whole house, Vogel wondered where Mattia slept. Maybe on the sofa he had seen in the living room, or else in the same bed as his mother, but he wasn't convinced.

He was about to turn on his heels and make a closer inspection when he spotted a barely noticeable rectangle on the wooden wall of the corridor.

A door.

Vogel went to it and pushed it with the palm of his hand. It opened onto a bare brick staircase leading down between two walls of rock, presumably to the cellar.

It was dark down there.

Vogel took out his mobile phone and lit the screen to light his way, then started cautiously to descend. The stairs were steep and worn at the edges. There was a slightly musty odour, although there seemed to be no damp. Reaching the foot of the stairs, he moved the phone about to light the space.

It wasn't a cellar but a basement room. From the way it was furnished, he deduced that it was Mattia's bedroom. Or rather, his den.

There were no windows or ventilation. Down here, the noise of the rain was a single, distant sound. A forlorn sound, like a lament.

On the right, against the wall, was a camp bed. It was unmade and there was a mountain of blankets on it. This room was much colder than the rest of the house, Vogel thought. But a teenager probably adapted well to it, just to have a little independence.

In front of him, Vogel saw a table. And on the wall over the table hung photographs. They were enlarged frames taken from videos.

Anna Lou was in all of them.

Vogel approached to get a better look. There were about thirty of them, all close-ups. The girl had been captured at various moments, always with a spontaneous expression. She almost never smiled in these images. But they revealed a hidden beauty, Vogel thought. Something that wasn't usually visible to the naked eye. It was as if, in his crazy photographic project, Mattia had been able to capture something that nobody else had ever been able to see. Not even Bruno Kastner, who didn't consider his daughter pretty enough to interest a kidnapper.

On the surface stood a no longer very modern PC. Next to it, a camcorder.

Vogel lifted it to take a closer look. Apparently, in his hurry to escape, Mattia had left behind the one object he was inseparable from. Then Vogel noticed something else.

A cuddly pink toy kitten on a shelf, probably the one the boy had taken away from the street outside the Kastners' house the night they had spotted him. Vogel took it down and examined it. The boy had taken a souvenir, which would be enough to incriminate him in the eyes of the media. Vogel felt a shudder, and at that exact moment he heard a noise behind him. It hadn't been just an impression, it was real.

Something had moved on the bed.

Vogel put down the kitten and turned slowly. He saw the mass of blankets shifting. A figure emerged from beneath them. Mattia was wearing his hooded top, the hood pulled down over his head, and it was impossible to make out his face.

Vogel saw him get up slowly. He was much taller and stronger than he remembered. All at once, Vogel understood. The boy hadn't run away at all, he had been hiding in his house all the time. The bugs placed outside would never have been able to record his presence down here, protected as the basement was by God alone knew how many metres of earth and rock.

Vogel had both hands full, the camcorder in one and the phone he was using to light the place in the other. He wouldn't

94

have time to take the gun from his holster, because the boy was very near and in the seconds it would take Vogel to put the things down Mattia would have jumped him. So he tried to use another kind of weapon, one with which usually he was good at navigating his way. 'So this is what you like to do, is it?' he said, smiling conspiratorially and nodding towards the camcorder. 'I bet you're good.'

The boy didn't reply.

Vogel could feel the intensity of his gaze beneath the hood. 'I can make you famous, you know? Your videos could end up on TV, and you'd get all the attention you deserve. I have a lot of friends who are journalists, their papers would pay a lot for the stuff. They'd all be talking about you. Think of your mother: she'd never have to work again. She could have a real house and all the things she can't afford now. And it would be you who gave her those things. It's easy to do that, Mattia. We just have to get out of here. Then you can take me to where Anna Lou is. Or rather, we could go there with the TV crews. You'll be the star, nobody will laugh at you, they'll all respect you . . .'

He didn't know if Mattia was actually thinking this over. Long seconds went by during which nothing happened. Vogel hoped his words had struck home. Then the boy moved, taking a small step in his direction. Instinctively, Vogel retreated. Mattia stopped. Then he took a second step. Vogel's side hit the edge of the table. Again, the boy stopped.

Then Vogel understood. The boy wasn't trying to scare him, or to attack him. He was simply asking him for permission to advance.

No, not towards me, Vogel thought. Towards the computer.

He shifted to allow Mattia to reach the table. The boy went

to it and switched on the PC. It took a couple of minutes for the system to fire up. Once it was working, Mattia opened a file called simply *She*. A number of icons appeared on the screen, each linked to a different video. 'She' was Anna Lou.

The boy searched with the mouse for what interested him and clicked on one of the icons.

Standing behind him, Vogel stared at the screen, wondering what he would see.

The video started. It showed Anna Lou walking along the street, carrying the same brightly coloured satchel with which she had disappeared and a bag with her ice skates. She was walking alone on a sunny day, without realising that she was being filmed. She passed an old white four-by-four. Then the image changed, and Vogel realised that Mattia had made a montage of different scenes. In this shot, Anna Lou was with her friend Priscilla. They were chatting outside school. Another change: Anna Lou was selling sweets for charity with other members of the brotherhood in the forecourt of the assembly hall. As he was wondering about the meaning of this montage, Vogel again saw the white four-by-four from the first scene. It might have been there in the second scene, too, although he hadn't noticed it.

The following sequences confirmed his suspicions.

Anna Lou with her parents in a picnic in the mountains – the white four-by-four was there in the car park. Anna Lou coming out of the house together with her little brothers – the white four-by-four was visible a few metres away, parked at the kerb.

The images continued. Vogel turned to look at Mattia. He was concentrating on the screen, which lit up his face. In following Anna Lou, the boy had noticed something.

That he wasn't the only one following her.

In every case, the distance was too great to make it possible to see the driver's face or read the licence plate. With the right software, of course, they'd be able to blow up the images. But Vogel was convinced it wouldn't be necessary. 'You know who he is, don't you?' he said.

Mattia turned in the direction of the shelf on which stood the cuddly kitten. He indicated it with his eyes, then nodded weakly.

Yes, he knew who he was.

23 February

Sixty-two days after the disappearance

The night everything changed for ever, the snow was still falling outside the window, spreading a false innocence that was unable to completely deceive the darkness of the night.

The radiator in Flores's office emitted a kind of gurgle. A guttural sound, almost alive. It was like a human voice, a voice hidden in another dimension, trying in vain to communicate a message.

Vogel had broken off his story and was staring at a point on the wall amid the photographs and the framed testimonials.

Flores realised that the special agent's attention had been drawn to one of the stuffed fish, silver in colour and with a pink stripe on its back. '*Oncorhynchus mykiss*,' he said. 'Also known as rainbow trout. Originally from North America, but also from some Asian Pacific countries. Many years ago, it was introduced into Europe, and is found in small mountain lakes. To survive, it needs fresh oxygenated water.' Flores had deliberately wandered off-topic. He didn't want to force Vogel to continue. His main task was to be a mediator, to act as a conduit between the individual in front of him and his inner conflict. In Vogel's case, instinct told Flores that the special agent was feeling remorse, and was trying desperately to hide from himself whatever had happened before the road accident, whatever it was that had stained his clothes with somebody else's blood.

Then Vogel lost interest in the fish and started talking again. 'The media establish roles,' he said. 'The monster, the victim. The victim must be protected from any possible attack or suspicion. He or she has to be pure. Otherwise, there's the risk of providing the person who has harmed them with a moral alibi. Sometimes, though – and it's pointless denying it – some victims have played their part in what happened. There have been macroscopic faults, genuine provocations, or else stupid actions which eventually set off a reaction. I remember the case of an office manager who deliberately mispronounced the name of one of his employees. He did it in front of everyone, but meant it as a joke. One morning, the employee showed up for work at the usual time, but with an automatic pistol.'

'Is that the case with Anna Lou Kastner?' Flores asked.

'No,' Vogel said sadly.

'Special Agent Vogel, why don't we try to forget that business for a while and concentrate instead on what happened this evening?'

'My bloodstained clothes. Right . . . '

Flores couldn't come straight out and ask him whose blood it was, he had to get there step by step. 'It would be useful to know where you were before the accident and where you were going afterwards.'

Vogel made an effort. 'I was going to the Kastners' house . . . Yes, I was going to their house to return a token.' He lowered his eyes to the bracelet he had on his wrist.

'But why so late?'

Vogel thought about this, too. 'I had to talk to them, tell them something . . .' But then the memory seemed to fade in his mind.

'Something?'

'Yes, but . . .'

Flores waited for the memory to be unblocked. He wasn't at all sure that Vogel was pretending. It seemed more likely that there was some kind of obstacle preventing the special agent from coming out with whatever he had inside him. What did he have to tell the Kastners that was so important? Flores had the impression that, whatever it was, it must have something to do with what had happened months before. That was why he now tried to make him start again from there. 'Did you really search for Anna Lou, or else did the fact that you thought she was already dead lead you to search only for a corpse that would serve as evidence to nail a possible killer?'

Vogel smiled weakly. It was a clear admission.

'Why didn't you say so straight away? Why nurture false hopes?'

Vogel paused, apparently to reflect. 'When asked in a recent survey what the purpose of a police investigation should be, most of those questioned said "to arrest the criminal". Only a very small percentage said that the purpose of a police investigation should be "to establish the truth".' Vogel leaned forward in his armchair. 'Did you understand what I just said? Nobody wants the truth.'

'Why do you think that is?'

Vogel thought this over for a moment. 'Because arresting the criminal fools us into believing that we're safe, and when it comes down to it that's all we want. But there's a better answer: because the truth involves us, makes us complicit. Have you noticed that the media and the public – in other words, all of us – think of the perpetrator of a crime as if he weren't human? As if he belonged to an alien race, gifted with a special power to do evil? We don't realise it, but we make him . . . a hero.' He emphasised this last word. 'In reality, the criminal is usually an ordinary man, devoid of creative impulses, incapable of distinguishing himself from the mass. But if we accept that he's like that, then we have to admit that, deep down, he's a bit like all of us.'

Vogel was right. Flores's eyes fell for a moment on the dog-eared corner of an old newspaper amid the mess on his desk. He knew exactly how long the paper had been there and the reason he hadn't thrown it away.

There was a name in the headline.

The name of the monster in the Kastner case.

In the course of the days, weeks and months, other papers and files had been heaped on top of that newspaper. It is the fate of news to be buried alive. Deep down, we all want to forget, Flores told himself. He would particularly have liked to forget Maria Kastner's heartbreaking weeping, which, with the passage of time, had become a muted, almost imperceptible lament. Flores had counselled the family initially, trying to help them come to terms with their grief. He had fought Bruno Kastner's silence and withdrawal, and tried to prevent Maria from gradually falling apart. He had done his job as best he could, as long as the brotherhood had allowed him. Then, little by little, he had distanced himself from the family.

'Special Agent Vogel, you said just now that you were on

your way to the Kastners' this evening to tell them something, but can't remember what it was.'

'That's right.'

'Which means you've also forgotten that nobody lives in their house any more.'

This seemed to strike Vogel like a punch in the face.

'You couldn't not have known that,' Flores went on. 'What happened, have you really forgotten?'

Vogel was silent for a while, then said under his breath, like a warning, 'There's something evil here . . . '

Flores felt a shudder go through him.

'Something evil has insinuated itself into your lives,' Vogel went on. 'Anna Lou was just a portal, a way for it to get in. A pure, naive girl: the perfect sacrificial victim . . . But there was something much more perverse behind her disappearance.' He shook his head. 'It's too late for salvation. That thing is here now and won't go away.'

Just then, a sudden violent blow made both men turn to the window. But what really terrified them was that nothing could be seen outside. It was as if their conversation had awakened a spectre in the fog, angered it so that it had intervened to silence them.

Flores stood up and went to check, opening both parts of the window. He looked around uncomprehendingly, the icy fog caressing his face. Then he glimpsed a dark patch beside the gutter.

It was a crow.

It must have awoken in the dead of night, assumed the light of the street lamps reflected in the fog was daylight, and taken to flight. Then it must have lost its way and smashed into the window pane.

Crows were the first victims of foggy nights. Dozens of them were found the morning after, in the fields and the streets.

Flores saw that the bird was still moving, its beak trembling slightly. It was as if it wanted to speak. Then it stopped for ever.

He closed the window and turned back to Vogel. For a second or two, neither man spoke.

'As I've already told you,' Flores said, 'I didn't think we'd ever see you up here again after what happened.'

'Neither did I.'

'The investigation was a disaster, wasn't it?'

'Yes, it was,' Vogel admitted. 'But it happens sometimes.'

If he wanted to know what Vogel had come back to Avechot for on a cold foggy night, Flores was going to have to force him to confront his ghosts. 'Don't you think you were to blame for the failure of the investigation?'

'I was only doing my job.'

'And what would that be?' Flores said provocatively.

'It's obvious: to make the public happy,' Vogel replied with a deliberately false smile. Then he turned serious again. 'We all need a monster, Doctor. We all need to feel better than someone.' The man in the white four-by-four, he remembered. 'I just gave them what they wanted.'

22 December

The day before the disappearance

'The first rule of every great novelist is to *copy*. Nobody admits it, but everyone is inspired by an existing book or another author.' Loris Martini looked at the class, trying to see if at least most of the pupils were paying attention. Some were laughing or chatting, and as soon as he turned, a couple threw paper pellets at each other, convinced the teacher wouldn't notice. But he liked to stay on his feet during his lessons, walking between the rows of desks. In his opinion, it stimulated concentration.

In general, though, the atmosphere this morning was one of boredom. It was always like this on the last day before the Christmas break. The school would be closed for two weeks, and the students already felt as if they were on holiday. He had to think of something to encourage participation. 'Another thing,' he said. 'It isn't the heroes who determine the success of a work. Forget literature and think about your video games for one moment. What do you like to do in a video game?'

The question reawakened the interest of the class. It was actually one of the boys who had been throwing paper pellets who was the first to answer. 'Destroy things!' he cried enthusiastically. They all laughed at the joke.

'Good,' Martini said encouragingly. 'What else?'

'Kill people,' a second student said.

'Excellent answer. But why do we like killing people virtually?'

Priscilla, the prettiest girl in the class, raised her hand. Martini pointed to her.

'Because in real life killing is forbidden.'

'Good, Priscilla,' Martini said. The girl lowered her eyes and smiled, as if she had received a great compliment. One of her classmates mockingly imitated her simpering reaction. Priscilla responded by showing him her middle finger.

Martini was well pleased: he had got them to the point he had been hoping to reach. 'You see, bad actions are the real driving force of every narrative. A novel or film or video game in which everything goes well wouldn't be interesting. Remember: it's the villain who makes the story.'

'Nobody likes the good guys.' This comment came from Lucas, who was noted for his poor grades, especially when it came to conduct, and for the skull tattoo peeking out from behind one ear. Maybe he felt implicated and saw this as an opportunity for revenge: no, nobody liked the good guys.

Martini felt a strange sensation whenever he managed to get somewhere with his class. It was a sense of relief. Not that it would have been easy to say what it meant. Reaching such a goal might seem a modest achievement to anyone else. But it wasn't modest to a teacher, it wasn't modest to Loris Martini. At that moment, he was perfectly conscious that he had sowed an idea in their minds. And that that idea might stay there. Notions could indeed be forgotten, but the spontaneous formation of thought followed a different route. The idea would follow them for the rest of their lives, maybe lurking in a corner of their brains and appearing suddenly when they needed it.

It's the villains who make the story.

That wasn't just literature. It was life.

When his colleagues talked about the class, they used expressions like 'human material', referring to the pupils, or else they were inclined to complain or to impose an iron discipline that was easily circumvented. On his first day, several of them had told him clearly that it was pointless having too many expectations because the average level was quite low. Martini had to admit that at the beginning of the school year, he hadn't nourished any great hopes for the results he would achieve from his 'human material'. But as the weeks had passed, he had found a way to overcome their distrust and little by little had started gaining their confidence.

In Avechot, there were only two values that counted. Faith and money. Even though many of their families were part of the brotherhood, the pupils mocked the former and worshipped the latter.

Money was a constant topic of discussion between them. The adults in the village who had got rich thanks to the mining company showed off their affluence, driving big cars or wearing expensive watches. They were the object of admiration and respect from the younger people, who at the same time tended to feel sorry for those – including their own parents in some cases – who couldn't afford certain luxuries.

The school was the place in Avechot where the difference between the two social categories into which the village was divided was most noticeable. The children of the better-off were always fashionably dressed and showed off their enviable gadgets, starting with the latest model of smart phone. All this was often a source of tension. There had been fights in the playground because of the scorn felt for those who were less privileged. There had even been cases of theft.

That was why, when Martini had presented himself to the class in his velvet jacket rubbed away at the elbows, his fustian trousers and his shapeless old Clarks shoes, he had aroused a great deal of mirth among the students. He had immediately grasped that he didn't enjoy their respect. And he had to admit: in that moment he had felt inadequate. It was as if he had been vainly pursuing the wrong objective his whole life – and he was now forty-three.

'I won't assign you any homework for the Christmas holidays.' Cries of jubilation rose from the class. 'Partly because I know you wouldn't do it,' he added, arousing a laugh. 'But in the intervals between smashing windows or robbing banks, I want you to read at least one book from this list.' He took a sheet from the desk and held it up. The discontent was general.

There was only one of the pupils who didn't say a word.

He had spent the whole lesson with his head bowed over his desk at the back of the class, writing or scribbling something in the big exercise book he always carried with him along with his camcorder. He had withdrawn into his own world, one nobody else could enter, not even his classmates, who responded by isolating him. Whenever Martini had tried to engage with him, he had been rejected.

'Mattia, what about you?' Martini now said. 'Do you mind reading at least one book in the next two weeks?'

For a moment, Mattia raised his eyes from his exercise book, said nothing and went back inside his shell.

Just then, the bell rang for the end of the lesson.

Mattia quickly grabbed his satchel and the skateboard he kept under his desk. He was the first to leave the classroom.

Martini addressed the students one last time before they left. 'Have a good Christmas, all of you . . . and try not to cause too much damage.'

In the corridors of the school, there was a frantic coming and going of pupils preparing to exit the building. Some were running, dodging Martini, who walked along at a normal pace with his usual vague air, a green corduroy bag over his shoulder. He heard someone calling him.

'Signor Martini! Sir!'

He turned and saw Priscilla coming towards him with a big smile on her face. Even though she got herself up like a delinquent, with that green parka that was too big for her and the boots that made her look taller, Martini thought she was very pretty. He slowed down and waited for her to catch up with him.

Priscilla did so. 'I wanted to tell you that I've already chosen the novel I'm going to read in the holidays,' she said with somewhat excessive enthusiasm.

'Oh yes, which one?'

'*Lolita*.'

'Why did you choose that one?' Martini was expecting her to say that, all things considered, the main character was like her.

'Because I know my mother wouldn't approve,' she said instead.

Martini smiled. When it came down to it, books were a form of rebellion. 'Enjoy the book, then.' He tried to get away, partly because he had been aware for a while now that Priscilla had a crush on him, and his colleagues had noticed it, too. That was why he always tried to avoid spending too much time with her in public. He didn't want anyone to think he was encouraging her.

'Wait, sir, there's something else.' She seemed embarrassed. 'Did you know I'm going to be on television tomorrow? I'm picking the numbers for the brotherhood's charity tombola. It's only a local TV channel, but you have to start somewhere, don't you?'

Priscilla had often expressed a desire to become famous. One day she wanted to take part in a reality show, the next day she wanted to be a singer. Lately, she had got it into her head that she'd like to become an actress. She didn't have any clear idea about how to achieve this, but maybe it was simply a cry for help, a way of telling everyone that she would like to get out of Avechot. It was likelier, though, that in a couple of years she would find a boy as messed-up as her who would make her pregnant and force her to spend the rest of her life here. After all, that was what had happened to her mother. Martini had spoken to the woman once, at a parent–teachers meeting. She was identical to her daughter, only older. Even though there was only fifteen years between them, Priscilla's mother had deep lines around her eyes and an ineluctable sadness in her gaze. Martini recalled that she had made him think of a belle of the ball who keeps dancing with her diadem on when the party lights have already been switched off and everybody has gone home. Priscilla looked a lot like her. From what he'd been able to ascertain, she was one of the most popular girls in the school. She was also a terrible gossip. She had read the graffiti written about her and her mother on the walls of the boys' toilet.

'Have you talked to anybody else about wanting to act?'

Priscilla turned her nose up. 'My mother wouldn't agree, because the people in the brotherhood have put it into her head that actresses aren't respectable. But she wanted to be a model when she was young. It's unfair of her to stop me following my dream just because she never managed to make hers come true.'

Yes, it was absolutely unfair. 'You should study acting, maybe that way you'd convince her.'

'Why, don't you think I'm beautiful enough to make it on my own?'

Martini shook his head good-naturedly in reproach. 'I took a drama course at university.'

'Then you could give me lessons! Please, please!'

Her eyes were shining with excitement. It was impossible to say no to her. 'All right,' Martini said. 'But you'll have to work hard, otherwise it's just wasted time.'

Priscilla took off her satchel and put it down on the ground. 'You won't be sorry,' she said, tearing a strip from a page of her exercise book and writing something on it. 'This is my mobile number. Will you call me?'

Martini nodded and smiled. He saw her walk away, as carefree as a butterfly. 'Happy Christmas, sir!' she called to him.

He looked at the number on the paper, written in pink ink. Priscilla had added a little heart. He put the paper in his pocket and continued to the exit.

On the forecourt in front of the school, some pupils lingered, laughing and joking, while others sped off on scooters. One of these was his rebellious pupil Lucas. As Martini searched for his car keys in his bag, the boy passed close to him, brushing against him playfully as he did so. Then he turned. 'When are you going to change that old crock, sir?'

His friends laughed. Loris Martini, though, had learned not to pay any attention to Lucas's provocations. 'As soon as I win the lottery,' he said in response.

At last, he found his keys in the bottom of his corduroy bag and unlocked the door of his old white four-by-four.

The twenty-second of December was one of the shortest days of the year. By the time Martini got home, the light was already starting to fade.

He walked in and saw her, stretched out on the wicker arm-chair by the window. She had a tartan rug over her knees and had fallen asleep with a book in her hand.

Clea was so beautiful in the glow of sunset that he felt a pang in his heart.

Her chestnut hair was tinged with fire, while half her face remained in shadow, as if in a painting. He would have liked to go closer and kiss her half-open lips. But his wife seemed so serene, he didn't have the courage to wake her.

He put his bag down on the wooden floor and sat down on the bottom step of the stairs that led to the upper floor. He joined his hands under his chin and gazed at his wife. They had been together for at least twenty years. They had met at university, where she was studying law and he was studying literature.

Future judges or lawyers usually don't mix with those who con-sider literature the only way to talk about the world, she had told him. She wore glasses with thick black frames, probably too big for her beautiful face, he had thought. Denim dungarees, a red T-shirt bearing the logo of the faculty, and a pair of white tennis shoes ruined by use. She was holding law books clutched to her breast. A rebellious lock of hair fell insistently over her forehead and she kept pushing it back. They were in the grounds of the university. It was a radiant spring day. Loris was wearing an old grey tracksuit. He had just finished his Thursday morning basketball training and was all sweaty. He had spotted her from a distance as she was on her way back to her room and had started running towards her, catching up with her before she could enter the women's dormitory. His hair was dishevelled. He leaned with one hand on the brick wall of the building. He was taller than her, but Clea didn't seem the least bit intimidated. She looked at him as if she wasn't afraid to tell him to his face what she thought. And she was serious.

Future judges or lawyers usually don't mix with those who consider literature the only way to talk about the world ... At first he had thought of it as a joke, a bit of flirtatious banter. 'Of course, but that doesn't stop future judges or lawyers from eating regularly,' he had retorted with a smile.

At that point, she had looked at him with suspicion. Her gaze contained a hands-off sign. Does this guy really think it's so easy to get me into bed? Loris had felt the sinister creaking of his own ego on the verge of collapse.

'Thank you, but I regularly eat alone,' she had replied, turning her back and hurrying up the steps leading to the entrance.

He had stood there, paralysed by surprise – or by disappointment. Who did the stuck-up bitch think she was? They had met a few evenings earlier at a party thrown by students in the Department of Natural Sciences. There was booze and stale sandwiches. He had immediately noticed her with her black sweater and her hair gathered at the back of her neck. He had spent ages looking for a pretext to approach her. The opportunity had presented itself when he had seen her talking with a guy he barely knew and whose name he didn't even remember – Max or Alex, it didn't matter. He had approached with the excuse of saying hello to him, in the hope that he would introduce them. The guy had taken his time: maybe he, too, had designs on her. In the end, he had introduced them only to save her the embarrassment of standing there in silence while they conversed.

'I'm Loris,' he had said immediately, holding out his hand, as if she might escape him at any moment.

'Clea,' she had replied, frowning. Over the years, that frown would become familiar to him: a mixture of curiosity and scepticism. She was looking at him the way primates were watched at the zoo, but at that moment Loris had found her gaze adorable.

They had exchanged enough basic information to start a conversation. Which faculty do you attend, where do you come from, what are your plans after university? Then they had looked for an interest in common, a thin thread from which to begin to weave a relationship. He had formed an impression of her: she was naturally beautiful but proud enough not to exploit her beauty, intelligent but without necessarily feeling any desire to humiliate other people, progressive and tolerant and, last but not least, proudly independent.

He had concluded that the one thing they had in common was basketball.

Loris had started naturally to hold forth about tactics and players, Clea knew all about statistics and scores. The university championship held no secrets for her.

So they had talked all evening, and he had even managed to make her laugh a couple of times. He was sure that inviting her out wouldn't be a problem, but he didn't want to overplay his hand. Next time, he had told himself. Because with a girl like that, you mustn't rush things.

But what happened that morning outside the women's dormitory was completely unexpected. She had given him the brush-off, coldly, almost with disgust. In fact, definitely with disgust. And Loris had silently told her to go to hell.

The rejection, though, had proved difficult to digest. In the days that followed, he had thought about it a lot, sometimes shaking his head in amusement at the absurdity of it all, but sometimes with anger. Without realising it, a little worm had got into his mind and was digging a hole that needed to be filled.

He couldn't forget her.

It was then that he made the craziest decision of his life. In a department store, he bought a blue suit, a white shirt and an absurd red bow tie. He pushed back his unruly lock of hair, invested a figure out of all proportion to his finances in a bouquet of red roses, made sure he was outside the lecture theatre where a class in comparative private law was being held at nine in the morning, and waited. When, at the end of the class, the mass of students burst into the corridor like a river in full spate, Loris stood his ground. He remained stoically still in the midst of the current, waiting to meet a specific pair of eyes. When it happened, Clea immediately realised that he was there for her. She walked up to him without hesitation.

Gravely, Loris held up the flowers. 'Will you allow me to invite you out for dinner?'

She looked at the gift, then peered at him with a frown. Unlike the first occasion, when he had asked her in his track-suit, sweating after a game of basketball and with the air of someone who takes a positive answer for granted, Loris had this time taken the trouble to demonstrate to her how much he respected her and how much he wanted to go out with her, at the risk of appearing ridiculous. Clea's face lit up in a smile. 'Of course,' she said.

As he remembered that episode, watching her sleeping with the winter sun settling like a caress on her face, it struck Loris Martini that he hadn't seen a smile like that on her lips for a long time now. It was a painful thought.

They had arrived in the valley six months earlier. She had been the one to suggest moving there. He had found a vacancy in Avechot and they had moved without too many second thoughts. There was nothing to guarantee that a little village in the mountains was the right place to start over again, but so be it. Clea had been determined to move, but now Martini feared that his wife wasn't happy. That was why he studied her at a distance, trying to catch the signs of something not being right. Maybe it had happened too quickly. Maybe in the end all they'd done was run away from something.

The thing, he told himself. Yes, it's all the fault of *the thing*.

Clea started to wake up. First she opened her eyes slightly, then she let go of the book she was holding in her lap and opened her arms to stretch. Halfway through the gesture, she noticed him and stopped. 'Hey,' she said with a slight smile.

'Hey,' he replied, remaining seated on the stairs.

'How long have you been there?'

'I only just arrived,' he lied. 'I didn't want to disturb you.'

Clea pushed away the tartan rug and looked at her watch.

'Oh, I've slept quite a while.' Then she folded her arms over her breasts with a shiver. 'Isn't it a bit cold here?'

'Maybe the heating hasn't come on yet.' Actually, he had moved the timer forward a couple of hours that morning, because the last bill had been quite high. 'I'll see to it immediately, and I'll also light the fire,' he said getting up from the step. 'Any sign of Monica?'

'I think she's up in her room,' Clea replied, with an anxious expression. 'At her age, it's not good to isolate herself the way she does.'

'How were you at her age?' he asked, trying to downplay this.

'I had friends,' she replied irritably.

'Well, I had a spotty face and spent all my time strumming a guitar. Just think, I thought that learning to play the guitar would help make other people accept me.'

Clea, though, didn't buy it. She was genuinely anxious about her daughter. It isn't healthy for Monica, she told herself, pensively. 'Do you think she's hiding something from us?'

'Yes, but I don't think it's a problem,' Martini said. 'At sixteen, it's normal to have secrets.'

23 December

The day of the disappearance

At six in the morning, it was still dark.

Martini had woken early. While his wife and daughter slept, he made himself coffee and drank it standing up, leaning against a cabinet in the kitchen, savouring the warmth of the drink in the yellowish glow of the light over the dining table. Slowly, lost in thought. Then he put on thick clothes and hiking shoes. The previous evening, he had told Clea he would be going up to the high mountains.

He left home about seven. Outside, it was cold but pleasant. The air was brisk and the smell of the woods wafted down into the valley, ousting for a while the unpleasant odours that came from the mine. As he loaded his rucksack in the four-by-four, he heard someone call his name.

'Hey! Martini!'

His neighbour was waving at him from the other side of the street. Loris replied to the greeting. From the start, the

Odevises had been friendly to him and Clea. Husband and wife were the same age as them, although the couple's children were much younger than Monica. From what Martini had gathered, he was involved in the construction business, but his money had come from the sale of land to the mine. They got along well. He was a little arrogant but fundamentally harmless. His wife was an intangible, finicky woman, who seemed to have come out of an advertisement for Fifties housewives.

'Going anywhere nice?' Odevis asked.

'I'm heading up to the pass, then continuing along the east slope. I've never explored it before.'

'Damn, maybe next time I'll come with you. I could do with losing a few kilos.' He laughed and patted his prominent stomach. 'Today, I'm taking my baby out for a ride.' He pointed to the open door of his garage and the blue Porsche parked inside. It was the latest in a long line of expensive toys he had purchased, because Odevis loved to spend his money and show off what he had bought with it.

'Maybe next time I'll come with *you*,' Martini replied.

Odevis laughed again. 'So, are we still on for Christmas?'

'Of course.'

'We really do want to have you join us.'

Clea had accepted the invitation without consulting him, but Martini didn't blame her for it. His wife spent her days at home, and it was understandable that she wanted to socialise a little. And he had the impression the Odevises were also in search of new friends. Maybe because of their new lifestyle, their relations with their old acquaintances had cooled.

'Well, have a good hike,' Odevis said, walking to the Porsche.

Martini returned the farewell and got ready to climb into

his old white four-by-four, which by now had accumulated too many kilometres and was beginning to display unmistakable signs of fatigue, in the form of noisy vibrations and overly dense exhaust fumes. He started the engine and set off towards the mountains as the darkness of the night started to fade.

By the time he got back, it was dark again. He opened the front door and was assailed by the unmistakable aroma of soup and roast meat. It was almost eight o'clock and that smell was the prelude to a reward that was well deserved after an exhausting day.

'It's me!' he called, but nobody replied. In the corridor, the only light came from the kitchen. The noise of the extractor hood must be preventing Clea from hearing him. Martini put down his rucksack and took off his hiking boots in order not to dirty the floor. He had mud everywhere and there was a makeshift bandage on his left hand. He was still bleeding. He hid his hand behind his back and headed in his stockinged feet for the kitchen.

As he suspected, Clea was completely absorbed in her cooking, though glancing every now and again at the portable TV set that stood on a shelf. Martini came up behind her. 'Hi,' he said, trying not to startle her.

Clea turned for a moment. 'Hi,' she replied before again looking at the TV. 'You're late.' She said it almost casually, not as an accusation. Her mind seemed elsewhere. 'I've been trying to call you on your mobile all afternoon,' she added.

Martini searched in one of his jacket pockets and took out the phone. The display was off. 'The battery must have run out in the mountains and I didn't notice. I'm sorry.'

Clea didn't even listen to him. Yes, her tone of voice was

different. Loris always knew immediately when something was worrying her. He went closer to her and lightly kissed her neck. Clea reached out a hand to caress him, but didn't take her eyes off the TV screen. 'A girl has gone missing in Avechot,' she said, pointing at the local news. The noise of the hood covered the voice of the newsreader.

Martini leaned over her shoulder and peered at the screen. 'When did it happen?'

'A few hours ago, in the afternoon.'

'Well, maybe it's a bit too early to say that she's missing,' he said to reassure her.

Clea turned to him, an anxious look on her face. 'They're already searching for her.'

'Maybe she just ran away. Maybe she quarrelled with her family.'

'Apparently not,' she retorted.

'Kids that age are always running off. I know them, I deal with them every day. You'll see, she'll come straight back as soon as her money runs out. You always take things too much to heart.'

'She's the same age as our daughter.' That was why she was so worried, Martini realised now. He put his arms round her waist, pulled her to him and spoke to her softly as only he could do. 'Listen, it's just a local channel. If it was something serious, all the news bulletins would be talking about it.'

Clea seemed to calm down a little. 'You may be right,' she admitted. 'Anyway, she attends your school.'

Just then, the image of a teenage girl with red hair and freckles appeared on the screen. Martini stared at her, then shook his head. 'She's not one of my pupils.'

'What happened to you?'

Martini had forgotten all about his bandaged hand and Clea had just noticed it. 'Oh, nothing serious.'

She took his hand to get a better look at the injured palm. 'But you seem to be bleeding a lot.'

'I slid down a ridge, and to stop myself I grabbed hold of a branch sticking out of the ground and cut myself. But it's superficial, nothing to worry about.'

'Why don't you go to A and E? It might need stitches.'

Martini pulled his hand away. 'Oh, no, there's no need for that. It's nothing, don't worry. I'll clean the wound now and change the bandage, and you'll see, everything will mend by itself.'

Clea folded her arms and looked at him grim-faced. 'Stubborn as usual. You never do what I tell you.'

Martini shrugged. 'Because then you get angry and that makes you even more beautiful.'

Clea shook her head, but any impulse to blame him was about to transform into a smile. 'Wash yourself, anyway: you stink like a mountain goat.'

He raised his injured hand to his forehead and gave her a military salute. 'Yessir!'

'And hurry up, dinner will be ready soon,' Clea admonished him as he walked towards the hallway.

In the living room, husband and wife looked at each other in silence. The dinner was getting cold on the table.

'I'm going up now,' Clea said. 'She'll listen to me.'

Martini reached out his hand to stroke hers. 'Let her be, she'll come down soon.'

'I called her twenty minutes ago. Then you went and knocked on her door. I'm tired of waiting.'

He would have liked to tell her that that would only make things worse, but he was always afraid of interfering in the delicate dynamic between mother and daughter. Clea and Monica had found a way of communicating that was entirely their own. They often clashed, frequently over stupid matters. But most of the time they reached a kind of tacit armistice, because both were proud but knew they had to continue living under the same roof.

They heard the door of Monica's room close, then her steps on the stairs. Monica came into the living room, dressed entirely in black, including a cardigan that was too big for her. She had put on black eye make-up, which made her generally sweet face look decidedly nasty. Maybe that was why she put it on, Martini thought. He would often tell his wife that the girl was going through a Gothic phase, but Clea always retorted that this period had already lasted too long. 'She looks like a widow, I can't bear it,' she would say. Mother and daughter were identical, not only in appearance. Martini found in them the same youthful attitude, the same way of approaching the world.

Monica sat down at the table without deigning to look at them. Head bowed, with a fringe falling over her eyes like a protective screen. Her silences always seemed like defiance.

Martini cut the roast and served the portions, saving the last one for himself. As he did so, he tried to distract Clea's attention so that she wouldn't go into attack mode, but it was obvious from her expression that she was on the point of exploding. 'So, how was school today?' he asked his daughter before the quarrel could break out.

'Same old same old,' was the terse reply.

'I heard there was a surprise maths test.'

'Yeah.' Monica was playing with her fork, constantly moving

the food about on the plate and raising only small mouthfuls to her lips.

'Did you sit it?'

'Yeah.'

'What mark did you get?'

'Six.' The lazy tone was deliberately provocative, as was the laconic nature of the replies.

Martini couldn't blame her. When it came down to it, she was the only one who hadn't had a say in the matter of the move to Avechot. Nor had they given her too many explanations about the reason. Monica had had no choice but to endure her parents' absurd, incomprehensible decision, but she was too clever not to realise that she had been asked to pay the price for their running away.

The thing, Martini remembered.

'You should find something to do, Monica,' Clea went on. 'You can't spend all afternoon lounging about in your room.'

Martini could see that his daughter wouldn't reply. But his wife had no intention of letting go.

'Take up a hobby, anything. Go skating, join a gym, choose a musical instrument.'

'And who'll pay for my lessons?' Monica had looked up from her plate and now her eyes were boring into her mother. But Martini knew that the accusatory question was actually addressed to him.

'We'll find a way, won't we, Loris?'

'Yes, of course.' He didn't sound encouraging. Monica was right: on his salary, they couldn't afford it.

'You can't spend all your time alone.'

'I could always go to the brotherhood. That's free.' Her voice was bitingly sarcastic.

'All I'm saying is that you need to make friends.'

Monica pounded the table with her fist, making the dishes clatter. 'I had friends, but guess what? I had to say goodbye to them.'

'Well, you'll soon make new ones,' Clea prevaricated. Martini detected a slight surrender in her, as if she had no counter-attack for this.

'I want to go back, I want to go home,' Monica said.

'Whether you like it or not, this is our home now.' Once again, Clea's words were strong, but the tone in which she had uttered them betrayed weakness.

Monica stood up from the table and ran upstairs, going to ground again in her room. From below, they heard the door slamming. There was a brief silence.

'She didn't even finish her dinner,' Clea said, looking at her daughter's still full plate.

'Don't worry, I'll go upstairs later and take her something.'

'I don't understand why she's so hostile.'

But Martini was sure that Clea understood perfectly well. Just as he was sure that, out of spite, his daughter would reject the food he brought her. It didn't use to be like that. Once upon a time, he had managed to mediate between mother and daughter. Now he felt he was just the strange awkward fellow who lived with them, shaved his face rather than his legs, didn't lose his temper over trifles one week in the month and occasionally tried to have his say. The role of the taciturn but understanding father had always worked with Monica before. Then something in their family had broken.

He was convinced, though, that he could fix it.

He saw that Clea was on the verge of crying. He could

always tell when her tears came from nervousness. Right now, they were tears of pain.

It's because of the missing girl, he told himself. She's thinking the same thing could happen to our daughter, because she doesn't know her as well as she used to.

Martini felt guilty. Because he was only a secondary school teacher, because he had a wretched salary, because he hadn't been able to offer a better life to the two women he loved most in the world and, last but not least, because he had shut his own family up in the mountains, in Avechot.

Clea resumed eating, but the tears started sliding down her cheeks. Martini could no longer bear to see her in that state.

Yes, he would fix everything. He vowed that he would make everything right.

25 December

Two days after the disappearance

On Christmas morning, the centre of Avechot was full of people. They all seemed to have decided to leave it to the last moment to buy their presents.

Martini was wandering amid the shelves in a bookshop, peering at the inside flaps of novels, looking for something to read over the holidays. He had homework to mark and had fallen behind with writing the end-of-term reports, but even so, he didn't want to give up on a little time for himself. Actually, there was a lot to do around the house. Odd jobs he'd been constantly postponing and which he was sure Clea would remind him to complete. Like the gazebo in the garden. When they'd chosen to live here, his wife had fallen in love with that small patch of green behind the house, which she was thinking of using to grow vegetables or plant roses. The gazebo was dilapidated, but Loris had suggested turning it into a greenhouse. Unfortunately for him, Clea had welcomed the idea with rather too much enthusiasm. She didn't want him to wait for the summer before refurbishing it, she'd rather he got it ready that very winter. He would have to spend quite a few hours out there in the cold, but it would be worth it just to see the grateful smile on her face.

Just then, Clea walked into the shop and searched for him along the aisles. She was carrying a small bag tied with a ribbon, and her eyes were sparkling.

'So, have you found them?' he asked once she had joined him.

She nodded enthusiastically. 'Exactly the ones she wanted.'

'Good,' he said approvingly. 'That way she'll stop hating us . . . for a while, at least.'

They both laughed.

'And what would you like?'

She put her arms round him. 'I've already had my present.'

'Come on, there must be something else.'

'"I possess or pursue no delight, save what is had, or must from you be took."'

'Stop misquoting Shakespeare and tell me what you want.'

He noticed that the smile had vanished from his wife's face. Clea had spotted something over his shoulder. Martini turned.

Not far from them, the bookshop owner was putting up a flyer behind the till, bearing the face of the missing girl.

'I can't begin to imagine how the Kastners must feel,' a customer said. 'All these hours not knowing what's happened to their daughter.'

'It's a tragedy,' another said.

Martini gently took his wife's chin between his fingers and made her turn back to face him. 'Would you like us to go?'

She nodded, biting her lower lip.

Before long, he was standing by a full trolley. They had

taken advantage of the Christmas special offers to do at least a month's worth of shopping. After a great deal of insistence from her husband, Clea had made up her mind to go to a clothes shop and pick out a present. He waited for her, hoping to see her come out with something. As he stood there, he looked down at his bandaged left hand. It had hurt all night and he'd been forced to take painkillers, but they hadn't been strong enough to let him sleep. This morning, he'd changed the dressing again, but he needed an antibiotic because there was a risk of the wound getting infected.

A familiar face in the distance made him forget about his hand.

Priscilla was sitting on the back of a bench next to a hot-dog stand. She was with her friends, just hanging about. They were joking, but seemed bored. Martini stared for a long time at his prettiest pupil. She was chewing gum and every now and then biting her nails. A boy whispered something in her ear and she gave a wicked smile.

'It took all my imagination to find anything I really liked in that shop.' It was Clea, jolting her husband out of his reverie. She showed him a small red bag. 'Ta-da!' she announced.

'What is it?'

'A scarf made of the finest acrylic.'

Martini gave her a kiss on the lips. 'I never doubted you'd criticise even the present you picked out for yourself.'

Clea took him by his good hand and pushed the trolley. She looked happy.

'It's what I always say.' Odevis was speaking as he stirred the fire in the large stone hearth with a poker. 'In business, you have to grab the opportunities.'

Loris and Clea were sitting on one of the white sofas in the living room. There was an equally white fur rug at their feet and a glass coffee table. Behind them, the table was still lavishly spread with the leftovers of Christmas lunch, and the ornamental red candles were slowly burning down. There was also a big decorated tree that almost reached the ceiling. In general, everything in the house was opulent, verging on gaudy.

'In all modesty,' Odevis went on, expanding on his theory, 'I've always known where the money goes. It's a matter of instinct. You either have it or you don't.'

Martini and his wife nodded, because they didn't know what else to say.

'Here's the coffee,' Signora Odevis announced radiantly, bringing in a silver tray with small cups.

Martini couldn't help noticing that she was still wearing the gold and diamond necklace her husband had given her as a present, even though she must have known this wasn't the time or place to show it off. The presents had been unwrapped just before lunch, right there in front of them. The Odevises had been unconcerned about the embarrassment this would cause their guests. They had wanted to display their treasures. Martini was still angry about it, but Clea hadn't yet given him the signal that they should go. He wondered why not. Maybe his wife really cared about their friendship with these rich country bumpkins.

As they chatted, the couple's children, a boy and a girl aged ten and twelve respectively, played with a games console connected to a large plasma screen. The game – a war game, of course – was too loud, but nobody told them to turn it down. Monica, meanwhile, was slumped in an armchair, her legs over the armrest, her brand-new red combat boots in full view. Her parents' Christmas present hadn't broken through her shell, and now, not having said a word for the last three hours, she was fiddling with her mobile.

'Some people say the mine has killed the economy of the valley, but that's bullshit,' Odevis went on. 'In my opinion, people just weren't clever enough to take advantage of it.' He turned to Clea. 'By the way, I've heard you were a lawyer before you moved to Avechot.'

'Yes,' she admitted with some difficulty. 'I worked for a law firm in the city.'

'Haven't you thought of doing the same thing here?'

Clea avoided looking at her husband. 'It's hard in a place you don't know well.'

The truth was, it would be too expensive to set up a practice.

'Then let me make you an offer.' He smiled at his wife, who encouraged him to continue. 'Come and work for me. There's always a need for someone to look over our legal paperwork. You'd make a perfect secretary.'

Taken aback, Clea said nothing. She was in a difficult position. There had been a number of arguments with her husband over her insistence on looking for a job. Martini didn't want her to settle for working in a shop, and being a secretary wasn't much of a step up from that. 'Thank you,' she said at last with a polite smile. 'But for now, I'd rather devote myself to our home. There's still such a lot to do. It seems like a house move never ends.'

Martini noticed that his daughter had suddenly lost interest in her mobile. After contemptuously raising her eyes to heaven, she was now staring at him as if blaming him for everything.

The job offer and the refusal had created an uncomfortable

atmosphere among those present. Luckily, the house phone rang at that moment, distracting them. Odevis went to answer it, exchanged a few sentences with whoever was on the other end, hung up and grabbed the plasma set's remote. 'He said I should watch something on TV.'

He changed channels, heedless of the protests from his children, who had been deprived of their video game.

The distressed faces of Maria and Bruno Kastner appeared on the screen.

The missing girl's father was holding up to the camera a photograph of his daughter in a white tunic with a wooden crucifix. The mother was staring straight into the camera. 'Our daughter Anna Lou is a kind girl, those who know her know that she has a good heart: she loves cats and she trusts people. That's why we're also appealing to those who've never known her in her first sixteen years of life: if you've seen her or have any idea where she is, help us to bring her home.'

In the Odevises' living room, as in other Avechot homes probably, the festive atmosphere vanished. Martini turned slightly to his wife, who was staring at the woman on the screen, her eyes wide with fear, as if looking at herself in a mirror.

Then, when Maria Kastner spoke directly to her daughter, the Christmas warmth evaporated completely, leaving only a cold sense of presentiment in everyone's heart. 'Anna Lou . . . Mummy, Daddy and your brothers love you. Wherever you are, I hope that our voice and our love reach you. And when you come home, we'll let you have the kitten you want so much, Anna Lou, I promise you . . . May the Lord protect you, my child.'

Odevis switched off the television and poured himself a

glass of whisky from the drinks cabinet. 'The mayor says a police big shot has arrived in Avechot to head the investigation. One of those guys who's always on TV.'

'At least something's being done,' his wife said. 'I didn't get the impression the local authorities were all that serious about the search before.'

'The only thing they're good at is handing out fines.' Odevis knew that all too well: he'd received several for speeding in his Porsche.

Martini listened, drinking his coffee, but said nothing.

'In any case,' Odevis continued, 'I don't believe this story everyone's telling, the little saint who's only interested in her home and her church. I think this Anna Lou had something to hide.'

'How do you know that?' Clea said indignantly.

'Because that's the way it always is. Maybe she ran away because someone got her pregnant. It happens at that age. They have sex and then, when it's too late, they're sorry.'

'So where do you think she is now?' Clea asked, hoping to demolish such an absurd version of events.

'How am I supposed to know?' he replied, opening his arms wide. 'She'll come back eventually, and then her parents and that brotherhood lot will try and hush everything up.'

Clea grabbed her husband's hand, the bandaged one. She squeezed it, heedless of the wound. Martini bore the pain. He didn't want his wife to get into an argument. There was always a lot to learn from people as narrow-minded as Odevis. And indeed, Odevis now came out with his own masterpiece of logic.

'If you ask me, it's something to do with one of those immigrants. They're always coming to me, looking for work. Don't get me wrong: I'm no racist. But I don't think they should let all these people in from countries where sex isn't allowed. They're bound to want to relieve their frustrations on our daughters.'

For some reason, Martini thought, racists always felt the need to preface their remarks with a declaration that they weren't racists. Clea was about to explode, but luckily Odevis turned to him. 'What do you think, Loris?'

Martini considered this for a moment before replying. 'A few days ago, when Clea and I talked about this business, I told her Anna Lou had probably run away from home and everything would soon be sorted out. But now I think too much time has gone by . . . What I mean is, we can't rule out the possibility that something may have happened to the girl.'

'Yes, but what?' Odevis insisted.

Martini knew that what he was about to say would increase Clea's anxiety. 'I'm a parent, and even in a desperate situation a parent always likes to look for a glimmer of hope. But I think the Kastners should start to prepare for the worst.'

His words made everyone fall silent. It wasn't so much the meaning of the words as Martini's tone. He sounded convinced, with no room for doubt.

'Shall we do this again next year?' Odevis suggested, standing with one arm around his wife's shoulders at the door of their splendid, gaudy villa.

'Of course,' Martini said, although he didn't sound convinced. Monica had already gone back inside their house, while he and Clea had lingered to say goodbye to their neighbours.

'Good,' Odevis said. 'It's a deal.'

Martini and his wife left, their arms around each other. As

they crossed the street, they heard the door close behind them. Clea pulled away from her husband a little too abruptly.

'What's the matter? What have I done?'

She turned. She was angry. 'It's because he offered me a job as a secretary, isn't it?'

'What? I don't understand . . . '

'Just now,' she said, as if stating the obvious, 'when you said all those things about Anna Lou's family. About the Kastners preparing for the worst . . . '

'What of it? It's what I think.'

'No, you said it on purpose. You wanted to punish me because I wasn't firm enough about turning down Odevis's offer.'

'Please, Clea, don't start this now.'

'Don't tell me to calm down! You know perfectly well how this business has affected me. Or have you forgotten that we have a sixteen-year-old daughter and that all this is happening in a place *we* decided to bring her against her will?'

Clea had folded her arms and was shaking, but Martini knew it wasn't just from the cold. 'OK, you're right. I was wrong.'

She looked at him and saw that he was genuinely sorry. She came up to him and placed her head on his chest. Martini put his arms around her to warm her. Clea looked up, seeking his eyes. 'Please tell me you didn't mean those things.'

'I didn't mean them,' he lied.

27 December

Four days after the disappearance

They arrived in groups or alone. Some even brought their families. There was a constant but orderly toing and froing. They would approach the house and lay a kitten – a cuddly toy, a rag doll, a ceramic figurine – on the ground. The glow of the candles was reflected on their faces. They would stand silently in that oasis of light and warmth surrounded by the dark and the cold and find solace.

Clea had seen the images of this impromptu pilgrimage to the Kastners' house on television and immediately asked her husband to take her there. Monica had stayed at home but had given her mother one of her favourite dolls to take as an offering to the missing girl.

A cuddly pink kitten.

Clea and her daughter had become much closer in the past few days. That was the power of evil when it happened to somebody else, Martini thought. It had a healing effect on the lives of strangers, helping them to rediscover the true value of what they had. Afraid of losing it, they would hasten to keep it safe before someone or something could take it away. The Kastners hadn't been quick enough. It was their thankless task to be the beginning of the chain, to pass the message on to others.

Martini was parked a hundred or so metres from the little house where Anna Lou had grown up. A police cordon was stopping cars from getting any closer. People were streaming in on foot. Clea had joined the small crowd and he waited for her in the car.

His bandaged hand resting on the wheel, Martini watched the scene through the windscreen.

There were the network vans and the TV news correspondents, each lit by the beam of a small spotlight. They talked about the past and the present, because they knew nothing about the future. But that was the way to grab an audience, letting a sense of mystery hover over every story. TV reporters, photographers, pressmen had come running, attracted by the smell of grief, which was stronger than the smell of blood – and no blood had flowed in Avechot yet. Other people's grief produced a strange fragrance: strong, pungent, but at the same time attractive.

Then there were the ordinary people. Many were simply being nosey, but there were a significant number who came there to pray. Martini had never been a man of faith, so he was always astonished at how people could trust blindly in God at times like these. A sixteen-year-old girl had gone missing and her family had been going through hell for several days. A truly kind God would never have allowed this, and yet it had happened. So why, then, should the same God who had allowed this to happen make things right again? Even assuming He existed, He wouldn't do that. He would let things take their course. And since it was the law of nature that creation should be preceded and followed by destruction, in the eyes of God Anna Lou Kastner could be sacrificed. Maybe that was the key: sacrifice. Without sacrifice, there would be no faith, there would be no martyrs. They had already started to make her into a saint.

Just then, a group of kids from the school walked past the white four-by-four and Martini recognised Priscilla. She was following the others, her back hunched, her hands in the pockets of her parka. She looked sad.

Martini thought for a while, then reached out for the wallet in the back pocket of his trousers and opened it. In one of the folds was the note on which Priscilla had written her mobile number the day before the holidays in the hope of getting acting lessons from him. Martini stared at it. Then he grabbed his mobile and tapped in a message. When he had finished, he raised his eyes to watch the girl and waited.

Priscilla was chatting to a friend when something drew her attention, presumably a sound or a vibration. Martini saw her take one hand out of her parka pocket and look at her display screen for a long time. As she read the text, her face assumed a look of surprise mixed with nervousness. Then she put the phone back in her pocket without saying anything to the others. But it was obvious she was still thinking about it.

Clea's form appeared in the passenger window as she walked back to the car from the house. Martini leaned over to open the door. She got in. 'It's heartbreaking,' she said. 'The girl's parents just came out to thank people. It was so moving. You should have come, too.'

'Better not,' he said evasively.

'You're right, it's not in your nature. But you could still make yourself useful.'

Martini saw the supplication in his wife's eyes. 'What did you have in mind?'

'I've heard they're organising search parties in the mountains. You've been on long hikes all over that area in the past six months, haven't you? So you could—'

'OK,' he interrupted with a smile.

Clea flung her arms around him and planted a big kiss on his cheek. 'I knew it. You're a good man.'

Martini started the engine. As he manoeuvred out of his parking spot, he glanced once more in Priscilla's direction, without his wife noticing.

She was chatting with her friends again, as if nothing had happened.

And she hadn't replied to his text.

31 December

Eight days after the disappearance

The search parties were following a specific procedure.

The volunteers advanced slowly over the ground in long lines, no more than twenty men in each group, with at least three metres between them, just like the rescue teams who go searching for people missing in an avalanche. But instead of using a stick to poke in the snow, they had been instructed to use their eyes, moving their gaze from one corner to the other of their allocated area and tracing the lines of an imaginary grid.

Obviously, the aim wasn't just to find a buried body: there were already dogs for that. Mainly, they were looking for clues, anything that might lead to the victim's current location.

Anna Lou, though, wasn't officially a victim yet, Martini thought as he walked with the others down a slope in the middle of the woods. And yet she was. It was as if she had been promoted in the field. By now, everyone was convinced there wasn't going to be a positive outcome. And in fact, deep down, everyone was rather cynically hoping for a negative one. A dramatic ending is what the public expects. Everyone wants to be upset.

Martini had been taking part in the operation for a few days now. The teams were always led by a police officer. In order not to lose concentration, the men took turns, each turn lasting thirty minutes. The shifts lasted a total of four hours.

On the last day of the year, Martini was on the early afternoon shift. It was the shortest, because the sun inevitably set behind the mountains at about three, putting an end to things for the volunteers, who didn't have night-vision equipment.

The first few times, the search had taken place in almost total silence, the men being careful not to miss anything. Gradually, though, an atmosphere of camaraderie had developed. Some felt it was all right to make conversation or, worse still, bring food or beer with them as if it was a picnic. Even so, nobody dared stop them.

Needless to say, there was no sign of Anna Lou. Or of her mysterious abductor.

In order to keep his promise to his wife that he would do his best, Martini hadn't socialised with anyone. He always kept himself to himself, and didn't respond when the others expressed opinions – opinions that struck him as no better than idle gossip anyway.

Today, he noticed that the atmosphere was different. Everybody was putting in a real effort. The reason was the presence of Bruno Kastner. The missing girl's father had taken part in the search before, but Martini had never met him. After attending an event in the brotherhood's assembly room, Kastner had joined the last group. Watching him,

Martini noticed that although he was clearly tense, he also had an incredible inner strength. He wasn't afraid of finding a clue that might indicate there was no hope for his daughter. Because that might also mean a kind of liberation for him. Martini asked himself how he would act in Kastner's place. There was no answer to the question. You had to experience the excruciating sensation of loss for yourself.

At the end of the operation, the volunteers returned to base camp. A tent had been set up in the clearing in the middle of the woods, where the group leaders took it in turns to deliver their reports. The areas that had been explored were marked on a large map. Some, especially those least accessible, required further investigation by the teams. Then they would outline the timetable for the following day.

The volunteers, who had parked their cars a short distance away, were getting ready to go home. Martini was leaning against the boot of his white four-by-four, taking off his muddy boots.

'All right, listen up, everybody,' the group leader said in a loud voice. They all immediately gathered around him. 'I've spoken to the incident room down in the valley, and they say the weather forecast isn't good. It's going to rain for at least forty-eight hours, starting tonight, so we'll need to suspend our search until the second of January.'

The men didn't take this well. Some of them had travelled many kilometres to get here, leaving their families behind and paying their own expenses. This was a blow to their morale.

The group leader tried to placate them. 'I know you don't think it'd be any problem for you, but the conditions of the terrain are really going to become impossible over the next few hours.'

'The mud will cover up any tracks,' someone pointed out.

'Or reveal them,' the group leader replied. 'Either way, we can't do our best if there are these limitations. Trust me, it'd only be a wasted effort.'

In the end, he managed to convince them. Martini watched as they walked back sadly to their cars. But on their way, they passed another group of people.

In the middle of this group stood Bruno Kastner.

As they passed him, each of them stopped to shake his hand or give him a silent pat on the back. Martini could have joined them and shown the man he felt just as much solidarity with him as they did, but he didn't. He stood motionless by his four-by-four. Then, without anyone taking any notice of him, he got in. He was the first to drive away.

He was standing in the corridor in his dressing gown and slippers. He had been knocking insistently on the bathroom door for a good ten minutes. Only the distorted sound of a rock song came from inside, but no answer. Martini was starting to lose patience. 'Just how much longer are you going to be?' He saw Clea coming up the stairs, carrying a stack of clean laundry. 'She's been locked in there for an hour,' he said. 'What the hell does a girl do in the bathroom that long?'

Clea smiled. 'Make herself look beautiful, you idiot.' Then she added in a low voice, 'She's been invited to a party tonight.'

'Who invited her?' Martini asked, surprised.

'What do you care? It's a good sign, isn't it? She's starting to make friends.'

'Does that mean we'll be spending New Year's Eve on our own?'

'Have you got any plans?' Clea asked with a wink, proceeding to the closet.

'We can still afford a pizza and a bottle of wine.'

And he took advantage of the fact that Clea had her hands full as she passed him to pinch her bottom.

Monica left home at about eight. She was still wearing black, but tonight at least she had allowed herself a skirt. Seeing her like this, it struck Loris Martini suddenly that his daughter would soon be a fully grown woman. It would happen overnight, without warning. The little girl who used to huddle in his arms during thunderstorms wouldn't ask for his protection any more. He knew, though, that she would always need it. He just had to find a way to take care of her without her noticing.

While Clea was in the shower, Martini dropped by the pizzeria on the corner and ordered two take-away capricciosas. When he got back home, he found his wife lying on the sofa in her soft flannel pyjamas, a blanket over her legs. 'I thought this was going to be an adventurous kind of evening, not a cosy one,' he said.

He put the pizzas down on a coffee table, took her face in both hands and kissed her. They kissed for a long time, savouring the taste and the warmth, then, without saying a word, she led him upstairs, to their bedroom.

How long had it been since they'd last made love like this? Martini wondered, staring up at the ceiling as they lay side by side, naked. Oh, sure, there had been other occasions when they'd had sex after *the thing*. But this was the first time he hadn't thought about *the thing* while they were doing it. It hadn't been easy to regain their old complicity or even just the desire to do it again. At first, they'd made love angrily, as if out for revenge. It was a way of reproaching each other for what had happened without having to argue. They had always ended up worn out.

But this evening had been different.

'Do you think our daughter's happy?' Clea asked out of the blue.

'Monica's a teenager. All teenagers suffer.'

'Don't joke about it, I want a proper answer,' she said reproachfully. 'Did you see how happy she was when she went out tonight?'

She was right. There had been a palpable euphoria in the house such as had been absent for too long. 'There's one thing I've realised after what happened to that girl, Anna Lou,' he said, and he saw her grow more attentive. 'There's always too little time to get to know your children. The Kastners are probably wondering now where they went wrong, what mistake they could possibly have made to bring them this suffering, when in their lives they took the small detour that led them to this point ... The truth is, we don't have the time to ask ourselves if our children are happy, because there's something more important to do: asking ourselves if we're happy for them and making sure our mistakes don't impact on them.'

Clea may well have thought he was laying the blame on her, but she didn't let on. Instead, she kissed him again, grateful for his reflections.

Shortly afterwards, they sat half-naked at the kitchen table, eating cold pizza and drinking the red wine Martini kept aside for this kind of occasion, from odd glasses. He told her anecdotes about his colleagues and pupils, just to make her laugh. It was like being back at university, when they would run out of money at the end of the month and find themselves sharing a tin of tuna in the one-room apartment they'd moved into.

God, he loved his wife so much, he'd do anything for her. *Anything.*

They were so close tonight, they didn't even notice that it was after midnight and the New Year had begun. It was the driving rain outside that brought them back to reality.

'I'd better call Monica,' Clea said, getting up from the table and grabbing her mobile. 'In this downpour, you may have to go and pick her up.'

The university student vanished and she was once again the wife and mother she'd become over the years. Martini witnessed the transformation as she waited silently for an answer at the other end of the line. Then he saw her pull more tightly around her that old cardigan she'd stolen from him and now wore only at home. She wasn't cold, but scared.

'I can't get a connection,' she said anxiously.

'It's only just past midnight. Everyone'll be calling to wish each other a happy New Year. The network must be over-loaded. That's normal.'

But Clea didn't listen to him. She kept trying, over and over, in vain. 'What if something's happened to her?'

'Now you're being paranoid.'

'I'm going to call the place where the party's being held.'

Martini let her. Clea found the number and called. 'What do you mean, she didn't turn up?' There was something heart-rending in her voice now. As her mind ran through a whole series of catastrophic scenarios, her facial expression quickly built up a crescendo of negative emotions. By the time she had hung up, her anxiety had turned to terror.

'They say she never turned up.'

'Calm down,' Martini said. 'Let's try and think where she might have gone.'

But when he tried to go closer to her, she waved him away with a peremptory gesture.

'You must find her, Loris. Promise me you'll find her.'

He got into the car and drove around Avechot, not knowing where to go. The thunderstorm raging over the valley had emptied the streets of pedestrians. The rain stopped him from seeing clearly, and the four-by-four's windscreen wipers couldn't keep up with the torrents of water.

He soon realised that Clea had infected him with her own agitation. He, too, found himself drawing a macabre comparison between Monica and Anna Lou.

No, it's not possible, he said to himself, trying to dismiss the idea from his mind.

It had only been twenty minutes since he'd left home, but it felt like an eternity. Soon, he was sure, his wife would call and ask if he had any news. He had nothing to tell her.

Monica gone, vanished into thin air. The police raising the alarm. The news broadcast on television. The search parties in the woods.

No, it won't happen. Not to her.

But the world was full of monsters. Unsuspected monsters.

He thought about Anna Lou's father, remembered him as he received encouraging pats on the back, remembered his knowing look. Because a parent always knows the truth, however impossible it is for him to admit it. That morning, he'd tried to put himself in Kastner's shoes, but couldn't. What now?

I must find her. I promised. I can't lose Clea. *Not again.*

He had to keep a clear head, hard as that was. Then it occurred to him to go back to the starting point. The party.

Within five minutes, he had arrived at the door of a house from which muffled noise and powerful, rhythmic music emerged. He rang the doorbell, then knocked repeatedly, his hair and clothes getting soaked as he did so. When at last somebody took notice and opened the door to him, he stormed in.

There were at least seventy young people crammed together in the living room. Some were dancing, others lay sprawled on the sofas. The music was too loud for talking, but alcohol had made everyone more relaxed. The half-light and the thick cigarette smoke made it hard for him to spot any familiar faces.

At last, he recognised a couple of his pupils. One of them was Lucas, the rebel with the skull tattoo behind his ear.

'Happy New Year, sir!' he said as Martini approached, and blew his liquor breath into his face.

'Have you seen my daughter?'

The boy pretended to think about it. 'Let's see ... What does she look like? Can you describe her?'

Martini put his hand in his pocket and removed a picture of Monica from his wallet.

Lucas took the picture and studied it. 'She's pretty,' he said, to provoke him. 'She might have been here tonight.'

But Martini was in no mood for jokes. He grabbed Lucas by his sweaty T-shirt and pushed him violently against the nearest wall. He'd never before acted like this, at least not in public. A few people turned towards them.

'Hey, guys, there's a fight!' someone announced, and many of those present gathered round.

All Martini was doing, though, was staring into Lucas's eyes. 'Have you seen her, yes or no?'

The boy wasn't used to being treated this way, and it was obvious that he would have liked to respond in kind. Instead, he said with a menacing smile, 'I could report you for this.'

Martini refused to be intimidated. 'I'm not going to ask you again.'

Lucas abruptly shook off his teacher's hands. 'I know where she is,' he admitted, then added triumphantly, 'But you're not going to like it.'

It had stopped raining by the time Martini reached the house. The lights were off inside. The sound of the doorbell echoed in the silence. Shortly afterwards, a light came on in the corridor.

Martini saw the scene through the frosted glass of the door. It was like a mirage or a bad dream.

A young man with a bare, very smooth chest opened the door. He was barefoot and wearing nothing but tracksuit bottoms. Behind him, Monica's head peered out of one of the rooms. She was dressed, but her rumpled hair told another story.

As they drove back home in the four-by-four, neither of them said a word for a long time. Martini had called his wife to tell her everything was all right, and that he was coming home with their daughter, but had preferred not to add anything else.

'The party was a bore, so we left,' Monica said as if to justify her actions. Her father said nothing. 'We fell asleep and lost all track of time. I'm sorry.'

Martini gripped the wheel angrily, heedless of the pain in his left hand. 'Have you been smoking?' he asked.

'What do you mean?'

'You know what I mean. Was that grass?'

She shook her head, although she knew it was pointless to lie. 'I don't know what it was, but I swear nothing else happened.'

Martini tried to remain calm. 'Anyway, you'll have to explain yourself to your mother now.'

He parked the white four-by-four in the drive. Clea was in the doorway, her cardigan pulled tight about her. Monica got out of the car first. Martini watched her as she ran to the house. Her mother opened her arms wide and clasped her to her chest. It was a liberating hug. Martini sat watching the scene through the windscreen, afraid to interrupt this moment with his presence. He thought back to what had happened to his family just six months earlier, when he had been on the brink of losing everything.

The thing.

No, it would never happen again.

3 January

Eleven days after the disappearance

The forecasts had been accurate. The rain hadn't stopped for two whole days.

But the third morning was illumined by a pale sun that had been crouching behind a thin blanket of off-white clouds.

Martini had decided this was the right day to devote himself to the gazebo in the garden. He wanted to distract Clea from the business of the missing girl, and dusting off the idea of a vegetable garden and a greenhouse struck him as the most appropriate move. His wife had nothing to do with herself, and spent her days watching TV programmes that dealt exclusively with the case of Anna Lou Kastner. In the absence of an official, verified truth, everyone felt they had the right to present their own version. It was the only thing being talked about right now on TV. And it wasn't only the experts giving their verdicts. Starlets and others from the showbiz world were invited on, too. It was indecent. The most absurd, most fantastic theories were being put forward, the most insignificant aspects of the story of Anna Lou dissected, analysed and discussed as if at any moment such discussions might lead to the solution of the mystery.

The impression was that the circus of chatter might go on ad infinitum.

The TV was constantly on in Martini's house, and so this morning he had got in his car and gone to the DIY store. He had bought a roll of plasticised canvas and another of flexible sheet metal, as well as a whole lot of nuts and bolts and steel vices to hold the tie beams in place. As he was loading everything into the capacious boot of his four-by-four, Martini had been disrupted by a sound.

The scraping of a skateboard on the asphalt.

He turned and saw Mattia just a few metres from him. 'Mattia!' He raised his arm to greet him.

Mattia didn't see him at first. When he did, he had a strange reaction. He slowed down, then accelerated and sped off.

Martini sighed. For the life of him, he couldn't understand the boy. He got in his car to drive home.

He always avoided the route through the village, instead taking a ring road that skirted the centre. The traffic usually flowed quite well, but this morning there was a whole line of slowly moving cars ahead of him. Maybe there had been an accident. They were frequent at the crossroads a bit further on. After a while, indeed, he caught sight of the flashing lights of a police patrol car. As he advanced, though, he couldn't see any damaged vehicle.

It wasn't an accident. It was a roadblock.

They were common in Avechot these days. It was all because of the missing girl. Quite apart from the fact that they were a great bother, Martini couldn't see the point of these road-blocks. It was a bit like shutting the stable door after the horse has bolted, he thought. But he suspected that the police, under a constant media spotlight and with the mystery deepening with every passing day, had to show the public they were at least doing something.

There were no side roads to turn onto in order to avoid the roadblock, and it would have looked suspicious to do a U-turn. So Martini resigned himself and patiently waited his turn. But as he moved slowly forward, a particular kind of anxiety grew inside him. There was a tingling in his fingertips, and a strange feeling of emptiness in his stomach.

'Good morning, may I see your papers please?' the uniformed officer said, leaning down to the open window.

Martini had everything ready. He handed over his licence and registration.

'Thank you,' the officer said, then walked away towards the patrol car.

Martini sat watching the scene. There were only two police officers. The second was in the middle of the road with a signalling disc, motioning the cars to stop. The officer he had spoken to had got in the car and was dictating the details of the documents into his radio. Martini could see him clearly through the rear window. But, after a while, he also began to wonder why they were taking so long. Maybe it was only an impression, maybe it happened to everyone who was stopped, but all the same the suspicion grew in him that something wasn't right.

At last, the officer got out of the police car and came walking back towards him. 'Signor Martini, could you follow me please?'

'What's going on?' he asked, perhaps a little too alarmed.

'Just a formality, it'll only take a few minutes,' the officer replied softly.

They had escorted him to the little police station in Avechot. There they had made him sit down in some kind of records office. Apart from the filing cabinets and the files lined up on the shelves, there was a jumble of everything in the room: obsolete computers, lamps, writing materials, even a stuffed bird of prey.

There were also a table and two chairs. Martini kept looking at the empty chair opposite him, wondering who would occupy it. Forty minutes had already passed since he had arrived, and still no one had come in. The silence and the smell of dust were draining.

The door opened suddenly and a man of about thirty in a jacket and tie entered the room. He was holding Martini's registration certificate and driving licence. He looked mild-mannered. 'I'm Officer Borghi,' he said, smiling. 'Sorry to have kept you waiting.'

Martini shook the hand held out to him. Faced with such politeness, he relaxed a little. 'That's all right.'

Borghi sat down on the empty chair and placed the documents on the table, giving them a quick glance as though he hadn't had time to check them earlier. 'So, Signor . . . Martini,' he said, reading the name.

Martini wondered if this was just a trick to make him think that there was nothing to fear, because the officer had known from the start what his name was. 'Yes, that's me,' he confirmed.

'I imagine you must be wondering why we stopped you. We're doing some random checks. This'll only take a few minutes.'

'Is it about the missing girl?'

'Do you know her?' the officer asked abruptly.

'She's the same age as my daughter and attends the school where I teach, but honestly I don't remember her.'

The young officer paused for a moment and Martini had the impression that he was studying him. Then Borghi resumed speaking with the same cordiality as earlier. 'I'm going to ask you a typical police question.' He smiled. 'Where were you on the twenty-third of December at five in the evening?'

'In the mountains,' Martini immediately replied. 'I was away for several hours and got back home in time for dinner.'

'Are you a climber?'

'No, I love hiking.'

Borghi gave a grin of approval. 'Good heavens. And whereabouts did you go hiking on the twenty-third?'

'I went up to the pass and then chose a route on the eastern slope.'

'Was anyone with you? A friend, an acquaintance?'

'No, nobody. I like walking alone.'

'Did anybody see you, another hiker, someone looking for mushrooms perhaps, anyone who could confirm where you were?'

Martini thought about this and said, 'I don't think I came across anybody on the twenty-third.'

Another silence. 'What did you do to your hand?'

Martini looked at the bandage on his left hand, as if he had forgotten it. 'I slipped. Actually, that was the day it happened. I took a wrong step, and to break my fall I instinctively grabbed hold of a branch that was sticking out of the ground. It's taking quite a while to heal.'

Borghi studied him some more. Martini felt a sense of

unease. Then Borghi smiled again. 'Good, we're finished,' he said, and gave him back his papers.

Martini was surprised. 'Is that all?'

'I told you it'd only take a few minutes, didn't I?'

Borghi got up and Martini followed suit. They shook hands. 'Thank you for your time, Signor Martini.'

For dinner this evening, Clea had made roast chicken and fried potatoes, the family's favourite dish. When something wasn't going well, or when they wanted to reward themselves, the Martinis always tucked into a nice chicken.

He didn't know why his wife had chosen chicken tonight, maybe it was to celebrate the fact that things were on an even keel with Monica again. He hadn't told Clea what had happened on New Year's Eve, hoping his daughter would. She hadn't had the courage to do so, but her sense of guilt had led to a rapprochement with her mother.

There was a new atmosphere in the house. At last, the dinner table was the scene of lively chatter. The subject was the neighbours. The Odevises were the object of amused scorn. Clea and Monica were laughing at them, couldn't stop talking about them. Fortunately, Martini thought. That way, they wouldn't notice his silence.

After leaving the police station, he had driven home feeling quite relaxed. But, as the hours had passed, strange questions had started to take shape in his head. Why had they let him go so soon? Was he really to believe that Officer Borghi's kindness was genuine? Had the fact that he had no way of proving his own 'alibi' for the day of the disappearance roused their suspicions?

After dinner, he tried to correct some of his class's

homework, but his mind continued to wander. He went to bed about eleven, aware that sleep would be a long time coming.

Everything's going to be fine, he told himself as he slid under the blankets. Yes, it'll all be fine.

'Are you a climber?'

'No, I love hiking.'

'Good heavens. And whereabouts did you go hiking on the twenty-third?'

'I went up to the pass and then chose a route on the eastern slope.'

'Was anyone with you? A friend, an acquaintance?'

'No, nobody. I like walking alone.'

'Did anybody see you, another hiker, someone looking for mushrooms perhaps, anyone who could confirm where you were?'

'I don't think I came across anybody on the twenty-third.'

'What did you do to your hand?'

Vogel stopped the video of the interrogation, freezing a close-up image of Loris Martini. He turned to Borghi and Mayer. 'No alibi, and a wound on the hand,' he said triumphantly.

'But he has an unblemished record,' Prosecutor Mayer objected. 'There's nothing to suggest he's capable of a violent act.'

Having viewed all Mattia's videos, Vogel had become convinced that the boy really had supplied them with the lead they were looking for. He was their star witness. He and his mother had been taken to a protected location.

Then they had immediately started keeping track of Martini. They had practically never let him out of their sight in the last seventy-two hours. They had watched him from a distance, filmed him in secret, noted down everything he did.

Nothing unusual had emerged, but Vogel had certainly not been expecting that they would find ironclad proof so soon. And besides, it was often necessary to give things a little push in these cases. That was why he had arranged that morning's fake roadblock. First, though, he had brought Mattia out of his refuge and explained to him exactly what he should do when he saw Martini on the street. He needed facial recognition.

While Martini had stood there wondering why the boy had sped away when he saw him outside the DIY store, Vogel had been watching him from an unmarked police car, analysing his every expression.

Taking him to the station and making him wait alone in a dusty records room for forty minutes had been a way to put pressure on him. Borghi had played his part well. He had been polite, he had appeared satisfied with the answers. But the questions hadn't been formulated in such a way as to force the suspect into contradicting himself, only to arouse doubts in him.

All this would bear fruit in the following hours, Vogel was convinced of it.

Mayer was rather less so. 'Do you know how many of the people we've questioned informally in the last few days have no credible alibi for the twenty-third of December? Twelve of them. And four of those twelve actually have criminal records.'

Vogel had expected the prosecutor's scepticism. But as far as he was concerned, Loris Martini fitted the profile. 'Invisibility is a talent,' he said. 'It requires self-control and a lot of discipline. I'm convinced that Martini has often committed terrible acts in his mind, wondering each time if he would be capable of them in reality. Monsters aren't born. It's like with love, you need the right person ... When he met Anna Lou, he finally realised what his true nature was. He fell in love with his own victim.'

Borghi listened to this exchange without commenting. If he were to trust his own instinct, he would have sworn that the teacher had seemed much too calm during their encounter.

'You said a while back that Anna Lou probably knew her kidnapper and had no qualms about going with him,' Mayer said. 'But we're not even sure the two of them did know each other.'

'Martini teaches in the same school the girl attended. She must have known him by sight at least.'

'Anna Lou may well have known who he was, but would she have trusted him? It takes much more than a casual acquaintance to persuade a girl to get in a car when it's dark out. Especially if the girl in question has been brought up to spend as little time as possible with anyone outside the brotherhood. And I don't think this Martini fellow is a member.'

'Then how do you explain Mattia's videos?'

'That footage isn't proof, not yet anyway, as you know perfectly well.'

But it'll become proof, Vogel thought.

And he gave another glance at the still image of the man's face.

Yes, Loris Martini was perfect.

5 January

Thirteen days after the disappearance

The yellow light of dusk formed a kind of blue aura around the contours of the mountains.

Martini was driving along the main road in the four-by-four, his wife beside him. The heating was on and rumbled a little, but the car was pleasantly warm. Clea had stopped talking some minutes earlier and seemed to be enjoying the lethargy of this relaxed atmosphere. Every now and again, Martini would turn to her and she would respond to his gaze with a smile. 'That was a good idea of yours,' she said. 'We hadn't been to the lake in ages.'

'Not since last summer,' he replied. 'But I think it's lovelier in winter.'

'I agree.'

They had spent the entire day by a lake located high in the mountains. To reach it, you had to hike for a couple of hours. It wasn't a difficult route, unlike those he usually took. Clea wasn't used to hiking, which was why he had chosen that itinerary. In the woods, little rivers and streams intersected with the path, which was cleared frequently to allow hikers to reach their goal. The unusual absence of snow in the region made the climb easier. The reward, once you got to the top, was the view of a small valley surrounded by rocky peaks, not far from a huge glacier. At the foot of this was a very clear stretch of water, its surface sparkling with golden light. All around, a forest of rhododendron trees, whose foliage in summer was bright red. Next to the lake was a mountain hut where you could eat. The menu consisted of only three dishes, all local. Martini and his wife went there for the vegetable soup and black bread in particular. The hours had passed quickly, and by the time they had got back to the car, it was almost dark.

'What are you thinking?' Clea asked. It seemed a harmless enough question.

'Nothing.' He was sincere. The thoughts that had been disturbing him, even just a day earlier, had all faded, and now he was calm again. But he hadn't told her about the roadblock, or about the interrogation – if you could call it that – that he had been subjected to.

'You should cut your hair,' she said, passing a hand through his layer of chestnut curls.

Martini liked his wife's little attentions. They made him think she hadn't given up on him. 'You're right, I'll go to the barber tomorrow.'

They were happy, but also tired. They both looked forward to getting home and having a nice shower. Martini, though, noticed that the fuel gauge had lit up on the dashboard. 'I have to fill her up.'

'Can't you put it off until tomorrow?' Clea asked. She really didn't want to stop.

'Unfortunately not.'

About ten kilometres further on, he spotted a service station. When he turned off the road, though, he realised that it was full of cars and camper vans. Strange – usually this wasn't a busy area. The missing girl, he thought. They've come here to snoop.

There was a party atmosphere. They had come in groups and the clamour of people and children was almost unbearable. When his turn came, Martini served himself from the self-service pump. Then he went inside the restaurant to pay. He queued at the cash desk, where a young girl was trying her best to keep things moving. On a shelf high up in a corner near the ceiling was a TV set. The voices of the people crowding the place drowned out the sound of the set, but images from the umpteenth item about Anna Lou Kastner flashed on the screen. Martini snorted in annoyance and looked away.

At last, it was his turn to pay. 'I filled her up from number eight,' he told the cashier.

'You're from around here, I suppose,' the girl said, checking the amount on a computer. Her tone was exasperated.

'How do you know that?'

'I saw you snorting just now.' Then she added in a low voice, 'My boss is happy with all these people, he says it's good for business, but I go home in the evening with my feet burning and a headache you wouldn't believe.'

Martini smiled. 'Maybe it won't last much longer.'

'Let's hope not, but today was a special day: the TV channels seem to have gone mad. All they do is show the same images.'

161

'What images?'

But the cashier had been distracted from her activities and the queue was getting longer. 'Sorry, you did say number eight?'

'Yes, that's right.'

She turned to the window of the restaurant, through which his white four-by-four could clearly be seen. Then she looked at Martini again with a puzzled expression on her face.

'Is there some problem?'

The cashier looked up at the television set. Martini did the same.

On the screen were images from an amateur video. Anna Lou captured at various moments: walking alone along the street with her brightly coloured satchel and a bag with her ice skates; in the company of a friend – Martini immediately recognised Priscilla; coming out of her house with her younger brothers. In each case, the image froze and there was a zoom in on a white four-by-four always visible in the background, a few metres away.

Martini realised that this was what the networks had been showing all day. It was the same thing that had drawn all these people to Avechot. A lead at last. A white four-by-four just like his.

No, it wasn't 'just like' his: it *was* his.

The scoop was due to the famous TV reporter Stella Honer. Superimposed on the screen were the words THE TURNING POINT: SOMEONE WAS FOLLOWING HER.

Martini left a fifty-euro note on the counter – a lot more than he had to pay – and quickly left the queue, ignoring the cashier's stunned expression. He hadn't yet reached the exit when he saw someone pointing at something through the windows.

'Hey, that's the car!' someone else cried.

In the meantime, a small group of men had formed outside, behind the four-by-four. They were checking the licence number. Luckily, Clea, still sitting inside, was busy sending a text message and hadn't noticed a thing. Martini started walking faster, while those present all turned to watch him. When he got to the four-by-four, he quickly climbed in.

'What's going on?' Clea asked, seeing how agitated he was.

'I'll tell you later,' he said. Without wasting any more time, he put his key in the ignition. His hands were trembling so much, the car wouldn't start. Meanwhile, people had surrounded them – men, women and children. In their eyes was the same mixture of surprise and fear he had seen in the cashier's eyes. If one of them decides to do something, the others will follow suit, Martini thought, terrified. At last, he managed to start the car and pull out. He immediately turned onto the main road, then glanced in the rear-view mirror. They were still there, standing staring at him threateningly.

'Why won't you tell me what's going on?' Clea asked again, alarmed.

He didn't have the courage to turn and look at her. 'Let's go home.'

On their way home, he couldn't avoid the barrage of questions his wife threw at him. He tried to explain the situation, even though he didn't entirely understand it himself.

'What do you mean, they stopped you?'

'Two days ago. It was a roadblock.'

'Why didn't you tell me?'

'Because I didn't think it was important. They stopped a lot of people, not just me. People I know,' he lied.

When they finally reached their destination, Martini expected to find the police waiting. Instead, the street outside their house was strangely deserted. There wasn't a soul in sight, but he still hurried his wife out of the car. 'Quick, let's get in the house.'

They walked in to find their daughter standing in the middle of the living room, staring at the TV screen. 'Mummy, what's going on?' She was scared. 'They're saying the missing girl . . . Someone was following her . . . They keep showing a car that looks like ours.'

Clea embraced Monica, not knowing what to say, then looked to her husband to say something. But Martini couldn't move from the corridor. 'I don't know, I don't understand,' he murmured. 'There must be some mistake.'

The white four-by-four appeared on the screen.

'But that's our car.' Clea was incredulous and upset.

'I know, it's crazy,' Martini said as Monica started to cry. 'I told you: I was at the police station, they asked me some questions and then let me go. I was convinced there was no problem.'

'You were convinced?' There was accusation in Clea's tone.

Martini seemed increasingly agitated. 'Yes, they asked me where I was when the girl disappeared. Things like that.'

Clea fell silent for a few seconds, as if trying to remember. 'You were in the mountains that day. You came back in the evening.' She sounded calm enough, but deep down she was starting to realise that her husband didn't have an alibi. 'Yes, they made a mistake,' she said firmly, because she couldn't imagine any other hypothesis. 'Now call the police and demand an explanation.' Determined as she was, though, there was uncertainty there, too.

At last, Martini managed to advance into the living room. He reached the telephone and dialled the number. At the other end, they answered after a moment or two.

'This is Loris Martini. I'd like to speak to the officer I saw the other day, please. I think his name was Borghi.'

As he waited for them to put him through, he turned and looked at his wife and daughter. They clung together, confused and afraid. It hurt him to see them in that state. But the worst of it was the feeling that this embrace excluded him. It was as if they had already decided to keep their distance from him.

Minutes passed, then a voice said, 'Borghi here.'

'Can you tell me what's going on? Why my car is on TV?' Martini was beside himself.

'I'm sorry,' Borghi said in a flat tone. 'There was a leak. It shouldn't have happened.'

'A leak? Am I accused of something?'

There was a brief silence at the other end. 'I can't tell you anything else. We'll call you, but my advice is to get yourself a lawyer. Good evening.'

Borghi abruptly hung up, and Martini stood there, the receiver stuck to his ear, not knowing what to do, although Clea and Monica were begging for an answer.

Just then, a flash lit up the room for a moment.

It hadn't been a hallucination. All three looked around, uncomprehendingly. The flash came again, then again seconds later. It was like a storm, but with no thunder to follow the lightning.

Martini went to one of the windows and looked out. His wife came up behind him.

The flashes were coming from the street. Figures, as dark as shadows, were moving around the house. Every now and again they let off a flash. They were like Martians, curious and menacing.

They were news photographers.

6 January

Fourteen days after the disappearance

During the night, the network vans had taken over the street outside the Martini house. Those who had arrived first had monopolised the best positions from which to capture the quiet house which would now appear on TV in an endless loop, twenty-four hours a day.

Along with the crews, the photographers and reporters, groups of onlookers had taken up position beyond the cordon the local police had put up for safety reasons. That cordon wouldn't be enough to protect either him or his family if the crowd decided to apply summary justice, Martini thought as he peered out of the window at about nine in the morning.

It had been a difficult night. None of them had got a wink of sleep. Monica had collapsed just before dawn and Clea had withdrawn into a tormented silence. Martini couldn't stand it any more. He had to do something. 'Borghi said they'd get in touch, but I have no intention of waiting,' he told his wife. 'I haven't done anything, and they don't have anything on me, or they would have arrested me by now, don't you agree?'

Thinking about this, Clea seemed to regain a little confidence. 'Yes, you have to go to them and clarify your position.'

Martini shaved and put on his best suit and even a tie, determined to go out there and show himself for what he had always been to those who knew him: a respectable man. When he stepped through the door, he was greeted by a barrage of flashes. They came from all directions, like a bombardment. He shielded his face with one hand, but only so as not to be blinded. Then he headed for the four-by-four, but thought better of it. After those videos, it wasn't wise for him to be associated with the vehicle. And besides, it would be difficult to get out of the street with so many people there. So he decided he would walk.

A police officer saw him and called out, 'Signor Martini, it may be better for you to go home.' It wasn't an order, he was simply advising him not to confront the crowd because it might be dangerous.

Martini ignored him and kept walking until he was beyond the cordon. Cameramen and reporters armed with microphones were on him in a moment.

'Why was your car in all those places Anna Lou went?'

'Did you know her well? Were you following her?'

'Have the police summoned you for questioning?'

'Do you think she's been murdered?'

Martini said nothing and tried to continue on his way, but they were slowing him down. In the meantime, the members of the public who were there were starting to yell. Martini could not hear the curses directed at him, but in the crowd that surrounded him he saw several angry faces. They hadn't yet come closer, but their intentions were obvious. When the first object was thrown at him, Martini couldn't even tell what it was. He only heard the dull thud it produced as it fell on the asphalt a small distance from him. Immediately, others started doing the same. More objects came flying over: beer cans, coins. Afraid of being hit, the reporters moved a few steps away, freeing a space around him and thus making him an easy target.

Martini raised his arms to protect himself, but it was pointless. The police who were there wouldn't do anything to contain the public anger. Just then, there came a screech of tyres. Martini had bent down to avoid the things raining down on him, but raised himself just enough to see a Mercedes with darkened windows coming to a halt a few metres ahead of him. The rear door opened wide and a man wearing a very elegant pinstripe suit held out his hand. 'Get in!' he said in a loud voice.

Even though he had no idea who the man was, Martini couldn't help but accept the invitation. He got in and the car set off again quickly, rescuing him from a certain lynching.

First, the well-dressed man handed him a box of Kleenex. 'Clean yourself up.' Then he said to his driver, 'Take us somewhere we can talk quietly.'

Martini realised there was a yellowish substance on his clothes. From the smell he knew it was mustard. 'They threw all kinds of things at me out there.'

'You shouldn't confront the crowd like that. If you do that, you provoke them, don't you understand?'

'What should I do, then?' Martini asked, angrily.

'Put your trust in me, for example.' The man laughed, then

held out his hand and introduced himself. 'Giorgio Levi, attorney at law.'

Martini looked at him suspiciously. 'You're not from around here.'

The man laughed again. 'No, I'm not.' He had a deep, sincere laugh. Then he grew serious. 'The way suspicion spreads in a community is just like an epidemic, did you know that? It doesn't take much for the contagion to become uncontainable. People aren't looking for justice, they simply want a culprit. They want to put a name to their fear in order to feel safe. In order to continue harbouring the illusion that everything's fine, that there's always a solution.'

'Then maybe I should accuse the media and the police,' Martini said.

'I wouldn't advise that.'

'So what can I do?'

'Nothing,' was the curt reply.

'In other words, I should let them destroy me without reacting?' He was incredulous and indignant.

'It's a war you can only lose, so it's pointless to fight it. The sooner you realise that, the better. No, we must concentrate on your image as an honest man, a good husband, a good father.'

'But on TV they're saying I'd been following the girl for almost a month before she disappeared. That's absurd!'

'Not *you*. Your *car* was following her. From now on, be very careful about the words you use. All that's visible in those videos is your four-by-four.'

'The reporters are also saying it was a pupil of mine who took that footage.'

'Yes, his name's Mattia.'

Martini seemed surprised.

'Let's say those videos are merely an absurd coincidence,' Levi went on. 'You and Anna Lou live in the same place, so it's plausible. But there's something else I need to warn you about.'

The Mercedes stopped. Through the window, Martini recognised the open space behind the cemetery, where the young people of Avechot sometimes went in their cars to have sex or smoke marijuana.

'The policeman who's after you is called Vogel.' He had uttered the name in a worried tone. 'I wouldn't call him a particularly good detective. He doesn't know much about criminology and isn't interested in things like forensics or DNA. He's someone who uses the media to get what he wants.'

'I don't understand.'

'Vogel knows those videos aren't proof of anything. Apart from anything else, they were made by a young man obsessed with Anna Lou, a young man with a criminal record for violence, who's taking psychoactive drugs and is being cared for by a local psychiatrist, a man named Flores. In other words, this Mattia isn't a reliable source. Vogel can't use him. That's why you're still free.'

'Aren't they afraid I might run away?'

Levi laughed again. 'Where could you go? You've been on national television, Signor Martini. Right now, the whole country knows your face.'

Martini took a closer look at the man. He was older than him, but looked younger than his years. Maybe it was because of his hair, which was still thick and the original colour. Women probably found him attractive. He gave off a pleasant scent of eau de Cologne, but it wasn't just that. His calm, his self-confidence instilled trust. 'So what are you doing here?'

'I'm here to defend you, obviously!' the lawyer replied with a smile.

'But how much is it going to cost me to hire you?'

'Not a cent,' Levi said, raising his arms. 'I'll get my payment from the publicity for the case. But there will be expenses.' He started to list them: 'For the moment, a private investigator to conduct an investigation parallel to that of the police. And then, if the case comes to court, we'll need experts of various kinds, as well as legal researchers.'

Martini tried in vain to imagine what the cost of all that might be. 'I have to talk to my wife.'

'Of course.' The lawyer slipped a hand into the leather bag that was by his feet and took out a white box: it was a brand-new mobile phone, still in its wrapping. 'From now on, use this to contact me, because it's very likely your phone's being tapped. And don't leave home if you can't move about safely.'

Vogel was adjusting his cashmere tie in front of the mirror in his hotel room. He had bought it before leaving for Avechot, savouring in advance the moment – and the occasion – he would wear it.

Below, a small crowd of reporters were waiting for him. He liked the idea of keeping them waiting, considering how much grief they'd caused him in the last few months.

The case of the Mutilator, he recalled.

He'd had to pay the price for that, but now he was back on track, and those bastards were at his feet again, hoping that he would throw them a few crumbs to momentarily appease their insatiable appetites.

The Mutilator had been a mistake, he had to admit. But it

was a mistake he would never make again. Just enough time had passed for him to restore his reputation and again become the idol of the media. He was one step away from recovering the power he'd once had, which was why he needed to proceed with caution.

Stella had used Mattia's videos well. That montage, zooming in on the teacher's four-by-four, was a masterpiece. And Officer Borghi had proved a valuable ally, too, more valuable than he would ever have expected. The young man might have a future, he would make sure he had him along on his next cases. The problem, though, was Prosecutor Mayer. The conceited bitch. There was nothing worse than an idealistic prosecutor. But he'd be able to tame her, all he had to do was massage her ego, make sure she felt the warmth of the spotlight. Nobody could ever resist that, even if it sometimes got so hot it burned you.

He had got burned himself in the Mutilator case. But the worst was over.

There was a knock at the door. It was Borghi. 'Sir, you have to go down. We can't hold them back any longer.'

Soon afterwards, Vogel appeared in front of a noisy audience anxious for news, who had gathered in the dining room of the hotel. The chairs were all occupied and many reporters were standing. At the back of the room were the TV cameramen.

'I don't have a lot to tell you, unfortunately,' he said into the cluster of microphones by way of introduction. 'I think we can get through this in a few minutes.' Some protested, but Vogel was too much of an expert to be drawn into a collective interview. He would say only what suited him.

'Why haven't you arrested Martini yet?' a newspaper reporter asked.

'Because we intend to accord him all the protections guaranteed by the law. For now, he's only a suspect.'

'Apart from the videos of the white four-by-four, have you found any other link to Anna Lou Kastner?' a female correspondent in a blue tailored suit asked.

'That's confidential information,' Vogel replied. It was one of his favourite phrases: not a confirmation, but not a denial either. He wanted them all to think that the police had an ace up their sleeves.

'We know Signor Martini recently moved here with his family.' This time, it was Stella Honer speaking. 'His wife gave up her job as a lawyer and followed her husband to Avechot. Do you think they were running away from something?'

Vogel was pleased with the question: Stella was good at homing in on unexpected aspects of whatever story she was covering. 'We're investigating Signor Martini's past, but for the moment all I can tell you is that he appears to be beyond reproach.' This defence of Martini was calculated: it would make the public, who had already made their choice and didn't like to be contradicted, more indignant than ever. 'It was actually all of you who ruined his reputation with your leaks,' he said shamelessly. 'I have nothing else to tell you.'

'Then why did you summon us?' someone complained.

'To reprimand you. We can't stop you from broadcasting the news, but you need to be aware that every piece of information that comes out without the consent of the police may harm the investigation and, worse still, may harm young Anna Lou Kastner. The fact that she isn't here with us doesn't mean we can ignore her.' He made sure these last words were addressed directly to the TV cameras. Then he moved away from the microphones and headed for the exit, while the questions kept coming. But Vogel wasn't listening to them any more. He was distracted by the vibration of his mobile. He took it out and looked at the text on the display.

I need to talk to you. Call me on this number.

It must be some reporter in search of a scoop. He decided to ignore the message and immediately deleted it irritably.

'Actually we didn't see much of them. The wife and daughter seemed all right, but I never liked him.' Odevis's face could barely be contained within the portable TV set in the Martinis' kitchen. 'To be quite honest, I was always aware of a kind of . . . well, a strange attitude. For instance, the morning poor Anna Lou went missing, we ran into each other as he was leaving the house. I said hello to him but he didn't so much as look at me. He put a rucksack in the boot of that rundown old four-by-four of his and . . . Yes, he was in a real hurry, I mean, like someone who has something to hide.'

Listening to his neighbour's incredible lie, Martini felt like punching the wall unit. But he stopped just in time, realising it was his bandaged hand.

From her seat at the table, Clea switched off the TV with the remote. 'That nasty wound hasn't healed yet. I told you to get it seen to by a doctor.' She said this with quiet resignation.

Martini was still seething with rage. 'That bastard.'

'Why, what did you expect?'

Martini tried to regain his self-control. He went and sat down next to his wife. It was after eleven at night, and the house was silent. The kitchen table, lit by the lamp in the middle, was like an oasis of light surrounded by darkness. On it, bills and receipts were piled, as well as a copy of the latest tax statement. Clea had run the figures through the calculator at least ten times. The result was always the same.

'There isn't enough money to pay for everything Levi's planning,' Martini had to admit, disconsolately.

'Then let's put off paying the rent for a while.'

'Oh, sure. And how will we live when they throw us out?'

'We'll figure that out when it happens. In the meantime, you could ask my family for a loan.'

Martini shook his head, as if to underline the fact that the situation they found themselves in was absurd and everything was happening too quickly. 'We'll have to do without Levi, we have no option.'

'We're out of food.'

'What's that got to do with it?'

'I went to the supermarket today. Some people recognised me. I got scared and left without buying anything.' Seeing the anger reappear on her husband's face, Clea took his hand. She talked to him in a low voice, the tone full of pain. 'Monica has been insulted on the internet. They've forced her to close her Facebook profile.'

'They're just crooks and losers looking for attention, I wouldn't worry about that.'

'Yes, I know . . . But in a few days she'll have to go back to school.'

She was right. With all the other things that were happening, he hadn't thought of that.

'You can't let them lynch you like this without reacting. Any direct accusation against you also affects us.'

Martini heaved a sigh. 'All right, I'll tell Levi to proceed.'

Someone rang the bell. Martini and his wife looked at each

other in silence, unsure who it could be at this hour. Then he got up from the kitchen table and went to open the door.

'Good evening, Signor Martini,' Borghi said, standing in the doorway. Behind him, there were at least five patrol cars with their lights on, a police van and a breakdown lorry. A big show for the media. Cameramen and photographers were capturing the scene. 'I have here a search and arrest warrant.' Borghi showed him the document.

Clea came up behind her husband, but stopped when she saw all those police officers outside the house.

'We also have to take your prints and get body samples,' Borghi went on. 'Do you agree to doing that here, or would you like us to go somewhere more appropriate?'

Martini was disoriented. 'No, it's all right, let's do it here.'

Borghi turned towards the waiting police officers and gave a signal for them to approach the house.

Martini was sitting in the middle of his own living room. Three forensics technicians wearing white coats and rubber gloves were busy around him. While one took saliva samples with a swab, another performed a subungual scrub on his right hand in search of organic material belonging to Anna Lou. The third was concentrating on the left hand. He took off the bandage, then proceeded to take a sample of tissue from the wound, which hadn't yet healed. Finally, he photographed the cut with a special model of reflex camera, from which it was possible to extract very large images.

Martini underwent all this without any reaction, as if dazed.

All around him, police officers were searching through his things, the memories of a life. There was a constant coming and going. Some officers left the house with transparent bags containing the most varied objects: kitchen knives, shoes, even gardening tools. In the drive, the four-by-four was being loaded onto the breakdown lorry while the whole neighbourhood, awoken by the noise, stood watching, winter jackets over their pyjamas, and commenting on the scene with expressions of disgust.

From one corner of the living room, Clea was observing her husband, Monica clasped in her arms. She had been forced to get her daughter out of bed. They both looked very shaken. For the umpteenth time, Martini felt guilty.

9 January

Seventeen days after the disappearance

They had picked the best forensics technician they could find to work on Martini's car.

He was a funny-looking little middle-aged man. The two things that made him especially odd were that, although he was almost bald, he wore his hair in a ponytail and that the skin visible under his white lab coat was totally covered in tattoos. His name was Kropp.

'We've carried out all the available tests,' he said, trying to justify himself to Vogel and Mayer. 'That's why it took so long.'

The police had requisitioned a garage in Avechot to allow the team to work in the best conditions. Inside, the room had been entirely covered in plasticised tarpaulin. A large white waterproof sheet had been spread on the floor and the car had been positioned on an elevator. The technicians were still at work, taking the four-by-four apart piece by piece. The components were divided into various categories and passed through highly sophisticated machines.

'So, anything?' Vogel asked impatiently. 'Yes or no?'

But Kropp was in no hurry and explained everything very calmly. 'The first thing I can tell you is that the car was recently cleaned, but only the interior.'

Obviously, this was music to Vogel's ears.

'There are residues of detergent and solvent,' Kropp continued, 'which makes me think someone was trying to remove traces of something.'

Vogel turned to Mayer. 'Of course. I mean, why only clean the interior unless you have something to hide?'

'Any blood or other bodily fluids?' Mayer asked, clearly not satisfied with the findings.

Kropp shook his head, and his ponytail fluttered between his shoulder blades.

'So what you're saying is that there's nothing to prove that Anna Lou was in this car, right?' Mayer said.

'Were you really hoping we'd find blood?' Vogel asked.

'DNA. I expected there to be the girl's DNA.'

Vogel wanted to ask her where she got her pig-headedness from. Was she in earnest or was she just trying to upset him? 'Can't you see it's a good thing we haven't found anything?'

'Why should that be? You'll have to explain.'

'Clues aren't always tangible. An empty space, for example, is a clue: it means there was something in that space before that's now gone. We need to ask Signor Martini why he decided to clean only the interior of his car.'

'What you're talking about isn't a fact, it's an opinion – *your* opinion, to be precise. There are a thousand reasons why a sensible person might decide not to wash the bodywork of his car, especially if he lives in the mountains and goes on frequent excursions. The mud, snow and rain would make the car dirty again within days. It makes more sense to clean the interior, because passengers travel in it.'

Mayer was doing everything she could to get on his nerves, but Vogel had to admit that he did admire her stubbornness. What he couldn't understand was why she was always trying to undermine the evidence. That was going against her own interests. That teacher was all they had so far. The investigation had already cost millions in taxpayers' money, and people would soon be demanding that Mayer justify the expenditure. 'The mechanism we've set in motion has to bring results, no matter what,' Vogel tried to explain calmly. 'Our job is not to judge evidence and clues, but to take them before a judge and a jury.'

'You're right,' Mayer replied determinedly. 'Our job is not to judge the evidence but to *find* it. I repeat: we need DNA.'

Kropp, who had so far followed this exchange with a certain indifference, now decided to intervene. 'Actually, we did find some DNA.'

They turned towards him, wondering why he hadn't said anything sooner.

'There is something, something quite strange,' he went on. 'The DNA of a cat. Or rather, *cat hairs.*'

'Cat hairs?' Vogel echoed in disbelief.

'From a tabby. Brown and ginger. There was quite a lot on the seats and the rugs.'

'The Martinis don't have a cat,' Mayer said.

Anna Lou loved cats, Vogel would have liked to say, but didn't, because just then Borghi came into the garage, talking on his mobile and looking around for Vogel. He seemed worried about something.

'Excuse me,' Vogel said and walked towards the young officer.

By the time he reached him, Borghi had finished his phone call. 'We have a problem,' he said in a low voice.

Anna Lou's mother, barefoot and in her nightdress, was busy collecting the notes and removing the dead flowers from the array of kittens people had left outside her house several days earlier. The pilgrimage had ground to a halt as soon as news had spread that there was a suspect. Pity had been replaced by morbid curiosity, and nobody really cared about the missing girl's fate any more. Not even the media, who had vanished along with the public. When Vogel and Borghi arrived, there were only a handful of photographers still relentlessly shooting the scene.

'Get rid of them,' Vogel immediately ordered Borghi. He walked up to Anna Lou's mother. 'Signora Kastner, I'm Special Agent Vogel, remember me?'

She turned and looked at him as if in a daze. The drizzle had soaked her nightdress, making it all too obvious that she wasn't wearing anything else underneath it.

Vogel took off his coat and put it over her shoulders. 'It's cold out here. Why don't we go into the house?'

'I must finish tidying up,' she replied, as if it were the most important task in the world.

Vogel showed her the little bead bracelet Anna Lou had made and which she had put on his wrist on Christmas Day, during his first visit to their house. 'Do you remember the promise you asked me to make you? Well, I have some news for you . . . But why don't we talk indoors?'

Maria Kastner seemed to consider this for a moment. 'That

man, the teacher . . . Do you really think it was him? I mean, I don't think he looks like the type. I think he's innocent . . . Because if he was keeping Anna Lou prisoner, you'd have found out where my little girl is by now, wouldn't you?'

Vogel searched for an answer to this. The woman was obviously refusing to come to terms with reality. 'He's under surveillance,' he said.

'But the days are passing. Anna Lou might be hungry. If the man's under constant surveillance, who's taking her her food?'

For the first time in his career and his life, Vogel was speechless. Luckily for him, Bruno Kastner arrived just then, apprised of what was happening outside his house. 'I'm sorry, I was working,' he said. He took his wife by the arm and led her to the front door. 'It's the sleeping pills her psychiatrist prescribed her.'

'Signor Kastner, I need your wife to be as lucid as possible. Maybe the dosage should be reviewed.' He was thinking the media might take advantage of the woman's confused state of mind to attribute unfounded statements to her.

'I'll mention it to Dr Flores,' Bruno Kastner assured him, his back already turned to Vogel.

Vogel stood watching as the man tenderly led his wife into their house. Then he looked again at the little bead bracelet on his wrist.

Stella Honer was in the living room of a modest but respectable house. The sofa on which she was sitting had had a faded cover flung over it, either to conceal the original, damaged upholstery or to protect it from wear and tear. As usual, Stella looked impeccable. Grey tailored suit, a red silk scarf round her neck. She had a microphone in her hand.

The camera moved back to reveal the person sitting beside her.

Priscilla wasn't dressed in her usual fashion, but looked decidedly more sober. Well-pressed jeans with no tears, a white blouse. The three ear studs had disappeared, as had the black eyeliner that gave her such a hard look. She wore no make-up and looked quite girlish. She was clutching a handkerchief.

'So, Priscilla, can you tell us what happened?' Stella asked gently.

The girl nodded, trying to pluck up courage. 'I was at the vigil outside the Kastners' house. I'd brought a cuddly toy kitten for Anna Lou. I had some friends with me, we were all upset by what had happened. Suddenly, I noticed I had a text message ... It was from Signor Martini.' The girl broke off, unable to proceed.

Stella realised that she had to help her along. 'Why were you surprised?'

'I ... I had a lot of respect for Mr Martini, I thought he was an OK guy ... but after what happened ... '

Stella let the silence last, in order to allow her viewers to fully process the girl's words. She was good at creating suspense. 'What did the text say?'

Just as she had been instructed before the live broadcast, Priscilla took the mobile out of her jeans pocket and read the text, with trembling hand and voice. '"Do you fancy coming by my house tomorrow afternoon?"'

There was another pause for effect, deliberately orchestrated by Stella, this time because she'd seen a tear form in the girl's left eye, even though she was trying not to cry. *Not yet.* So, to give her a moment to pull herself together, she gently took the mobile from Priscilla's hand and showed it to the camera. 'We're often accused of only telling half-truths, doctored in order to manipulate the public. But this is no journalistic invention. Look: this really happened.' She gave the viewers enough time to read the message, then turned back to her guest. 'And what did you think, Priscilla?'

'Nothing at first. It was just weird, that's all. But then when they said on television that Signor Martini was a suspect, I thought about Anna Lou. The same thing could have happened to me . . . '

Stella nodded gravely and put her hand on Priscilla's. As expected, her gesture triggered a reaction: Priscilla started to cry. Stella asked no more questions, but cleverly let the camera linger on the girl's face.

'It's just the fantasies of a little girl who always wanted to be on television,' Martini said, his voice cracking with desperation.

But his wife was more angry than anything else. 'And in the meantime, this *little girl* has cost you your job! What do you suggest we do now?'

Two days after the end of the Christmas holidays and the start of the new term, the principal had called Martini to tell him he was suspended from teaching – and without pay.

'How are we going to pay for your defence? We're already riddled with debt and you start fooling around with a pupil? A child?'

'I know Priscilla. That humble look, those clothes – they're all an act!'

Vogel was enjoying this exchange, sitting comfortably in his makeshift office in the school gym's changing room. He was wearing headphones, had both feet up on the table, and was rocking in his chair, hands folded in his lap. Until now, bugging Martini's house hadn't yielded results, but it looked as if something might be happening at last. Vogel seemed entertained by the couple's argument. He had been the one to persuade the school principal to take action against Martini before Stella Honer's interview with Priscilla provoked the anger of parents and pupils alike – anger that would obviously be partly directed at the principal. Being the spineless bureaucrat he was, he had been all too easy to convince.

'Why did you send her that message?' Clea asked.

'She'd asked me to give her acting lessons. Think about it – if I'd wanted to take advantage of her, I'd hardly have been stupid enough to invite her to our house, would I?'

Clea fell silent. For a moment, she seemed to have been swayed. But then she resumed, and there was real pain in her voice. 'I've known you half my life, so I know you're a good man . . . but I'm not sure how innocent you are.' Her words fell like a bombshell, and were followed by another brief pause. 'You're intelligent enough to understand the difference between the two things: even good people make mistakes sometimes . . . Wherever I go, I get hostile looks. I'm constantly afraid somebody might hurt you or us. Monica can't leave the house, she's lost the few friends she had and she can't stand it any more.'

Vogel knew what was about to happen. He'd wanted it, planned it.

'Whatever mistakes you've made, big or small,' Clea went on, 'I'll stand by you for the rest of my days. I promised that, and I will. But your daughter isn't bound by any vows. So I'm going to take her far away from here.'

Vogel felt like rejoicing, but contained himself.

'You mean far away from me.' Martini's response wasn't a question, more a bitter observation.

Clea did not reply. There was silence, interrupted only by the sound of a door opening and closing. Vogel took his feet off the table and leaned forward, putting his hands tightly over his headphones to concentrate on the silence.

Martini was still in the room. He could hear him breathing. The breathing of a hunted man. A man who couldn't be thrown in jail yet but was already imprisoned by his own existence, unable to escape.

Vogel had created a void around him. Now that even his wife and daughter had abandoned him, he would crumble. The man was finished.

But then something happened that Vogel hadn't anticipated. Something absurd, senseless.

Martini started to sing.

He sang softly, in a muted voice. Such cheerfulness definitely jarred with what had just transpired. Vogel listened, perplexed, to the surreal song. It was a nursery rhyme. He could only catch a few words.

It was about little girls and kittens.

10 January

Eighteen days after the disappearance

Levi had called him on the 'secure' phone he'd given him a few days earlier and asked to see him. Then he had sent his own driver to pick him up from his house. The reporters had immediately chased after the Mercedes, but had had to give up when Martini had got out of the car and walked through the gate of a private residence.

The lawyer had rented it in order to keep a close watch on the case.

When Martini stepped inside, he was faced with an unexpected scene. The living room had been turned into an office, where a small handful of colleagues were already hard at work. Some were studying law books and files, others were on the telephone, discussing defence strategies. They had even put up a noticeboard with the findings so far. They were so busy, they didn't notice him.

Levi was waiting for him in the kitchen.

'Did you see how I've organised things?' he boasted. 'It's all for your benefit.'

Martini thought of what it would cost him and the fact that he no longer had a job. 'Frankly, I'm losing hope.'

'You shouldn't,' Levi said, motioning him to a chair. He himself remained standing. 'I heard your wife and daughter left yesterday.'

'They're at my in-laws'.'

'Honestly, it's much better like that, trust me. There's a tense atmosphere building up, and I think it's going to get worse over the next few weeks.'

Martini couldn't suppress a bitter smile. 'And you have the nerve to tell me not to lose hope?'

'Of course. It's what I expected.'

'It's that Vogel, isn't it? He's behind all this.'

'Yes, he is, but that's what makes him predictable. He's simply following the usual script. The man's incapable of any kind of inventiveness.'

'And yet everybody listens to him.'

Levi went to the refrigerator and took out a small bottle of mineral water. He unscrewed the top and offered it to Martini. 'The only thing that can save you is to remain clear-headed and keep your nerve. So please stay calm and leave everything to me.'

'That policeman has ruined my life.'

'But you're innocent, aren't you?'

Martini looked down at the bottle. 'Sometimes even I have my doubts.'

Levi laughed, although Martini hadn't been joking. Then he put his hand on his shoulder. 'Even Vogel has a weak point, and that's exactly where we'll hit him . . . And it's going to hurt him – a lot.'

Martini looked up at Levi with what might have been a glimmer of hope in his eyes.

'Have you ever heard of the Derg case?' the lawyer asked.

'I don't think so,' Martini replied.

'It was a case that caused a big stir in the media, right up until about a year ago. But you might remember Derg better by the name the papers saddled him with: the Mutilator.'

'Oh, yes, I've heard of him ... though I don't usually take much interest in news stories about crime.'

'Well, for a long time the police were hunting for this man who hid small explosive devices in the products on supermarket shelves: a box of cereal, a tube of mayonnaise, tinned food. A lot of people were injured when the devices went off. Some lost fingers, one his entire hand.'

'My God. Did he ever kill anybody?'

'No, but it would have happened sooner or later: the Mutilator would have got tired and tried something spectacular. That's what everybody was expecting. If you remember, there was widespread panic. But before anybody could get killed, Vogel came up with a seemingly harmless bookkeeper who was fond of model-making and electronics: Signor Derg. As luck would have it, Derg had lost his right index finger as a child. At the time, everybody said it was just an ordinary domestic accident. What actually happened was that his mother had cut off his finger with poultry shears as a punishment. She was mentally ill and frequently mistreated her son.'

'Oh, Lord ... ' Martini said.

Levi pointed at him. 'You see, you're thinking exactly what everybody else thought, that Derg was the perfect culprit.'

'That's true,' Martini admitted. 'It's quite plausible that he'd be violent as an adult after what had happened to him as a child.'

'That's how monsters are created. In the Derg case, there wasn't any evidence either – only clues. Vogel put on a show for the media and persuaded the prosecutor to incriminate Derg. But in the end, the bookkeeper was exonerated.'

'How?'

'The explosive used by the Mutilator was rudimentary. Any amateur could have assembled it with products found in a local hardware store. But there's a problem: it leaves a chemical trace on anyone who handles it. There were no traces of it on Derg . . .'

'And this was enough to exonerate him?'

'No, of course not. The most important clue against him had been found during a police search. In his apartment, Derg had a biscuit tin that was identical to the one in which the Mutilator had hid one of his devices. On top of that, its serial number showed that it had been bought in one of the very same shops where the maniac had struck – a shop Derg had always denied ever visiting.'

'So how—'

'This is where it gets interesting. Whoever planted that tin in his house to frame him hadn't checked the date on the biscuits. They were manufactured when Derg was in prison, awaiting trial, which means he couldn't have bought them. As a result, he was released and the case against him was immediately dropped.'

Martini thought about this. 'And what about Vogel?'

'Vogel saved face by shifting blame onto one of his subordinates, a young officer who was dismissed. He always does that: he finds a scapegoat he can sacrifice if need be . . . Still, after Derg, the media started to be suspicious of Vogel's tip-offs and gradually consigned him to obscurity.'

'Until now,' Martini said. 'I'm his chance to grab the spotlight back.'

'Except that when that happens, we'll show him up for what he is: a fraud.'

Martini seemed to have regained a degree of confidence. 'I'll get out of this, then.'

'Yes, but at what price?' Levi's tone turned serious again. 'Derg spent four years in jail, waiting for his trial to end. During that time, he had a stroke and lost his job, his friends and his family.'

Martini realised that Levi's speech was heading in a specific direction. 'What can I do to avoid that?'

'Forget you're innocent.'

Martini didn't understand what he meant, but the lawyer dismissed him with a handshake and no further explanation.

'I'll be in touch soon,' he promised.

Borghi had spent a sleepless night. He had tossed and turned, endlessly recalling the scene he'd witnessed outside the Kastners' house: that poor, dazed woman wandering in her nightdress amid the kittens people had brought for her daughter, trying to make sense of her grief.

Cats are the answer, he told himself.

The brown and ginger hairs that had been found in Martini's 4 × 4 made no sense. When he'd first heard about them, Borghi had followed the same thought process as Vogel.

The Martinis didn't have a cat. Anna Lou desperately wanted one.

In his sleepless state, Borghi had concluded that the key to solving this riddle lay with the girl. And yet everybody had lost interest in her. They no longer wondered what had happened

192

to her. The media, the public and the police had moved on to questions of a different kind. How did the teacher kill her? Did he rape her first? They took it as read that she had been murdered and, although they wouldn't openly admit it, they were busy feeding their own prurient imaginations with gory details.

Nobody, however, was asking 'Why did he kill her?'

The motive an apparently harmless teacher in a small town in the mountains might have for murdering a girl as invisible as Anna Lou remained an unexpressed question. And yet it was bound to be crucial.

Why did he kill her?

By dawn, Borghi had realised that she had to be their starting point. Anna Lou Kastner. What did they know about her? Only what friends and relatives had said. But was that enough? There was a lesson he had learned at the police academy.

That victims, too, have voices.

It was all too easy to get resigned to the fact that victims were no longer able to provide their own version of events. But they could. The past usually spoke for them. Only, somebody needed to listen to it.

That was why, after discovering that the school attended by Anna Lou had a video surveillance system to discourage bullying and vandalism, Borghi shut himself in a kind of closet packed with old-fashioned video recorders and spent hours checking the footage featuring the girl. It showed everyday scenes in which Anna Lou appeared in all her innocence. The classrooms weren't covered, but the canteen, the gym and the corridors were, and whenever she appeared in any of these she was always the same. Shy, reserved, but capable of responding with a smile to those who spoke to her. There was nothing unusual in her behaviour.

The system was reset every two weeks, which meant that the recordings were erased and the tapes reused. Fortunately, the Christmas holidays had interrupted the cycle, and more than two weeks had been preserved.

The two weeks or so before her disappearance.

Still, there were hours and hours of footage. Borghi had adopted a method by which he would choose parts of the tape at random and search for the girl in them. He sat on a folding chair in front of a black-and-white monitor, a flask of coffee beside him, although the coffee had long turned cold. He had watched lots of scenes, none of them showing Anna Lou and Martini together. Right now, he was watching footage of the last school day before the holidays, which was also the day before the disappearance. His mobile phone rang.

'Why didn't you call me last night?' It was Caroline, and she sounded annoyed.

'You're right, I'm sorry. My work's taking up a lot of my time.'

'Is your work more important than your pregnant wife?' It wasn't a question, it was an accusation.

'Of course not,' he replied. 'I wasn't trying to defend myself, it's the truth. If I'm working, I can't call you, but I think of you constantly.'

At the other end of the line, Caroline sighed. Maybe it was one of her 'good' days, when her hormones weren't driving her crazy. But Borghi couldn't possibly say that to her, or she would hit the roof.

'Have you received the things I sent you?'

'Yes – thank you. I really did need a change of clothes.'

'My father saw you on television last night.'

Borghi could picture her smiling. That was why she wasn't angry: she was proud of him. 'Oh? How did I come across?'

'All I can say is that I hope our daughter takes after me.' They laughed. 'My mother would like us to stay here for a while after she's born.'

They had already discussed this at length. Caroline had said that her mother could help her in the beginning, but that would involve his moving there, too, and, however well Borghi got on with his in-laws, he didn't want to take the risk of living with them in case it turned out to be an indefinite stay. 'Can we talk about this when I get back? After all, the baby isn't due for some months yet.'

Caroline ignored him. 'Dad has already prepared a room for us at the end of the corridor. It was my brother's before he went to live on his own. It's out of the way, so we'll have our privacy.'

Caroline's tone suggested she had already decided for both of them. Borghi would have liked to respond, but just then he noticed something on the monitor and sat up straight on the folding chair. 'Sorry, Caroline, I have to call you back.'

'I can't believe that on one of the rare occasions we get to talk, you brush me off like this.'

'I know, forgive me.' He hung up without waiting for a reply. Then he focused on the video.

There on the screen, Anna Lou and the teacher were finally in the same frame.

The school corridor was deserted except for the girl, who was walking along carrying some books. Then Martini appeared from the opposite direction.

They walked past each other, almost touching.

Borghi rewound the tape and watched the scene again. One

thing in particular struck him. If the media got hold of this, there would be a big hoo-ha. He would have to inform Vogel.

At eleven that night, Martini was sitting on the living room sofa, in the dark. The voices of the crews camped outside his house could be heard inside. He couldn't make out what they were saying, but every now and then he heard laughter.

It's always strange when your life comes to a halt while other people's lives continue, he thought. That was how he felt. As if his life was at a standstill.

He had switched off the lights in order to stop the people out there from peering through the windows to see what the monster was up to. But there was also another reason. He wanted to avoid Clea and Monica's eyes, which kept following him around the house from their framed photographs. They had run away from him, and now he wanted to run away from them. Although he was angry, he could understand their point of view. When it came down to it, it was for their own good.

Suddenly there was a vibration and a little light came on. It was the mobile phone Levi had given him, which lay on one of the shelves. Martini stood up from the sofa and went to check it. There was a message on the screen.

The cemetery in half an hour.

Martini wondered why the lawyer was suggesting a meeting in such an unusual place instead of the house he had rented as his headquarters. Levi's words from that morning still echoed in his ears.

Forget you're innocent.

Maybe he would get an answer. So he concocted an elaborate plan to leave the house unseen. He went upstairs and got out an old jacket and a peaked cap that he felt would be good camouflage. He would avoid the reporters by leaving through the back door and climbing over the garden hedge.

It took him over half an hour to reach the cemetery because he was constantly stopping to make sure nobody was following him. The main gate was half open. He pushed it, walked in, and began advancing between the gravestones.

There was a full, grey moon in the sky. Martini wandered about for a while, certain that Levi would appear any second now. He noticed an intermittent red dot in the distance. He followed it as if it were a beacon pointing him in the right direction. As he drew closer to the light, he realised it was a cigarette, the tip of it lighting up and then fading whenever Stella Honer took a drag.

'Calm down, I'm here as a friend,' she immediately said in an amused tone. She was sitting on a gravestone, legs crossed, as if she was in someone's living room.

'What do you want?' he asked angrily.

'To help you, Loris.'

He was annoyed at being addressed in such a familiar way. 'I don't need your help, Signora Honer.'

'Do you want me to prove what a good friend I am? All right . . . Six months ago, your wife was about to leave you for another man. You moved here to try and start all over again.'

The thing, Martini thought. How did she know that?

'You see? We're friends,' Stella went on, seeing that Martini was more surprised than angry. Vogel, who had passed the information on to her, knew he would react that way. 'I could have used that, but I didn't . . . I know Clea's left and taken your daughter with her. If you want them back, you need to be smart.'

'When everything's been straightened out, they'll come home and we'll go back to our old life.'

Stella tilted her head and looked at him tenderly. 'Poor darling, do you seriously think that's what'll happen?'

'I'm innocent.'

'In that case, you haven't understood a damn thing.' In her mouth, it sounded like a threat. 'Nobody gives a hoot whether you're innocent or not. People have already decided. And the police will never leave you alone: they're spending tons of money on solving this case and they don't have the resources to afford another investigation – and especially not another culprit.'

Martini swallowed with difficulty but tried to appear calm. 'So you're saying it's me or it's nobody.'

'Precisely. There's only one reason you're still free: they haven't found a body, and without a body they can't officially charge someone with murder. But something will turn up sooner or later, Loris, it always does.'

'If I'm screwed, why would I need you, Signora Honer?' Once again he addressed her formally: it was important to establish boundaries.

She paused briefly and smiled. Her deep eyes gleamed in the moonlight. 'You need me in order to take maximum advantage of this business. You could get a lot out of the very same media that are currently hostile to you. Right now, an interview with you would be worth its weight in gold. And I want to buy it . . . Of course, the offer's only valid for as long as you're free. You'll be worth nothing any more once you're in jail.'

'Did Levi organise this meeting? That little speech he made this morning . . . ' Martini gave a grimace of disgust.

'Your lawyer's a practical man. If you want to hang on to the hope that you'll get out of this, you'll need enough money to pay for a whole other investigation, involving experts and private detectives.'

'Yes, he told me that.'

'And just where do you think you're going to find the money? And have you thought of what'll happen to your family while you're in prison? How will they manage?'

He should have lost his temper, but instead he started to laugh. Stella was quite surprised by this reaction, but Martini seemed unable to stop himself. 'I'm sorry,' he said eventually, managing to regain some self-control. 'This is so strange. As far as everybody's concerned, I'm the monster. They don't need any proof. Even my wife isn't sure. But you know what I say?' He took a deep breath, quite serious now. 'That I know *exactly* who I am. So there's no way I'm going to gain financially from a missing girl and her family's grief just to save myself or my wife and daughter. You can tell that to my lawyer.' He turned to leave.

'You're a fool, you know that?' Stella Honer said.

But for an answer, she had to make do with the sight of Martini's back as he walked away.

That evening, Vogel had had a light dinner in his hotel room and was now writing something down in his usual black notebook before going to bed. He was sitting in an armchair in his dressing gown, smiling to himself. He was certain that old weasel Levi had already started to move his pieces on the chessboard.

When he had heard that the lawyer was in town, he hadn't been hugely surprised. Levi always jumped on the bandwagon.

You expected him to turn up at any minute, although the exact details of his act could be a surprise. He might be the magician who astounds the crowd or the clown who comes in to distract the audience while the lion tears the tamer to shreds. In this case, Levi must surely have contacted Stella Honer and got her to persuade the teacher to throw himself to the wolves of his own accord.

Martini would agree. Because in the end, everybody agreed. Derg, too, had worn the mask of a monster for a while – long enough to make some money before again proclaiming his innocence.

If Martini went on television, things would be simpler for Vogel. The idiot would be sure to beg for the public's sympathy, but would only end up increasing their anger. And then everybody would demand his head on a platter – not just ordinary people, but also the police bigwigs and even the minister. And there would be nothing Prosecutor Mayer could do about it.

When his mobile started to vibrate, Vogel was surprised. He recognised the mysterious sender he'd had a text from four days earlier, after the press conference.

I need to talk to you. Call me on this number.

Again, he decided to ignore whoever it was and deleted the message without further thought. There was a knock at the door. Vogel wondered if the two events might be connected. Certain it was the mystery caller, he opened the door abruptly.

It was Borghi, looking rumpled and with dark rings under his eyes. He was carrying a laptop in a case. 'May I have a word?'

'Can we leave it until tomorrow?' Vogel said irritably. 'I was just going to bed.'

'I have to show you something,' Borghi said, patting the case. 'I think you should see it now.'

Moments later, the laptop was open on Vogel's bed and the two men stood staring at the screen.

'I found this on the school's video surveillance system,' Borghi said. 'Look what happens . . . '

He had watched this footage about twenty times, but this was Vogel's first time. Anna Lou was walking calmly along the deserted corridor. Then Loris Martini came towards her from the opposite direction. They passed very close to each other, then both vanished from the frame.

Borghi paused the video. 'Did you see that?'

'See what?' Vogel asked, still irritable.

'They didn't even look at each other . . . I can rewind it if you like and show it to you again.'

As Borghi reached out his hand to replay the sequence, Vogel grabbed him by the wrist. 'No need.'

'Why not?' He was surprised. 'One of the cornerstones of the accusation is that Anna Lou knew her kidnapper, remember? That's why she trusted him, why she went with him, why none of the neighbours saw or heard anything. You said that yourself.'

Vogel was unable to suppress a smile. The young man's naïvety was touching. 'And you think this proves that Anna Lou didn't know who Martini was?'

Borghi thought for a moment. 'Well, actually—'

'Actually, she may have known very well who he was. The reason she didn't look at him might be because she was shy.'

But Borghi couldn't accept this explanation. 'It's still a risk.'

'For whom? For us? Are you afraid that if the media found out about this video, they'd change their minds about Martini?'

Of course not, but Borghi was only now figuring it out. Everything had already been decided. Barring any sudden dramatic turn of events, they wouldn't change their minds about Martini. Simply because it wasn't convenient for them.

'Is that where you've been all day?' Vogel's tone was reproving but good-natured. 'While you were spending your time on this stuff, I also had some video footage checked.'

'What video footage?' Borghi asked in surprise.

'The footage from the security cameras in the Kastners' neighbourhood.'

'But you said you weren't interested in it, because it only showed the houses, not the street.' Everyone cultivates his own garden: Vogel had used those words at the first briefing. What was he hiding from him now?

But Vogel wasn't about to share his findings. He put a hand on Borghi's shoulder and walked him to the door. 'Get some rest, Borghi. And let me do my job.'

11 January

Nineteen days after the disappearance

'I have no intention of authorising any arrest.'

Mayer's words sounded final, decisive. Once again, Vogel had come up against the prosecutor's stubbornness.

'You're ruining everything,' he said. 'We need to arrest Martini, otherwise everyone will say we're tormenting an innocent man for nothing.'

'And isn't that the case?'

Vogel had brought her a crucial clue as a gift – enlargements of frames from the footage captured by security cameras in the Kastners' neighbourhood – hoping it would be enough to make Mayer change her mind. Obviously, it hadn't worked.

'I need concrete proof. What part of that don't you understand?'

'You need proof to sentence someone, but you only need clues to arrest them,' Vogel replied. 'If we arrest Martini now, he'll probably decide to cooperate.'

'You want to extract a confession from him.'

They had been going on like this for at least twenty minutes, shut up in Vogel's changing room-cum-office. 'Once Martini realises he's lost everything and has no way out, he'll talk to ease his conscience.'

They were both standing among the lockers, but Mayer kept tapping her high-heeled shoe nervously on the floor. 'I'm not stupid, Vogel, I've figured out what your game is. You're trying to back me into a corner and force me to make a decision I don't agree with. You're threatening to make me look ridiculous in the eyes of the public.'

'I don't need to threaten you in order to achieve my aim,' he said. 'I have rank and I have experience. They should be enough to add weight to my theory.'

'Just like in the Mutilator investigation?'

Mayer had mentioned this deliberately. In fact, Vogel wondered why she hadn't done so sooner. He smiled. 'You know nothing about the Derg case. You think you know, but you don't.'

'Oh, sorry, what is there to know? A man was thrown in jail because of a cleverly fabricated charge. He spent four years of his life in a narrow cell, in solitary. He lost everything – his family, his health. He nearly died from a stroke. And why? All because somebody skewed the investigation by planting a false piece of evidence.' There was contempt in the prosecutor's voice. 'What's to guarantee that won't happen again?'

Vogel refused to answer. Instead, he picked up the frame enlargements he had laid out on the table, which he had thought were his winning cards, and walked to the door, intending to leave the room immediately.

'Do you even remember when it was that you lost your integrity, Special Agent Vogel?'

Mayer's words reached him at the door and he came to an abrupt halt. Something was preventing him from leaving. He turned back to the prosecutor with a look of defiance. 'Derg was pronounced innocent by a court of law, and received generous compensation for four years' unfair detention . . . But if he wasn't the Mutilator, then how come the attacks suddenly stopped after he was arrested?' Without waiting for an answer, he walked out.

Outside, in the gym turned operations room, he was greeted by total silence. His men, who had obviously heard the argument, were staring at him, wondering if all the work and effort they had put in over the previous twenty days had been in vain.

But Vogel turned to Borghi and said, 'It's time we spoke to that teacher.'

It was an unusually sunny morning for January. It didn't seem like winter. Loris Martini had woken very early. In fact, it would be more correct to say that the thoughts assailing him had woken him. His anxiety could be summed up in a simple message.

The moment has come. They're going to arrest you.

But he didn't intend to waste this beautiful, sunny, oddly warm day. He'd made Clea a promise and he intended to keep it. So he picked up his box of tools and went into the garden, where reporters and nosy neighbours wouldn't be able to disturb him. There, shielded by tall hedges, he had begun to transform the derelict gazebo into a greenhouse.

As he worked hard with hammer and nails, he could feel the sun kissing the back of his neck, the small drops of sweat slowly running down his forehead, the effort toughening his muscles and his heart. There was something rejuvenating about it. But every so often, sadness would descend on him and stay there, silently, reminding him why he had come to this point, why he had lost everything.

It had all begun before Avechot. The little village in the mountains had seemed like the right place to start over again. Instead, it had been merely the sequel to a nasty episode.

The thing. Even Stella Honer knew about it.

Martini wondered how she had found out. The answer was staring him in the face, but he didn't see it at first. This often happens to men who are naïve. Especially those whose wives are stolen from them without their even noticing.

Of course. It was Clea's ex-lover who had sold the information. Elementary.

And to think that until now he had felt something like respect for the man. Maybe because Clea had chosen him and he trusted his wife's judgement. He knew it was absurd. But it was also a way of raising her in his estimation, because he couldn't bear to think that Clea had been so shallow.

We're always trying to save others in order to save ourselves, he thought. And perhaps playing the role of the understanding husband had helped him to avoid his duty to face the truth.

If Clea had cheated on him, it had to have been his fault, too.

On that distant morning in early June, a pupil's stupid prank had brought classes to an early end. The anonymous phone call claiming that there was a bomb in the school was typical of the end of the academic year, when pupils were trying to get out of the final exams in order to avoid failure. Everyone knew it was a hoax, but the safety procedures had to be followed. So they all went home early.

As Martini walked into his apartment, he was greeted by an unexpected silence. Usually when he got home, Clea and Monica were already there and made their presence known by the fact that the television or the stereo was on, or simply by their smell. Lily-of-the-valley for Clea, strawberry chewing gum for Monica. That morning, though, there was none of that.

On the bus ride home, Martini had thought about how to use those unhoped-for extra hours. He was supposed to be preparing the papers for the final exams, and that was exactly what he would do. But once he was in the apartment, he realised he didn't feel like doing that. He went to the refrigerator, made himself a salami and cheese sandwich, then sat down in an armchair and switched on the television at low volume. They were showing an old basketball match on one of the channels. He couldn't believe he had all this time just for himself.

He couldn't remember when exactly it happened, whether he had finished his sandwich or what score the game had reached, but he could still recall the sound that had insinuated itself between the commentator's voice and the noise of the bouncing ball.

It was like a flapping of wings, a kind of rustling.

At first, he merely turned his head, trying to work out where it was coming from. Then a gut feeling made him stand up. The sound hadn't been repeated, but all the same he went into the corridor. Four closed doors, two on each side. For some reason, he chose the bedroom door. He slowly opened it and saw them.

They weren't aware of him, any more than he had been aware of them earlier. In that small apartment, they had continued alongside each other, unawares, for several minutes. And they could have carried on like that if something hadn't occasioned their encounter.

Clea was naked, only her legs and pelvis covered by the sheet. Her eyes were closed, and she was lying in a position he knew well. Loris concentrated on the man beneath her, convinced he was looking at himself. But it was somebody else. And what was happening had nothing to do with him.

Beyond that, he remembered nothing.

Clea said she heard the door slam. It was only then that she'd realised what had just occurred.

When he returned home several hours later, she was wearing a loose white sweater and tracksuit bottoms that were too big for her. Maybe she was trying to hide her body – and with it, her sin. She was sitting in the armchair in which he had watched the match that morning. Knees pulled up to her chest, rocking back and forth. She looked at him with vacant eyes. Her hair was dishevelled, her face pale. She didn't make any excuses. 'Let's get out of here,' she said. 'Right away, tomorrow.'

In his aimless wanderings around town, he had searched for something to say to her, without finding it. Now he said just two words, 'All right.'

From then on, they had never mentioned it again. They had moved to Avechot a couple of weeks later. She had given up a job she loved and everything else, just so that she could be forgiven with his silence. And Loris had realised how terrified she was at the prospect of losing him. If only she knew that he was even more terrified than she was . . .

The worst thing, however, was finding out the identity of the man his wife had been cheating on him with. Like her, he was a lawyer, and he had the money and the means to help her escape the wretched life which was all her husband could offer her.

Loris had to come terms with a devastating truth: Clea deserved better.

And so they had taken refuge in the mountains, so as not to think about it again. But the sour residue of the betrayal remained and was slowly eating away at whatever love they still felt for each other.

That was why he had made that promise. *Never again*.

Now, beneath the undeserved sun of a January morning, he thought once again about *the thing*, hoping it really was over. When the phone rang in the house, he dropped the hammer on the grass dried by the winter and went into the kitchen to answer it.

'All right, I'll be there,' was all he said.

He opened the fridge. Inside, there was only a wrinkled apple and a four-pack of beer. He took one bottle out and went back to the garden. He opened the bottle with a screwdriver. Then he sat down on the dead grass, his back against one of the beams of the gazebo, and calmly sipped his drink, his eyes half-closed.

Once he had finished, he looked at his hand, still bandaged ever since the day Anna Lou Kastner had disappeared. He unrolled the bandage and checked the scar. It had almost healed.

Then he picked up the screwdriver with which he had opened the beer and did the same thing with his injury. He sank the point into his flesh and parted the sides. Not a single moan emerged from his lips. He had been a coward in the past, so he knew he deserved this pain.

The blood started gushing out, staining his clothes and slowly dripping on the bare soil.

The warm, sunny day was nothing but a memory now. In the evening, thick, compact clouds had swept into the valley, bringing heavy rain in their wake.

There was still a flashing sign wishing HAPPY HOLIDAYS to passing motorists on the window of the roadside restaurant. Christmas and New Year had been over for a while, but nobody had had time to remove it. They had been too busy lately.

At ten o'clock that night, though, the restaurant was empty.

Vogel had asked the elderly owner to put aside a booth for him, for a special meeting. Although he hadn't claimed any credit for the sudden increase in business over recent weeks, the man felt indebted to him anyway.

The glass front door opened, triggering a buzzer. Martini stamped his feet on the ground to shake the rain from his coat, then took off his peaked cap and looked around.

It was dark, except for the light over one of the booths against the wall. Vogel was already sitting there, waiting for him. Martini walked towards him, his Clarks shoes groaning in contact with the linoleum floor. He sat down at the pale blue Formica table, facing Vogel.

Vogel was elegantly dressed, as usual. He hadn't taken off his cashmere coat. On the table in front of him was a thin folder, on which he was drumming with the fingers of both hands.

It was the first time they had met.

'Do you believe in proverbs?' Vogel said, without so much as a hello.

'How do you mean?' Martini asked.

'I've always been fascinated by how simply they distinguish between right and wrong. Unlike laws. Laws are always so complicated. They should be written like proverbs.'

'You think right and wrong are simple?'

'No, but I find it comforting to think that someone else should see it that way.'

'Personally, I don't think the truth is ever simple.'

Vogel nodded. 'You may be right.'

Martini put both arms on the table. He was calm. 'Why did you want us to meet here?'

'No cameras or microphones, for once. No pain-in-the-neck reporters. No games. Just you and me . . . I want to give you the chance to convince me that I'm wrong, and that your involvement in this business is purely a misunderstanding.'

Martini tried to look confident. 'No problem,' he said. 'Where shall we start?'

'You have no alibi for the day Anna Lou disappeared, and on top of that, you injured your hand.' He pointed to the blood-stained bandage. 'I see it hasn't healed yet. Maybe it needs a few stitches.'

'My wife thinks so, too,' Martini replied, making it clear he didn't care for this pretence at concern. 'It was an accident, as I've said before. I slipped and instinctively grabbed a branch to break my fall.'

Vogel looked down at his folder without opening it. 'Strange, the forensics man noticed that the sides of the cut are identical . . . as if caused by a blade.'

Martini didn't reply.

Vogel didn't labour the point, but moved on. 'Mattia's videos, in which your car appears. You're going to tell me it's just a coincidence, and anyway it's impossible to see the driver's face. And the car was available to the rest of your family . . . By the way, does your wife have a driving licence?'

'I was always the one driving, leave my wife alone.' He had gone against Levi's instructions, but he didn't care. He didn't want Clea to be involved, not even if it would help improve his position.

'We've analysed the inside of the car,' Vogel went on. 'No trace of Anna Lou's DNA, but oddly enough, there were cat hairs.'

'We don't have a cat,' Martini said, somewhat ingenuously.

Vogel leaned towards him and spoke in a honeyed voice. 'What would you say if I told you that, thanks to the cat hairs, I can place you on the spot where the girl disappeared?'

Martini seemed not to understand, but on his face there was curiosity as well as fear.

Vogel sighed. 'There's something that struck me right from the start. Why didn't Anna Lou resist being taken? Why didn't she scream? None of the neighbours heard anything. I've reached the conclusion that she went with her kidnapper of her own free will . . . Because she trusted him.'

'Which means she knew him well. And that rules me out. She may have attended my school, but you won't find anybody who could testify they saw us talk to each other, let alone socialise.'

'As a matter of fact,' Vogel said calmly, 'Anna Lou didn't know her kidnapper. She knew his cat.' At last, Vogel opened the folder and took out the frame enlargement he had shown Mayer that very morning to persuade her to arrest Martini. 'We've examined the footage from the security cameras in the girl's neighbourhood. Unfortunately, none of the cameras point to the street. What is it they say? "Everyone cultivates his own garden." But it seems that in the days before Anna Lou disappeared, there was a stray cat roaming the area.'

Martini looked at the photograph. It showed a large tabby cat, ginger and brown, sprawled on the grass.

Vogel pointed at something. 'Can you see what's round its neck?'

Martini took a closer look and saw a bracelet made of tiny coloured beads.

Vogel slipped from his wrist the one that had been given to him by Maria Kastner and put it down next to the photograph. 'Anna Lou used to make them and give them to the people she liked.'

Martini seemed frozen, unable to react.

Vogel decided the moment had come to deal the knockout blow. 'The kidnapper used the cat as bait. He took it there several days earlier and let it loose, confident that Anna Lou, who loves cats and couldn't have one of her own, would be bound to notice it sooner or later . . . She not only noticed it, she adopted it by putting a bracelet round its neck. So from now on, my dear Signor Martini, I won't be constantly after you. If I manage to find that cat, you're done for anyway.'

A few moments passed in silence. Vogel knew he had him. He watched him, waiting for a reaction, anything that would tell him he wasn't wrong. But Martini didn't say a word. Instead, he stood up and calmly made for the exit. Before stepping outside, though, he turned to Vogel one last time. 'Talking of proverbs,' he said. 'Someone once told me that the devil's most foolish sin is vanity.' He left the restaurant, again triggering the buzzer on the door.

Vogel sat on for a while, enjoying the quiet. He was convinced that he had scored an important point. But Mayer was still a problem. He had to find a way to neutralise her.

The devil's most foolish sin is vanity.

Whatever did Martini mean by that? It could be interpreted as an insult. But Vogel wasn't sensitive. He knew perfectly well that you take the blows and then you hit back. And the teacher's hours were numbered.

He got up to go. As he was putting the photograph back in the folder, he suddenly stopped. He had noticed something on the table. He leaned down to see it better.

On the pale blue Formica surface, where Martini had rested his bandaged hand, there was a small, fresh bloodstain.

16 January

Twenty-four days after the disappearance

Little Leo Blanc had turned five a week before he vanished into thin air.

Back then, they hadn't had the kind of sophisticated tools the police had now. They would simply 'comb the area', as they used to say. The case would be entrusted to experienced officers who had long been familiar with the place and the people, who knew how to obtain information and had no need for forensic teams or DNA. It was hard work, carried out day after day, a matter of small steps and modest results, which put all together formed the basis of the investigation. What you needed more than anything was patience.

Patience was a quality that grew rarer with the advent of the media. The public demanded quick answers, otherwise they would switch channels, and so the networks would put pressure on the investigators, forcing them to do their work in haste. In such circumstances, it was easy to make a mistake. The important thing, however, was not to stop the show.

Leo Blanc, with his tragic story and brief life, would unwittingly represent an important watershed between what came before and what came afterwards.

One morning, his mother, Laura Blanc, a twenty-five-year-old widow who had lost her husband, Leo's father, in a road accident, came to the police station of the small town where she lived. She was desperate. She said somebody had broken into her house and abducted her Leonard.

Vogel was a low-ranking officer back then, only recently graduated from the police academy. So he had been given the most basic, most boring tasks, like filing reports or typing up complaints. All he had to do apart from that was watch his senior colleagues at work – and of course, learn. It was he who took down Laura's statement.

She claimed it was only that morning that she had realised she'd left in her car the carton of milk she'd bought the night before at a convenience store. She had run to fetch it before her son woke up and demanded his breakfast. After all, her car was parked only fifty metres away. Maybe because she was distracted, or maybe because the residents of the town all knew one another and usually didn't lock their doors even at night, Laura had left her door slightly ajar. And now she couldn't forgive herself.

Vogel followed the normal procedure and passed the statement on to the officer who was training him. They went together to the woman's house. There was no sign of a break-in, but they found that little Leo's room had been turned upside down. They concluded that the child had woken up, been frightened by the presence of a stranger, and tried to fight him off. But in the end, the kidnapper had succeeded.

Laura Blanc was in a state of shock, but still managed to reconstruct the exact process of events with the police. Only eight minutes had elapsed between her going out and returning, and during that brief window, she had exchanged a few words with a neighbour. It had been long enough, though, for the kidnapper to enter the house and take the child.

A manhunt immediately got underway. But things would have turned out differently if a television news crew hadn't been in the area, making a feature on migratory birds in the nearby marshes. A lieutenant had had the idea. The crew were asked to broadcast an appeal by Laura for information about her child.

After the appeal went out, things really heated up.

People started flooding the police with phone calls. Many were sure they had seen little Leo, and provided exact locations and circumstances. Some claimed they had seen him with a man who was buying him an ice cream, others with a couple on a train, some mentioned specific names. The majority of sightings turned out to be unfounded, but in any case, it was impossible to check them all. As a matter of fact, the mass of information raining down on the police team slowed the investigation considerably. But what was truly surprising was the number of people who called just to find out how the case was progressing. Similar calls jammed the switchboards of the networks, who decided to 'cover the story', as they put it, and send crews to the location.

Vogel saw all this happen over a very short space of time. As a young, inexperienced officer, he wasn't quite shrewd enough to grasp the nature of the revolution taking place before his eyes. Everything just looked very unreal. Transformed by the media, even the truth seemed different. Laura Blanc soon became a tragic heroine. When Vogel had first met her, she was an ordinary, rather plain girl, but now her appearance suddenly changed. With make-up and the right lighting, she started receiving letters from suitors eager to take care of her. Her son Leo was adopted as an ideal by all the mothers in the country. A five-year-old child had become an icon. People kept his picture at home and many new parents named their offspring after him.

Just as the solution to the mystery was starting to seem like a mirage, yet another search of the Blanc house revealed a fingerprint. It took two weeks to go through police records in search of a match. In the end, that, too, was found.

The prints were those of a man named Thomas Berninsky, a forty-year-old labourer with a history of molesting minors, who at the time happened to be working for a company that was building industrial warehouses in the area.

The hunt for Berninsky didn't take long. He was arrested and little Leo's bloodstained pyjamas were found in his possession. Berninsky confessed to having had his eye on the child for quite a while, and led the investigators to the abandoned rubbish tip where he had buried the little body.

This horrific end to the story shook the public. But a few people, high up in the echelons of the police and the networks, sensed that something had changed and that there was no turning back.

A new era had begun.

Justice was no longer a matter reserved for courtrooms but was everybody's, without distinction. And in this new way of seeing things, information was a resource – *information was gold*.

The death of a poor innocent child had led to the establishment of a business.

As an idealistic young officer, Vogel had no idea as yet that he would become part of this perverse mechanism and build his own brilliant career on the back of other people's misfortunes. All the same, he had come to a surprising conclusion. Laura Blanc had said she had left home in order to fetch the milk she'd bought the night before. Her house had been turned upside down dozens of times in police searches until they had found Berninsky's fingerprint.

But why had nobody ever found the famous carton of milk?

The adult Vogel, with years of experience behind him, was still wondering that. To this day, the possible answer sent a shiver through him. Laura Blanc had quickly rebuilt her life with a man she had met before the tragic events, a man who might not have wanted to take on the responsibility of somebody else's child. The idea that she had long been aware of the slow-witted Berninsky's intentions and might have actually made things easier for him would have been hard to sell to the media. Laura Blanc had deliberately left the house, Vogel was sure of it. But he knew that there were secrets that had to remain hidden. That was why he had never shared his suspicions with anybody. He would always remember them, though, whenever something unusual happened in a case.

And that morning at dawn, the case of little Leo came back to his mind as he sat in the service saloon beside Borghi, who had rushed to the hotel to pick him up.

Apparently, divers had found Anna Lou Kastner's brightly coloured satchel in a drainage channel.

At times, the house became claustrophobic and then he had to escape. Martini had grown skilful at throwing the reporters camped outside off the track. For example, he had learned that

219

the period between five and six, when the crews got ready for the first editions of the television news, was the best time to sneak out through the back.

There was a labyrinth of 'safe' streets he could take to get out of Avechot. Then he would go deep into the woods and savour the solitude of nature, certain as he was that he would soon lose the privilege of freedom. Five days had passed since the meeting with Vogel in the restaurant. The thought of the special agent chasing after a ginger and brown tabby cat struck him as decidedly ridiculous. The truth was, Martini wasn't the least bit afraid of what might happen to him. Although his scruffy appearance told a different story, Loris Martini hadn't given up. His long, unkempt beard and his body odour had become a kind of shield with which, he somehow deluded himself, he could keep other people at bay. Clea would have objected. She was always very particular and was constantly giving him advice about his appearance. This had been the case ever since the day at university when Loris had worn a blue suit and a ridiculous bow tie to ask her out to dinner. Form and appearance were important to his wife.

Martini missed Clea and Monica, but he knew he had to be strong for them, too. They hadn't been in touch since they had left, not so much as a quick phone call. Actually, he hadn't tried to call them, either. He wanted to protect them – protect them from himself.

The morning dew slowly glided down the leaves. Martini loved to stroke them and feel their cool wetness on his palms. As he walked, he spread his arms wide and half closed his eyes, enjoying a momentary bliss. Then he took a deep breath of the scented air. His mind filled with green as the night receded and day appeared. Forest animals came out of their hiding places, and the birds sang, happy to have escaped the darkness.

When the quartz watch on his wrist began to emit a brief, constant sound, Martini knew his two hours of freedom from the media were about to end and it was time to go home. But today, as he walked back towards Avechot, he saw a figure coming towards him on the opposite side of the road. He would have liked to avoid it, but there was no path to turn onto: he was surrounded by fields. He was obliged to keep walking, but he lowered his head and pulled his cap down so that the peak covered most of his face. Hands in his pockets, stooping slightly, he carried on along an imaginary line, determined to follow it faithfully. But the temptation to get a glimpse of the mysterious walker's face got the better of him, and when he recognised him his breath caught in his throat.

Bruno Kastner noticed him a few seconds later. He, too, felt something sudden and uncertain, because he slowed down.

Both were about to stop, but it was as if each expected the other to do so first. Kastner had an inscrutable but composed expression. Martini didn't think about his likely reaction, about what he might do to the alleged monster who'd kidnapped his daughter. Rather, strangely enough, he thought about what he might do in his place. And that scared him.

Their footsteps synchronised on the asphalt, the sound of one set of steps merging with the sound of the other. The time remaining before they met seemed to last forever. When they finally drew level with one another, there were only a couple of metres between them. But neither turned to look at the other. Martini stopped first, expecting something to happen.

But Kastner didn't slow down. On the contrary, he picked up the pace a little and vanished from sight.

Martini couldn't move. All he could hear was his own heart pounding in his chest. He kept sensing Bruno Kastner's presence behind him. For a moment, he wished the man would turn back and attack him. But that didn't happen. When he turned to look behind him, Kastner was nothing but a dot in the distance, on the edge of the woods.

Martini would never forget the encounter. That was the moment he came to a decision.

Anna Lou Kastner's brightly coloured satchel lay on the autopsy table in Avechot's small morgue. They had put it in there in the absence of a corpse. Even so, Vogel seemed to see the girl with her red hair and freckles lying there, naked, cold and motionless, beneath the overhead light that left everything else in semi-darkness.

Strokes of luck do happen sometimes, Vogel thought. Whoever had thrown the satchel into the drainage channel had first taken care to empty it and fill it with heavy stones, but that hadn't been sufficient. This find was definitive proof. That there was a maniac behind all this was no longer just a theory. It was real.

Right now, the satchel was Anna Lou. And it was as if the girl opened her eyes and turned to look at Vogel, who had been there for at least half an hour, alone, weighing up the possible implications of the find. A strand of red hair fell over her forehead and her lips moved, uttering a voiceless sentence. A message just for Vogel.

I'm still here.

Vogel thought about his visit to the Kastners' house on Christmas Day. He remembered the decorated tree, which, according to the girl's mother, would remain lit until her daughter returned – like a beacon in the darkness. He recalled the present tied with red ribbon, waiting only to be unwrapped. Now, that box would be replaced by a white coffin.

'We'll never find you,' he said softly. And immediately this conviction took root in him.

The devil's most foolish sin is vanity.

That was why it was time to act. To stop this from happening again.

At about nine in the morning, Loris Martini got in the shower. The hot water took away his accumulated tiredness. Shortly afterwards, standing naked in front of the mirror, he looked again at the reflection of his face, something he had carefully avoided doing in the past few days, and started shaving off his beard.

In the wardrobe, he looked through the few clothes he owned and chose the ones that best represented his state of mind. A beige corduroy jacket, dark fustian trousers and a blue and brown check shirt, to which he would add a dove-grey tie. When he'd finished tying the laces of his Clarks shoes, he put on his coat and slipped his canvas bag over his shoulder. Then he left the house.

The reporters and cameramen were surprised to see him appear in the doorway. The cameras were immediately turned on him as he casually walked down the drive to the road, through the cordon, and out into the streets of Avechot.

As he strolled along the main street, people stopped in disbelief and pointed at him. Customers came out of shops to witness the scene. But nobody said or did anything. Martini avoided meeting anyone's eyes, although he could feel the pressure of them on him.

By the time he got to the school, a small crowd had gathered behind him. Martini saw that apart from the gym, requisitioned as the police operations room, nothing had changed.

He went up the steps to the main entrance, sure that the vultures behind him wouldn't come any further. They didn't. Once inside, he recognised the familiar sound of the bell. According to the timetable, the literature class was at ten. So he made for his own classroom. Those teachers and pupils who were present in the corridor watched as he walked past them.

There was the usual chaos that prevailed between classes. The supply teacher the principal had assigned to the class would soon be arriving, but in the meantime, the pupils were taking advantage of the teacher being late in order to lark about.

Priscilla was dressed in her old clothes again. She had gone back to wearing heavy eye make-up and ear studs. 'I'm going to audition for a reality show,' she was telling her girlfriends excitedly.

'Is your mother OK with that?' one of them asked. 'Doesn't she mind?'

'Who cares if she does?' Priscilla replied, dismissing the question with a shrug. 'It's my life now, I've found my direction, and she just has to get used to it. I may have to find myself an agent.'

Lucas, the rebel with the skull tattoo, turned to somebody at the back of the classroom. 'What about you, loser, hasn't anybody offered you anything?'

This remark was followed by general laughter, but Mattia pretended not to have heard and carried on scribbling something in his exercise book.

The door opened. They didn't all turn at once. The few who

did fell silent. By the time Martini reached the teacher's desk, the silence was total.

'Good morning, kids,' he said to them with a smile. Nobody responded. They were completely taken aback, including Mattia, who looked terrified. A few seconds went by during which Martini looked at them one by one, still standing. Then, as if nothing had happened, he went on, 'Now then, in our last class, I was talking about narrative technique in novels. I told you that all writers, even the greatest, start off by drawing on what's been written before. The first rule is "copy", remember?' There was still no response. That was fine with him, Martini thought. The class had never been this attentive.

The classroom door opened again. This time, the pupils all turned. Vogel came in. Seeing what was happening, he raised his hand, almost apologetically, signalling to those present that they shouldn't mind him. Then he sat down at an empty desk and looked at Martini as if inviting him to carry on with the class.

'As I told you,' Martini went on, unperturbed, 'the real driving force in every story is the villain. The heroes and the victims are only instruments, because readers aren't interested in everyday life, they already have their own. They want conflict, because that's the only way they can be distracted from their own mediocrity.' He deliberately stared at Vogel. 'Remember: it's the villain who makes our mediocrity more acceptable, he's the one who *makes* the story.'

Out of the blue, Vogel began to applaud. He did it with great conviction, clapping his hands energetically and nodding with satisfaction. He looked around at the class, as if encouraging them to do likewise. At first, the pupils looked at each other, not knowing what to do. Then, timidly, some of them started imitating him. It was an absurd, paradoxical situation. Vogel stood up from his seat and walked up to the teacher's desk, still applauding. Once he was standing in front of Martini, just a couple of centimetres from his face, he stopped. 'Good lesson.' Then he leaned in towards him and whispered in his ear, 'We've found Anna Lou's satchel. No body yet, but we don't need one. Because your blood was on the satchel, Signor Martini.'

Martini didn't reply, didn't say anything.

Vogel took a pair of handcuffs from the pocket of his cashmere coat. 'Now we really must go.'

23 February

Sixty-two days after the disappearance

The night everything changed for ever, the mine was the only thing visible from the window of Dr Flores's office. Red lights flashed on and off at the top of the ventilation towers like little eyes, sentinels in the fog.

'Do you have family, Special Agent Vogel?'

For some reason, Vogel was looking at the nails of his right hand. He had been silent and withdrawn again for a while now, so he didn't immediately catch Flores's question. 'Family?' he echoed after a moment. 'Never had the time.'

'I've been married for forty years,' Flores said, although he hadn't been asked. 'Sophia has brought up our three beautiful children, and now she's totally devoted to our grandchildren. She's a wonderful woman, I don't know what I'd do without her.'

'What's a psychiatrist doing in Avechot?' Vogel asked, genuinely curious. 'In a small place like this, you're the last person I'd expect to find.'

'Suicides,' Flores said gravely. 'In this area there's the highest percentage of suicides in the country in proportion to the number of inhabitants. Every family has a story to tell. Fathers, mothers, brothers, sisters. Sometimes a son.'

'Why?'

'Hard to say. Those who come here from outside envy us. They think that in a quiet place like this, snug and safe in the middle of the mountains, life is always serene. But maybe it's the excess of serenity that's the real disease. It's not enough to be happy – on the contrary, it becomes a prison. To escape it, they take their own lives, and they always choose the most violent methods. It's not enough for them to swallow a few pills or cut their wrists, they tend to do themselves enormous harm, as if they wanted to punish themselves.'

'And have you saved a lot of them?'

Flores gave a brief laugh. 'I think what my patients need more than drugs is someone to unburden themselves to.'

'I bet you know all the right words to get them to talk. You've known them for so long, they find it easy to open up to you.'

He was right. Flores was good at probing people, because he knew how to listen and never imposed himself. He never lost patience, never raised his voice in an argument, not even to reproach his own children. He liked the fact that he was considered a well-balanced man. He thought of himself as a mountain medic, like those old-time doctors who were concerned as much with their patients' souls as their bodies and for that very reason were so good at curing disease.

'Maybe they aren't simply unhappy,' Vogel went on. 'Maybe the excess of serenity takes away their fear of dying, have you thought of that?'

'That may be the case,' Flores admitted. 'Have you ever

been afraid of death, Special Agent Vogel?' The question was deliberately provocative. He wanted to get him back to the reality of his bloodstained clothes and the reason he had returned to Avechot.

'When you're surrounded by other people's deaths, you don't have time to think about your own,' Vogel said bitterly. 'What about you? Do you often think about death?'

'Every day for the last thirty years.' He pointed to his chest. 'Triple bypass.'

'A heart attack? At such a young age?'

'I already had children then. Youth doesn't count for much when you have responsibilities. Thank heavens, I survived a difficult twelve-hour operation, and now I just have to remember to take my pills and have a check-up every now and again.' Flores always tended to downplay that episode, perhaps because he didn't want to admit how deeply marked by it he had been. But the night everything changed for ever would push everything in his previous life into the background, even that.

There was a knock at the door. Flores didn't tell whoever it was to come in. Instead, he stood up and left the room. It was an agreed signal. But Vogel didn't seem to give it any weight.

In the corridor, Prosecutor Mayer was pacing back and forth impatiently. 'Well?' she asked as soon as she saw Flores.

'He has moments of lucidity and others when he seems absent.'

'But is he pretending or not?'

'It's not as simple as that. He's started talking at great length about the Anna Lou Kastner case, and I'm letting him talk because I think we'll eventually get to last night's accident.'

What Vogel had been coming out with was more like a confession. But Flores kept that to himself.

'Be careful,' Mayer said. 'Vogel's a manipulator.'

'He doesn't need to manipulate me if he's telling the truth. And so far, I don't think he's been lying.'

Mayer, though, wasn't convinced. 'Is Vogel aware that Maria Kastner killed herself three days ago?'

'He hasn't mentioned it. I don't know if he knows.'

'You should confront him with it. After all, it's basically his fault it happened.'

Flores had immediately realised that Maria wouldn't be able to take the strain. But he had been prevented from doing anything. Since the suicide, the brotherhood had distanced themselves from Maria, condemning her for her sacrilegious act. They had even refused her a religious funeral. 'I don't think it'd serve any purpose bringing that up right now. In fact, it might be counter-productive.'

Mayer came and stood a few centimetres from Flores and looked him in the eyes. 'Please don't let him charm you. I made that mistake just once, and I still can't forgive myself.'

'Don't worry. If it's all an act, we'll find out.'

When he went back into the room with two cups of steaming coffee, Vogel was no longer sitting in the armchair. Instead, he was on his feet, looking closely at the stuffed rainbow trout that had aroused his curiosity earlier.

'I brought us some refreshment,' Flores said with a smile, placing one of the cups on the table.

Vogel didn't turn. 'Do you know why we never remember the names of the victims?'

'I beg your pardon?' Flores said as he sat down.

'Ted Bundy, Jeffrey Dahmer, Andrei Chikatilo ... We all remember the names of the monsters, but nobody ever remembers those of the victims. Have you ever wondered why? And yet it ought to be the opposite. We say we feel pity, compassion, but then we forget them. It serves our purpose.'

'Do you know the reason?'

'People will tell you it's because we're constantly bombarded with the name of the monster until we're tired of it. The media are bad, didn't you know that?' he said with a hint of sarcasm. 'But they're harmless, too. We can neutralise their effects by pressing a button on the remote. Except that nobody does it. We're all too curious.'

'Maybe what we care most about isn't the monsters, it's justice.'

'Naah,' Vogel replied, dismissing the idea with a gesture of his hand, as if it were obvious naïvety. 'Justice doesn't build an audience. Justice doesn't interest anyone.'

'Not even you?'

Vogel fell silent, nailed by the question. 'I knew Martini was guilty. There are things a police officer can't explain. Instinct, for example.'

'Is that why you pursued him, made his life impossible?' Flores felt that they had reached something of a turning point.

'When I saw Anna Lou's satchel on the autopsy table, something broke inside me. Prosecutor Mayer would have dropped the charges.' He fell silent again. Then, in a low voice: 'I couldn't allow that.'

'What are you trying to tell me, Special Agent Vogel?'

Vogel looked up at him. 'It wasn't going to be another Derg case. In the end, the Mutilator got away with it, everybody apologised to him, and he even pocketed millions camouflaged as compensation for unfair detention.'

Flores sat there as if paralysed, but he didn't want to force Vogel's hand.

'The evening we met properly for the first time, in that road-side restaurant, Martini had a bandage on his hand. The idiot hadn't even gone to have the injury stitched up, and it was still bleeding.' Vogel clearly remembered the moment when, as he was putting the photograph back in the folder, he had noticed the red bloodstain on the blue Formica table.

'The blood on the satchel,' Flores said, incredulously. 'So it's true. You falsified the evidence.'

17 January

Twenty-five days after the disappearance

It was just after midnight. A dark unmarked car drove in through the prison's security gates and came to a halt in a hexagonal courtyard surrounded by high grey walls that made it look like a well.

Two plain-clothes officers got out through the rear doors, then helped Martini out of the car. His movements were hampered by the handcuffs. It was only when he set foot on the asphalt that he finally looked up.

The starry sky was enclosed within a narrow, claustrophobic space.

Borghi was sitting in front. For once, he hadn't been driving. He was carrying a folder with the arrest warrant signed by Mayer and the transcript of the interrogation Martini had undergone that afternoon in the prosecutor's office. Martini had continued to deny the charges, but the evidence against him was significant.

Borghi preceded the two other officers and Martini into Block C. Then he handed the documents to the head warder as part of the handover process. 'Loris Martini,' he said, introducing him. 'The charge is abduction and homicide of a minor, with the aggravating circumstance of concealing a body.'

Obviously, the head warder knew who Martini was and why he was here, but it was the way things were done. So he merely asked Borghi to sign the admittance forms.

Once these formalities had been dealt with, Borghi turned one last time towards Martini, who seemed confused and disoriented and looked at the young officer with the imploring expression of someone who is trying to understand what is going to happen. Borghi didn't say a word to him, but turned instead to the other officers. 'Let's go,' he said simply.

Martini watched as they walked off. Then two hands grabbed him by the elbows and pulled him away. The two warders led him into a cramped little room, its walls encrusted with damp. There was a low iron stool and a drain cover in the middle of the sloping floor.

They removed his handcuffs. 'Strip off,' they ordered.

He did as he was told. When he was completely naked, they told him to sit down on the stool, then turned on the shower directly above him – he hadn't noticed it – and passed him a bar of soap. When Martini tried to stand so that he could wash himself more easily, they stopped him. It was against regulations. The water was lukewarm and smelled of chlorine. Finally, they gave him a white towel that was too small and almost immediately got soaked.

'Stand up and place both your hands on the wall, then lean forward as far as possible,' one of the warders said.

Martini was shivering with cold, but also with fear. He couldn't see what was happening behind him, but he could imagine it when he recognised the smack of a rubber glove. The bodily inspection lasted a few seconds, during which Martini closed his eyes as if to erase the humiliation. Having checked that he wasn't hiding anything in his rectum, they told him to sit back down on the stool.

Minutes passed in total silence. Nobody said anything and Martini was obliged to wait. Then footsteps were heard, and a doctor in a white coat came in, carrying a small folder. 'Do you have any chronic illnesses?' he asked without even introducing himself.

'No,' Martini replied in a thin voice.

'Are you on any medication?'

'No.'

'Are you suffering, or have you suffered in the past, from venereal disease?'

'No.'

'Do you use drugs?'

'No.'

The doctor noted down this last reply, then left without another word. The warders again grabbed Martini by the arms and forced him to stand. One of them gave him his prison uniform, which was of rough canvas, a washed-out blue in colour, as well as a pair of plastic shoes that were two sizes too small for him. 'Get dressed,' they told him. Then they led him in handcuffs along a corridor that seemed endless. They went through a series of doors that opened then closed behind them.

Although it was night time, the prison never slept.

From one of the cells there came a low, rhythmic, metallic

noise that soon spread to the others. The sound accompanied his passage with the warders, like a fanfare preceding a condemned man. Behind the barred doors, sinister whispers could be heard.

'Bastard.'

'Count the days, we'll get you.'

'Welcome to hell.'

This was the welcome reserved for those guilty of terrible crimes against minors. According to the prisoners' code of honour, their offence made them unworthy even of being behind bars. For them, there was an added sentence: they were marked out as dead meat.

Martini walked with his head bowed. His uniform was too big for him and kept falling down, but with his wrists handcuffed it was difficult to hold it up.

They came to a heavy iron door. One of the guards opened it and pushed him inside. The room was too cramped for one person, let alone for three. There was a camp bed, a steel toilet bowl in a corner and a wash basin on the wall. Through the small window, way up high, the moonlight filtered in, along with an icy draught.

A fourth person came in. He was a sturdy man of about fifty, the material of his uniform bulging with his biceps. 'I'm Chief Alvis,' he said. 'I'm in charge of solitary.'

Martini assumed Alvis would give him a speech about how things worked here. Instead, he handed him a brown woollen blanket, as well as a mess tin and a spoon – both of silicon, so that he couldn't use them to harm himself or anyone else.

'These objects, like the mattress on the bed, are the property of the prison,' he said, as if reciting. 'They are given to you intact. Any loss or damage will be your responsibility. Now sign here.'

He handed him a clipboard and Martini put his own name at the bottom of the brief list, wondering what value these objects could ever have to require such concern. It was only now that he realised the worst aspect of prison: the obsession with bureaucracy. Every aspect of life behind bars, down to the most insignificant, was regulated by forms and codicils. Every decision had already been made by someone else. To limit personal initiative to a minimum, every act was translated into a pre-ordained standard. And dehumanised. In this way, there was no space for emotion, compassion or empathy.

You were alone with yourself and your own guilt.

As the warders and Chief Alvis left the cell, Martini stood there holding the brown blanket, the mess tin and the spoon. The heavy iron door closed and the key turned in the lock.

Dead meat, Martini repeated to himself as silence fell in the cell.

Vogel had waited twenty-four hours before issuing a statement. He had wanted the clamour about the previous day's arrest to die down first, so as to have the limelight just for himself.

The police officer who had succeeded in getting a man charged with murder even in the absence of the victim's body.

Now he stood in front of a forest of microphones and TV cameras in the school gym which would still function for a while as an operations room, and was savouring the attention of the media. He had chosen a new outfit to present himself to the journalists. A dark jacket of smooth velvet, grey trousers, a regimental tie, a white shirt, a pair of star-shaped white gold cufflinks. He was still wearing Anna Lou's bead bracelet, intending to show it off like a trophy.

'The quiet, meticulous work carried out by the police has finally led to the result we were all hoping for. As you see, determination and patience always pay off. We haven't been thrown off course by pressure from the media and the public. We've worked in secret, out of the spotlight, in order to reach the objective we set ourselves from the start: to find out the truth about the disappearance of Anna Lou Kastner.'

It was paradoxical how he could twist the facts without feeling any embarrassment, Officer Borghi thought, standing to one side watching the scene. And although the truth Vogel spoke of didn't include any answer as to what had happened to the girl with the red hair and the freckles, he was still good at convincing everybody of the things he was saying. Because, deep down, he himself was convinced.

'At this point, our work in Avechot is over and we yield to the justice system, sure that Prosecutor Mayer will be able to make good use of the incontrovertible evidence revealed by the investigation.'

Mayer, who was beside him, looked away slightly from the cameras aimed at her. It was a small gesture, but to Borghi an eloquent one. Unlike Vogel, she couldn't lie to herself.

'How have the Kastners greeted the news of the arrest?' a reporter asked.

'I think they learned about it from television,' Vogel replied. 'I prefer not to interfere with the understandable grief they must be feeling right now. But I'll go and see them as soon as possible, to explain what happened and what will happen now.'

'Will you stop looking for Anna Lou?' The question came from Stella Honer.

Vogel, who had been expecting it, avoided replying directly to her. 'Of course not,' he immediately reassured everybody. 'We won't be satisfied until we've found the last missing piece of the puzzle. What happened to the poor girl has always been our priority.'

But those words – 'poor girl' – were also an official admission that he had given up hope of finding her, Borghi thought. It was the kind of dialectical trick employed to get them off the hook if they failed. On top of that, the funds to continue the search would immediately be reduced sharply once the floodlights had been turned off. No more forensic teams, dog units or frogmen. No helicopter flying between the mountains. The volunteers would gradually return home. But the first people to abandon Avechot would be the reporters. Within days, the circus would lower its tents, leaving behind a barren stretch of ground filled with waste paper. The TV crews would decamp, and the valley and its inhabitants would sink once again into their usual inexorable lethargy. Their old life would restart, disparities would re-emerge between those who had been lucky enough to possess land with fluorite beneath it and those who, on the contrary, had been impoverished by the mine. The hotels and restaurants that had temporarily reopened would gradually lose their customers, and the 'horror tourists' would choose other destinations, other gruesome crimes for their Sunday excursions with their families. Maybe the roadside restaurant would postpone closure for another year, but in the end even the owner of that would resign himself and realise that the best option was to shut up shop.

For Avechot, a brief season of unexpected, if occasionally tiresome popularity had come to an end. But nobody would ever forget that winter.

Vogel was about to dismiss the audience – he had to get back to the city as soon as possible, because he was due to appear on a well-known evening talk show – when Stella Honer again raised her hand. 'Special Agent Vogel, one last question,' she said, although he hadn't signalled to her to speak. 'After this major success, can we say that the Derg case was merely an unhappy interlude in your career?'

Vogel hated Stella's almost feral skill at targeting open wounds. He allowed himself a forced smile 'Well, Signora Honer, I know it's quite easy for you and your colleagues to distinguish between success and failure, but for us police officers there are shades of grey. The Mutilator – as you in the media dubbed him – never struck again. Maybe one day he will, or maybe not. But I like to think that we scared him so much that he'll think twice before planting another bomb.'

He had scored a point, now was the moment to escape. He walked away from the microphones before anyone else could detain him with any more uncomfortable questions.

As the main player in the drama headed for the exit, accompanied by the flashes of the cameras, Officer Borghi moved away from the wall at the back of the room to join him. Part of him was happy that it was finally over, but there was another part of him, a small but tenacious part, that couldn't resign itself to the outcome. For a while, he had genuinely thought he was part of something epic, a kind of battle between good and evil. But after Martini's arrest, he hadn't felt any sense of relief. When it came down to it, the case had been solved by a stroke of luck. The positive aspect was that now he could go back to Caroline and they could await the arrival of their daughter together. But he would miss the work. He would miss Avechot.

Borghi caught up with Vogel outside the gym. 'Do you want me to drive you to the hotel?' he asked.

Vogel looked up at the sky. 'No, thanks. I think I'll take advantage of the nice weather and have a little walk.' And he took his usual black notebook from his overcoat.

It was an action Borghi had seen him perform dozens of times in the course of the investigation. He was curious to know what Vogel wrote down so diligently. There was surely much to learn from those notes.

'Well, Officer Borghi, we have to say goodbye.' Vogel actually placed a hand on his shoulder, a fatherly gesture that wasn't at all like him. 'In the next case that presents itself, I'll ask for you to be assigned to my team.'

On this occasion, Vogel thought, things had gone well and it hadn't been necessary to lay the responsibility for failure on a subordinate. But Borghi could prove useful to him: the boy was sufficiently green to believe everything he was told.

'It's been an honour to work for you, sir,' Borghi said with conviction. 'I've learned a lot.'

Vogel doubted it. His investigative method was a mixture of tactics and opportunism. It couldn't easily be learned, and he wasn't ready to share his secrets. 'Well, good for you,' he said with a smile.

He was about to go when Borghi said. 'I'm sorry, sir, there's something I've been wondering . . . '

'Go on, officer.'

'Have you ever wondered why Martini should have

kidnapped and killed Anna Lou and hidden her body? I mean . . . what do you think was his motive?'

Vogel pretended to consider the question seriously. 'People hate, Officer Borghi. Hate is something intangible, it's hard to demonstrate and doesn't produce evidence that can be exhibited in a courtroom. But unfortunately, it exists.'

'I'm sorry, but I don't understand. Why should Martini have hated Anna Lou?'

'Not her in particular, but the whole world. Deep down, the teacher led a humble life, with not much to satisfy him. His wife had cheated on him with another man, he'd come close to losing his family and being left on his own – as, indeed, happened later. In the long term, when anger accumulates it has to find an outlet. I think Martini harboured a desire for revenge on other people. And killing Anna Lou, with her youthful innocence, was a perfect way to punish all of us.'

Borghi, though, wasn't completely convinced. 'Strange, because in the academy they taught us that hate isn't the prime motive for murder.'

Vogel smiled again. 'Let me give you a piece of advice you'll never again hear from a police officer. Forget everything you were taught and learn to consider every case on its own merits, or you'll never develop the instinct for catching criminals.'

He watched the cashmere coat as Vogel walked away. The instinct for catching criminals, he thought. As if it were the opposite of the instinct to kill.

Hate isn't the prime motive for murder, Vogel repeated to himself as he walked into his hotel room. What did that snotty-nosed kid know about murderers? And how had he dared to doubt his words? But he would never let his rage obscure the sense of well-being he had been feeling all day. Borghi had no future, that much was certain.

The clothes that had been hanging in the wardrobe all these days had already been placed on the bed. Each item in its own wrapper. Like the shoes, which had been slipped into cotton bags. Then there were the ties, the shirts, the underwear. The whole of it occupied the entire surface of the mattress, forming a perfect, very neat and very colourful mosaic. Soon, Vogel would transfer everything to his suitcase. But when he went to the bed, he noticed something that hadn't been there before.

On the bedside table, next to the TV set, was a package.

He approached it suspiciously. Someone from the hotel staff must have put it there while he was away. But there was no note with it. That struck him as strange. After a moment's hesitation, he decided to unwrap the gift anyway.

When he opened the box, he found a battered old laptop.

What kind of joke is this? he thought. He lifted the screen. There on the keyboard was a small piece of cardboard with a message on it, written in pen in a very neat hand.

He's innocent.

Beneath these words, there was a mobile phone number. It was the same number from which he had received two anonymous texts – I need to talk to you. Call me on this number – which he had erased, thinking they came from a reporter looking for a scoop.

Vogel was annoyed. He couldn't stand invasions of his private sphere. Nevertheless, he had to admit to himself that he felt a strange kind of curiosity about what was on the computer. Common sense told him to stop right there, but when it came down to it, it didn't cost anything to check.

He reached out his hand and turned on the laptop.

It took a while to come to life. The black screen turned blue. In the middle, just one icon, that of an internet browser. Vogel was about to click on it, but the connection was automatic. There now appeared an internet page with bare, rudimentary graphics. This must be an old website that had been around for years, he immediately thought, one that nobody visited any more but that continued to float like detritus on the surface of the internet.

The page even had a name.

The man in the fog.

Beneath that title was an array of six faces: all of young girls, all very similar, with red hair and freckles. Above all, they were very similar to Anna Lou Kastner.

At the other end of the line, the telephone rang several times. At last a hoarse female voice answered. 'You took your time, Special Agent Vogel.'

Vogel immediately went on the offensive. 'Who are you and what are you trying to prove?'

The woman remained calm. 'I see I have your attention at last.' These words were followed by a brief series of coughs. 'My name is Beatrice Leman, and I'm a journalist. Or rather, I was.'

'I'm not going to issue any statement about what I've just seen – whatever it is. So don't be under any illusions: you're not going to become famous because of this.'

'I'm not after an interview,' Leman replied. 'There's something I'd like to show you.'

Vogel thought this over for a moment. His anger didn't diminish, but there was something that told him he should listen to this woman. 'All right, let's meet.'

'You'll have to come to me.'

Vogel let out an irritated laugh. 'Why's that?'

'You'll see.'

The woman hung up before he could reply.

21 January

Twenty-nine days after the disappearance

Beatrice Leman was confined to a wheelchair.

It had taken Vogel four days to make up his mind to go and see her, but in the meantime, he had discreetly gathered information about her. As a journalist, she had mainly handled local news, but her articles had on several occasions embarrassed politicians and powerful people. She'd been a tough customer, but now she was past it. She no longer scared anybody.

At first, Vogel had decided to ignore her. She was just an old journalist looking to make a comeback and regain a modicum of fame. But then it had occurred to him she might get in touch with Stella Honer, for example. And Stella certainly wouldn't turn down the opportunity to exhume the Kastner case, not if it meant offering the public a juicy alternative version of the truth established by his investigation. It would be disastrous if someone gave credit to such ravings, especially in the light of the fact that he had falsified evidence in order to nail Martini.

Vogel didn't want anyone sticking their nose into the case, not now. So in the end he had decided to meet the woman.

Leman lived in a chalet just outside Avechot. She had never married and her only company was a horde of cats that swarmed all over the study that served as her den. When she greeted him, she struck Vogel as an embittered, disillusioned woman, her face furrowed by deep brown lines and her grey hair gathered into a bun. She was wearing a sweater covered in cigarette ash, and there were ashtrays filled with cigarette ends everywhere. A persistent odour of stale nicotine hung over the house, mixed with the pungent odour of cat urine. Leman must be so used to it, she could no longer smell it. Documents and old newspapers lay in heaps on shelves and on the floor.

'Welcome, Special Agent Vogel,' she said as she led him inside. There was a kind of path through the chaos that allowed Leman to move surprisingly easily with her wheelchair.

Vogel pulled his cashmere overcoat tight around him. He didn't want to touch anything, afraid of the dust and, above all, the germs there might be in the room. 'Frankly,' he said by way of introduction, 'I don't know what I'm here for.'

Leman laughed. 'As far as I'm concerned, the main thing is that you're here.' Then she took up position behind a desk and motioned to him to sit down on the chair in front of it.

However reluctantly, Vogel sat down.

'I see you haven't brought me back the laptop I sent you. It's the only one I have and I'd really like to have it back.'

'I thought it was a gift to me,' Vogel said ironically. 'I'll try to get it back to you as soon as possible.'

Leman lit a cigarette.

'Is that necessary?' Vogel asked.

'I've been paraplegic from birth because of a mistake by an

obstetrician, so I don't give a damn about what might harm other people.'

'All right, but let's get to the point. I have no time to waste.'

'I founded a little local paper and edited it for forty years. I did everything myself: from the news to the obituaries. Then the internet came along and rendered all my efforts obsolete. I had to close down for lack of readers. Now, people know in real time what's happening on the other side of the world, but don't know what the fuck is happening around the corner.' After this brief preamble, Beatrice took a heavy file down from one of the shelves, causing a small avalanche of documents and newspapers. She laid it on her lap, but didn't open it. 'As a journalist, you deal with hundreds of cases in your career,' she resumed. 'But there's always one that stays with you: you can't forget the names or the faces of the victims, and you carry inside you a kind of parasite that feeds on your sense of guilt. Maybe it's the same for you in the police.'

'Sometimes,' Vogel acknowledged, just to get her to continue with her story.

'Well, my solitary worm started to dig a hole for itself with the disappearance of Katya Hillman.' She lifted the file again and let it fall heavily on the table. 'She was the first.'

The thud echoed briefly in the cramped room. Vogel looked in silence at the voluminous file. He knew that once he started in on this, it would be hard to get out of it later. But he had no choice. He lifted the cardboard cover and began leafing through the file.

The first thing he came across was an old photograph of Katya Hillman. He had already seen it on the website, but now he gave it a closer look. The girl was wearing a blue smock: a school uniform. She was smiling at the camera. She had honest blue eyes. The other images of teenage girls with red hair and freckles followed. Vogel studied them one by one. They looked like sisters. There was the same innocence in their facial expressions. Predestined, he told himself. The curse of innocence had fallen on them.

As he looked through the file, Leman watched him, smoking her cigarette in silence, holding it between her fingertips and consuming it in slow, deep drags, letting the ash accumulate unsteadily at the end.

Vogel noted that along with the personal details of the supposed victims, there were numerous newspaper articles written by Leman herself and some perfunctory police reports.

'The girls all came from difficult family situations,' Beatrice said, breaking the silence. 'Violent fathers, mothers who suffered but never reported their husbands. Maybe that was why the police in Avechot and the other villages never investigated the disappearances too closely. It was almost natural for the girls to want to run away from those hellholes.'

'But you saw a connection between the cases. You thought there might be a single person behind them.'

'Girls aged fifteen or sixteen, with red hair and freckles. It all pointed to an obsession. To me, it was obvious. But nobody believed me.'

'The last disappearance was thirty years ago,' he said, reading the date on a report.

'Precisely,' Beatrice said. 'This Martini of yours wasn't living in Avechot then. In fact, he was still a child.'

Yes, Vogel thought, Stella Honer would love this story. Although he thought its similarity to the Kastner case was a mere coincidence, he couldn't just shrug his shoulders and leave. First he had to disabuse Leman of the notion that there might be a connection. And to do so, he had to know more. 'When Anna Lou went missing, why on earth did nobody in the valley apart from you bring any of this up?'

'Because people soon forget, didn't you know that? Years ago, I created the website I showed you, hoping to keep the memory alive, but nobody cares about those poor girls any more.'

'And why "the man in the fog"?'

Leman's voice, already deep thanks to her cigarette habit, became a low rasp. 'People vanish in the fog. We know they're there, but we can't see them. Those girls are still among us, Special Agent Vogel, regardless of whether something terrible happened to them, regardless even of whether they're dead. For some obscure reason, the man in the fog took them – because I'm sure we're dealing with one man. We know it's not Martini, so I can only assume he's still out there, in search of new prey.'

'It doesn't make sense,' he said. 'Why stop for thirty years, then start again?'

'Maybe he moved somewhere else and now he's come back. Maybe he struck again in other places and we don't know about it. We just have to look for girls with the same characteristics.'

Vogel shook his head. 'I'm sorry, I don't buy it. With all the fuss around the Kastner case, someone would have brought any similar cases to the attention of the police or the media.'

Leman was about to say something in reply, but broke off to cough. 'It's not just that file I wanted to show you,' she somehow managed to splutter. She opened a drawer in her desk and held out a package to Vogel. 'I got this a while ago, but if you look at the postmark, you'll notice it was sent the day Anna Lou disappeared.'

Vogel lost interest in the file and grabbed the package.

'As you can see, it was sent here but addressed to you. But since you didn't answer my texts, a couple of days ago I opened it.'

Vogel lifted the envelope to see the contents through the torn edge. Then he put his hand inside and took out a little pink book covered in pictures of kittens.

Anna Lou's *real* diary, he thought immediately.

The one she had hidden from her mother. The one they hadn't found. Presumably, she had kept it in the satchel that had ended up in the channel.

Vogel looked at the heart-shaped padlock that sealed it.

He tried to rationalise the situation. The only reason anyone could have had to send the diary to Leman was to draw attention to the case of the man in the fog. Who was he? And what did Martini have to do with any of it? A presentiment was growing in him that he had been mistaken about the teacher. And yet he had the same feeling he'd had with Derg. In that case, too, the conviction that he knew the identity of the culprit had driven him to falsify the evidence. Only, there, he hadn't made any mistake. Derg really had been the Mutilator, that was why he had stopped.

'What do you want in return?' he asked the woman, waving the diary. He was trying to be practical.

'The truth,' Leman said without hesitation.

'Are you after a scoop or what?'

'You're too clever, my friend. I'm just a simple woman.'

The devil's most foolish sin is vanity, Vogel told himself, thinking again about Martini's words and his own situation. Maybe he had indeed committed the sin of vanity, and now he would be punished.

'If I wanted what you're offering me now, I'd have gone to a network and sold them that diary for a lot of money.'

She was right. How stupid he had been not to think of it. But if she didn't want either fame or money, then what was she after? 'I promise you, if there's anything in here that'll make it possible to reopen the investigation and extend it to the other six missing girls, I won't hesitate for a moment.' He made it sound like a solemn promise.

'This is the last opportunity to catch the man in the fog,' Leman said. 'I'm sure you won't waste it.'

Clearly, she had fallen for it, hook, line and sinker.

The steel tables and chairs in the visiting room were bolted to the floor. The ceiling was low and voices echoed unpleasantly, making it almost impossible to talk. But right now, apart from four warders silently observing the scene from a distance, the only people in the room were Loris Martini and Attorney Levi.

Even though he had only been in prison for a few days, Martini looked exhausted. 'I'm very popular here. They're keeping me in solitary, but at night I can still hear the other prisoners threatening me from their cells. They can't get their hands on me, but they do everything they can to keep me awake.'

'I'll talk to the governor, or have you moved.'

'Better not. I'd rather not make more enemies. It's already difficult enough being a star.' He laughed bitterly. 'One of the warders implied it's better if I don't touch the food from the prison kitchen. I think even the warders despise me and he only said it to scare me. Well, he did scare me, because since then I've been living on crackers.'

Levi was doing his best to encourage his client, but seemed

seriously worried for him. 'You can't go on like this, you have to eat, you have to keep your strength up. Otherwise you'll never stand the stress of the trial.'

'Do you have any idea when it'll start?'

'They're talking about a month, maybe a bit longer. The prosecution has enough evidence, but we're getting ready to refute it point by point.'

'How will I manage without money?'

Levi spoke in a low voice so as not to be overheard by the warders. 'That's why I arranged for you to meet Stella Honer. It was stupid of you not to accept her offer.'

'So are you giving up on me?'

'Don't talk nonsense. I still think we have a chance. The case against you rests on the DNA evidence. If we can demolish it, the whole thing collapses. I've already found a geneticist who'll repeat all the compatibility tests on the bloodstains.'

Martini didn't seem convinced. 'I was told you've been a guest on TV, talking about me and my case.'

It sounded like an accusation, but Levi didn't seem to take it badly. 'It's important for people to hear your version. You can't be there, so I have to do it.'

Martini couldn't find fault with that. When it came down to it, Levi was getting his payment in the form of publicity. So it was fine to use his case for that. 'Have you heard from my family? How are my wife and daughter?'

'They're fine, but as long as you're in solitary they can't visit you.'

They wouldn't have visited me anyway, Martini thought.

'You'll see, when we get to the trial we'll refute the charges and the truth will come out.'

*

After leaving Beatrice Leman's house, Vogel had driven aimlessly all afternoon, using only secondary roads that led up
into the mountains. He needed to think, to clear his mind. He
had planned to leave Avechot days earlier, instead of which he
was stuck here, forced to do something he had never done and
was not sure he could do.

Investigate.

The man in the fog had screwed up his plans. And now he
was watching him, safe in his white blanket, and laughing at
him.

Anna Lou's supposed diary was on the seat next to him.
Vogel hadn't opened it yet because he wasn't convinced it
was the right move. First he had to weigh up the pros and the
cons. Maybe the solution was to throw it away or burn it and
forget everything. Maybe the man in the fog had no intention of making another appearance, maybe he only wanted
to scare him. Maybe. But would that be enough for him? He
must have planned this, too, Vogel told himself. That was
why he hadn't yet destroyed the evidence that could exonerate Martini. The thought had even flashed through his mind
that he could use the diary to take credit for the teacher's
release, but then someone might wonder, hypothetically, if he
hadn't falsified the results in this case as he had done with
Derg. The suspicion could put an end to his career. It didn't
even occur to him that an innocent man was in prison. That
wasn't any concern of his, not any more. If anything, he was
scared that the man in the fog really had decided to resume
his activities after thirty years. In that case, it would be events
that gave the lie to Vogel, because after Anna Lou he would
surely strike again. Another girl with red hair and freckles.
Someone's daughter. But this, too, was of no importance to

Vogel. He had to think of himself first. It wasn't cynicism, it was a matter of survival.

Outside, the sun had already started its inexorable descent into darkness.

After driving around for almost three hours, it was the fuel gauge that forced Vogel to stop. He parked in the open space by the mine's decantation basins. He got out and sniffed the dust-laden air. In front of him, a series of mounds of fluorite. In the dark, the mineral gave off a greenish glow, like an aurora borealis. There wasn't a soul about. Vogel went closer, opened his flies and started to urinate. As he emptied his bladder, he felt something like a series of small taps on his shoulder. Obviously, it was his imagination, but it felt as if someone was trying to attract his attention.

The diary was calling him from the car seat. You can't ignore me, it seemed to be saying.

When he had finished, Vogel went back to the car. He sat down and picked up the diary. He looked at it as if it were a relic. Then, driven by a sudden impulse, he grabbed the little heart-shaped padlock and pulled at it until it snapped. He felt cold and hot and nervous.

He opened the page at random and immediately recognised Anna Lou Kastner's handwriting.

'Shit,' he muttered. Then he started reading. The hope was to find something that led to Loris Martini – something that proved that he, and not the man in the fog, was indeed the killer of the missing girl. Obviously, it wasn't plausible that he could have sent the diary to Beatrice Leman. But it had been sent on the very day of Anna Lou's disappearance, so whoever had done it hadn't been trying to exonerate Martini, who at the time wasn't even a suspect. No, there had to be another meaning to it.

It was a signature.

That was why Vogel didn't find anything in it to connect Anna Lou to Martini. The secret she had been trying jealously to guard in her diary was something else entirely.

11 August: Met a really nice boy at the seaside. I only talked to him a couple of times, I think he wanted to kiss me. But he didn't. God knows if I'll see him again next year. His name is Oliver. What a nice name! I've decided that every day I'll write his initial in biro on my left arm, the arm nearest the heart. And I'll do it all winter, until I see him again next year. It'll be my secret, like a token that we'll meet again.

Vogel quickly leafed through the other pages. There were more passages referring to the mysterious Oliver, the object of Anna Lou's innocent fantasies, of desires that would never be realised.

'Oliver,' Vogel said to himself, thinking again of the initial that was now imprinted on the arm of Anna Lou Kastner's body. A little O drawn in pen, which was rotting away just as she was, and which nobody would ever discover.

Her secret died with her.

But there was something else in the diary. Vogel didn't immediately notice the little sheet of paper that had slid out from between the pages. He picked it up later from the mat under the seat. He opened it and read it, realising as he did so that it wasn't the girl who had slipped it in there.

The new clue in the hunt was a map.

22 January

Thirty days after the disappearance

He had spent a sleepless night.

The map was on the bedside table. Vogel had lain there the whole time staring up at the ceiling, motionless, the quilt pulled up to his chin. The questions and doubts that piled into his head were stopping him from thinking. A new game had begun, and he couldn't afford not to play it. The man in the fog wouldn't allow that. That was why there was only one thing to do.

Keep going.

Even though Vogel feared that the ending the monster had planned wouldn't be pleasant for him. For the first time in his career, he was afraid of the truth.

At about five, he decided he'd had enough of the hotel room. He had no choice now but to act. Only if he anticipated events would he be able to save himself. So he threw off the cocoon of blankets in which he had taken refuge and got out of bed.

Before dressing, he checked his service Beretta, the one he'd been carrying with him for years to keep up appearances. He had actually never fired a shot except at the rifle range, and he doubted he still could. Just as he didn't know if he could maintain the weapon in working order – in fact, he usually entrusted the task to some subordinate. When he picked up the pistol, it struck him as heavier than he remembered, but it was anxiety that was transforming the texture of things. He made sure that the magazine was full and that the barrel moved smoothly. But his hand was shaking. Calm down, he told himself. He dressed, although not in one of his usual elegant suits. He chose a dark sweater, casual trousers and the most comfortable shoes he had. Finally, he put on his coat and went out.

Almost all the reporters had abandoned Avechot. A couple of TV crews had stayed behind to cover the last stages of the case, but the correspondents had changed. The big names had gone. Still, Vogel harboured the fear that some trainee in search of a scoop that would gain him or her a promotion might notice his flight. So he was very cautious as he left the built-up area. He kept checking the rear-view mirror to make sure nobody was following him. As he drove, he clutched the map with one hand, trying to figure out where he was going.

In the middle of the map was a dot with a red X next to it. To help him find his way, he had bought a compass the previous evening in a shop selling mountaineering equipment. He tried not to think about what he would find. The place was situated to the north-west, in a relatively accessible area that had actually been gone over several times by the search teams, even quite recently. So why hadn't they noticed anything? The operation had been badly carried out, Vogel told himself.

Nobody had really been concerned about finding Anna Lou Kastner. And it was all his fault. He should have supervised things, instead of entrusting every specifically operational decision to the young and inexperienced Borghi, leaving himself free to court the media.

A red dawn was peering out from behind the tops of the mountains and starting to invade the valley like a river of blood. Vogel was near the spot indicated, but from here on the woods began. He was obliged to abandon his car and continue on foot with a torch. The ground sloped slightly and his shoes slid on the blanket of leaves covering the soil. He clutched the branches to stay on his feet. The tangle was so thick that a bramble lightly scratched his temple. Vogel didn't even notice. Every now and again, he would stop to check the map and the compass. He had to be quick, before the sun came up. He was terrified that someone might see him.

He came out into a small clearing. According to the map, he was close to the red X. If his career, his very life, hadn't been in the balance, it would have seemed like a joke. But, when it came down to it, it was. The man in the fog was making fun of him. All right, let's see what you've prepared for me, you arsehole.

He swept the ground with the beam of his torch, but couldn't see anything unusual. It was only when he aimed the light upwards that he noticed something. Someone had placed a box of biscuits on a branch. *The Derg case*, he thought immediately. Apparently, the man in the fog knew his weak points well. Vogel could even appreciate the irony of the reference to the Mutilator and the falsified evidence.

And he also knew where he had to dig.

He knelt at the foot of the tree, put on a pair of rubber gloves and cleared the ground of dead leaves. Then he started to move the damp earth, unconcerned about dirtying his clothes. He had no intention of going too far down, because if the body of Anna Lou Kastner was there, he didn't want to see it. He just needed confirmation. But after digging only a few centimetres, he already felt something. There in front of his eyes was part of an opaque piece of plastic. Vogel hesitated a moment, then grabbed it and pulled with all his might.

Out came the whole of the plastic. It was wrapped around something and hermetically sealed with insulating tape to preserve the contents.

He turned it over, trying to figure out what it could be. He shook it close to his ear and it produced a familiar sound, something like a child's rattle. Whatever the gift of the man in the fog was, it didn't seem like part of a human body. Let's have done with this, he told himself, anger now replacing his fear. He set about unwrapping the package. It took him quite a while to remove the plastic, which had been put on with great care. When he recognised the object, though, his worst fears materialised, making his throat tighten. This time, there was no irony.

The gift the man in the fog had intended for Vogel – the TV policeman – was a videocassette.

Solitary sharpened the senses. He had discovered that in his days of solitude. He wasn't allowed to read the newspapers or watch television, and his quartz watch had been taken from him. But from the smell that came from the kitchens he was able to guess when they were starting to make the meals, that way he knew that breakfast, lunch or dinner hour was approaching. The cell was an embryo, everything that entered it remained imprisoned – just like him. Now even the noises of the prison were familiar to him. He heard the clinking of the keys with which the warder who guarded the automatic gate in the corridor was equipped and that way he knew that the night shift had ended and that the night warder would be handing over to his morning colleague. It must have been around six.

His vision of what was happening outside was hampered by the heavy iron door, but from the light that filtered onto the ground through the crack it was possible to understand a lot of things. When he saw shadows cross the light, he knew someone would soon be entering the cell. He drew himself up and waited for the key to turn completely in the lock. Then the door opened and two figures appeared against the light.

Two warders he had never seen before.

'Take your things,' one of them said.

'Why, where are we going?'

Neither of them answered. Martini did as he was told. He picked up the brown woollen blanket, the mess tin and the spoon that were the gift of the prison, as well as the bar of soap and the little bottles of shampoo and aftershave that he had acquired from the commissary and which, right now, constituted his only property. Then he followed the officers.

Martini assumed that they wanted simply to move him to a different cell, instead of which they walked along the entire corridor of the solitary section, as far as the gate. And there – the first oddity – there was no one on guard. Another couple of corridors, then they took a lift and went down a couple of floors. All of this without encountering a soul – the second oddity. The warders couldn't all have simultaneously abandoned their positions. In addition, there was a strange silence coming from the cells. Usually, at this hour the prisoners were already on their feet and making a great commotion, demanding their breakfast. Martini thought again about the night he had just spent. Nobody had kept him awake with screams or threats. The third oddity.

They came to a security entrance and when Martini saw on the wall a sign saying BLOCK F, he realised they were about to enter the section for common prisoners and took fright. 'Hold on,' he said. 'I'm a special prisoner, I have to stay in solitary. It was an order of the judge.'

The two of them ignored him and pushed him in front of them.

Martini felt a sudden sense of terror. 'Did you hear me? You can't put me with the others.' His voice was shaking. The warders ignored his complaints. They grabbed him energetically by the arms.

They came to the door of a cell. One of the warders opened it, while the other said to Martini, 'You'll be here for a while, then we'll come back for you.'

Martini took a step forward, then hesitated. It was dark beyond the doorway and he couldn't see who or what was inside.

'Go on, go in,' the warder exhorted him in a reassuring tone.

A fleeting thought passed through Martini's mind. He was convinced that these men hated him, like everyone else in the prison. But why should they hurt him? Unlike the prisoners, they were obliged to respect the law. So he decided to trust them and went in. The door closed behind him and he waited without moving for his eyes to become accustomed to the darkness. Then he heard noises around him – little sounds, rustling.

Solitary sharpened the senses. He realised he wasn't alone.

When the first punch hit him in the face, Martini immediately lost his balance. The objects he was holding in his hands fell to the floor together with him. He was overwhelmed by a series of blows and kicks that came from every direction. He tried to shield himself with his arms, but couldn't evade the blows. He tasted blood, felt the burning of the cuts on his face. His ribs cracked and he couldn't breathe. But after a moment, he didn't feel anything any more. He was only a mass of flesh struggling pointlessly on the floor.

Dead meat.

There was no more pain now, only exhaustion. His mind surrendered before his body and he let himself go into a kind of torpor. Only his arms kept up a strenuous, futile resistance. Even though it was dark, his eyes clouded over. And when everything was about to vanish, a light came into his field of vision. It came from behind his back. He felt himself being forcefully grabbed and dragged away, beyond the doorway of the cell. He was safe, but he would never be safe again.

Then he lost consciousness.

He had gone to ground in the school's box room, where the video recorders from the antiquated surveillance system were kept. The only light came from the monitor that cast its reflection on Vogel's face, creating a mask of shadows.

He inserted the video cassette into the appropriate compartment, which swallowed it after a slight pressure. There followed a series of sounds while the mechanism captured the tape and stretched it around the spools. Then the video started.

First, there was the grey dust of static, which produced a loud, unpleasant rustling. Vogel adjusted the volume, because he wanted everything to stay in the room. Seconds went by, then the image abruptly changed.

A narrow beam of light was moving over an opaque surface. Dirty, cracked tiles. On the soundtrack, a series of taps on the camera's microphone. Whoever was filming was trying to adjust it as best he could. The camera moved along a wall and stopped in front of a mirror. The little light above the lens was sharply reflected. In the blinding glow, all that could be seen was the operator's hand, in a black glove. Then he took a step to one side, so that his face could also be seen. He was wearing a balaclava. The only human thing was his eyes – distant, indecipherable. Empty.

The man in the fog, Vogel told himself. He waited for him to say or do something, but all he did was stand there. Motionless. Only his breathing could be heard – calm, regular. It was lost in the echo of the small room in which he stood. A bathroom. What kind of place was this? And why had he wanted him to see it? Vogel went closer to the screen to get a better look and saw that behind the man a threadbare towel hung from a hook.

On it, two small green matching triangles.

Vogel was trying to figure out the meaning of this symbol when the man on the screen lifted his free hand from the camera and started a countdown on the fingers of his glove.

Three ... two ... one ...

Then the camera suddenly moved to one side. The face with the balaclava disappeared from the mirror and in its place a bright patch appeared in the background. The camera took a while to focus.

And then he saw her. And jumped back in his seat.

Beyond the doorway of the bathroom was a bedroom – a

bedroom in an abandoned hotel. Sitting in a corner at the foot of a filthy mattress, a thin figure. The light from the lamp above the camera made it look as if she was wrapped in a dazzling aura in the midst of the darkness that loomed threateningly around her. Her back stooped, her arms hanging loosely, a resigned posture. Her skin was very white. She was wearing only a pair of green knickers and a white bra that adhered almost completely to her chest. The underwear of a child. The camera moved in on her. Her red hair fell over her face in dishevelled strands. The only feature visible was her half-open mouth, a trickle of saliva emerging from one side of it. Every time she breathed, her thin shoulder blades rose and then slowly fell again. Outside her lips, the breath condensed because of the cold, but she wasn't shivering. It was as if she didn't feel anything.

Anna Lou Kastner seemed almost unconscious, her mind perhaps blurred by drugs. Vogel recognised her only by the little circle drawn on her left forearm. O for Oliver, the boy from the summer when she had discovered love. The secret she had confided only to her diary.

The camera lingered on her, pitilessly. Then the girl slowly raised her head, as if she wanted to say something. Vogel waited, but was afraid of hearing her voice. As she started to scream, the recording suddenly stopped.

The first thing he did was destroy the videocassette. He threw it in the school's gas boiler and waited until it had burned to a cinder. He couldn't risk anyone finding it in his possession. By now, he was paranoid.

He was about to get rid of Anna's diary, too, but then thought better of it. Beatrice Leman could testify that she had given it to him, so it wasn't a good idea to destroy it. And when it came down to it, it didn't contain any information that could compromise him. So he decided to keep it, but hid it in one of the lockers in the changing room that still served as his office.

Then he started to search on the internet. He had to track down the abandoned hotel where the footage had been shot. He was sure the video was an invitation. If he found Anna Lou's body in that room, he could always manipulate the scene in such a way as to put the blame for the murder on Martini.

That was what the man in the fog wanted, Vogel was now convinced of it.

Otherwise why lead him to the discovery of the truth? Why show him the video of the girl? If he had simply wanted to claim responsibility for the kidnapping, he would have sent it to the media, not to him.

Vogel searched through all the old hotels in Avechot, concentrating in particular on those that had closed down after the mine had opened and the tourists had deserted the area. In some cases, the websites still existed. He didn't have many details at his disposal. The most important was the two matching green triangles. And it was thanks to them that he found the right hotel.

The triangles were two stylised pines on an almost completely rusted sign.

Vogel had reached the gates that led into the grounds surrounding the building. It was after seven, and there was nobody about, partly because the hotel was in an isolated area, some distance from Avechot.

Vogel noted that the gates weren't closed, so he pushed them open and drove in. Then he got out of the car to close them.

He drove down the short drive with his lights off and parked under a portico, so that nobody should see the vehicle.

The hotel had four floors. The windows of the rooms were covered with wooden planks that had been nailed on, but those on the front door had been partly removed. He slipped into a passage and only then switched on the torch he had brought with him.

The sight that greeted him was depressing. Although it had ceased activity only five years earlier, the hotel looked as if it had been closed for at least fifty years. As if the world had ended here. The furnishings were almost non-existent. Skeletons of old sofas rusted in the shadows. Damp had attacked the walls, covering them with a greenish patina, and down them ran rivulets of dense yellow water. The floor was an expanse of rubble and pieces of mildewed wood. A smell of rottenness prevailed everywhere. Vogel walked past the reception desk, with the rack for the keys behind it, and found himself at the foot of a concrete staircase that had once been covered with an elegant burgundy moquette, scraps of which still clung to some of the steps.

He started climbing.

When he got to the first floor, he saw a plate indicating the numbers of the rooms in the corridors to his right and to his left – from 101 to 125, and from 126 to 150. Given that there were four floors, it struck Vogel that there were too many rooms to find the right one at first go. But he didn't want to linger in this place any longer than was necessary. Then he remembered another detail of the video that he had neglected until now. Before showing him Anna Lou, the man in the fog had made a kind of countdown with his hand.

Three . . . two . . . one . . .

It hadn't been a piece of theatre, a maniac's umpteenth joke. He had been telling him where they were.

Room 321 was on the third floor, towards the end of the left-hand corridor. Vogel stood in the doorway, pointing his torch inside. The beam of light explored the room and finally came to rest on the bottom corner of the filthy mattress on which Anna Lou had been sitting.

But there was nobody in the room – not even the *smell*.

And there were no signs that anyone else had been here. What's happening? Vogel asked himself. Then he noticed that the bathroom door was shut. He went closer and placed his hand on the door frame, as if he could perceive something with that gesture, a force field of death or destruction. It was from beyond that doorway that the monster had shot his macabre footage.

He wants you to open it, he told himself. In Vogel's head, the monster was now in charge.

So he grabbed the handle and slowly pushed it down until he felt the lock snap. Then he opened it wide.

He was overcome by a blinding light.

It was like an explosion, but without heat. A white shock-wave that pushed him back.

'Stay on him,' a woman's voice said. 'Do you have him?'

Someone replied, 'Yes, I have him!'

Vogel retreated, one arm raised to shield his eyes. Through the light, he saw a man with a TV camera and, behind him, a second figure who reached out an arm and placed something under his chin.

A microphone.

'Special Agent Vogel, how do you explain your presence here?' Stella Honer asked without giving him time to think.

Confused, Vogel continued to retreat.

'Our network has received a video showing Anna Lou with her kidnapper,' Stella went on. 'Did you know that the girl had been in this hotel?'

Vogel almost fell on the filthy mattress, but managed to keep his balance. 'Leave me alone!' he screamed.

'How did you find out, and why did you keep silent about it?'

'I . . . I . . .' he stammered. He was prevaricating. But he couldn't think of anything to say. It didn't even occur to him to act as a police officer should and demand to know what *they* were doing here. 'Leave me alone!' he heard himself scream again, and he couldn't believe it was his own voice – so shrill, so unsteady.

That was the moment Vogel realised that his career was over.

23 February

Sixty-two days after the disappearance

The night everything changed for ever, Flores watched as Vogel walked around the room, reviewing the stuffed fish on the walls.

'You know something, Doctor? Your fish all look alike.'

Flores smiled. 'Actually, they're the same fish.'

Vogel turned to look at him, incredulous. 'The same fish?'

'*Oncorhynchus mykiss*. They're all specimens of rainbow trout. There are only a few minor differences in colour and shape.'

'You mean those are the only fish you collect?'

'It's strange, I know.'

Vogel found the notion hard to accept. 'Why?'

'I could tell you it's a fascinating species, one that's not at all easy to catch. But that wouldn't be the truth. I've already mentioned my heart attack. Well, I was alone on the shore of a mountain lake when it happened. Something had just taken the bait and I was pulling it up with all my might.' Flores mimed the action. 'I took the acute pain in my left arm for a cramp due to the effort, and didn't let go. When the pain spread to my chest, then up to my sternum, I realised something was wrong. I fell back and almost passed out. All I remember is that next to me on the grass was that huge fish staring at me, gasping for air. We were both about to die.' He laughed. 'Stupid, don't you think? I was young, barely thirty-two, but that fish was also in the prime of its life. With what little breath I had left in my body, I managed to call for help. Luckily, a gamekeeper was passing in the woods.' He pointed to one of the specimens on the wall. 'And that's the trout.'

'And the moral of this story?'

'There isn't one,' Flores admitted. 'But ever since then, every time I've caught an *Oncorhynchus mykiss*, the specimen has ended up on these walls. I stuff them myself. I have a little workshop at home, down in the basement.'

Vogel seemed amused. 'I should have stuffed Stella Honer. That harpy screwed me good and proper. It never even crossed my mind that I might not be the only person Anna Lou's kidnapper had contacted.'

Flores again turned serious. 'I don't think your presence in Avechot tonight is pure chance. The road accident is, though. When you drove off the road, you were escaping.'

'That's an interesting theory,' Vogel admitted. 'But what exactly was I escaping from?'

Flores sat back in his armchair. 'It isn't true that you're in a state of shock. It isn't true that you've lost your memory. No, you remember everything. Am I right?'

Vogel sat down again and passed a hand over his cashmere coat, caressing the material as if wanting to savour its softness.

'I had to lose everything in order to think more clearly, more deeply. To think about something that, for once, wasn't just for my own advantage.'

'And what was this deeper thought that's changed your way of feeling?'

'A little O written in biro on a left arm.' Vogel mimed the action. 'The first time I read the passage in Anna Lou's diary, I didn't think about poor Oliver. I only remembered him later.'

'Poor Oliver?'

'Yes, that young man who couldn't summon up the courage to kiss her during the summer. He lost something, just like all the others – her family, those who knew her. But, unlike them, he doesn't know it, and never will ... If Anna Lou is dead, then the children she won't have also died with her, and the grandchildren: generations and generations that will never exist. All those souls imprisoned in nothingness deserved something better ... Revenge.'

Deep inside, Flores sensed that the moment of truth had arrived. 'Whose blood is it on your clothes, Special Agent Vogel?'

Vogel raised his head and smiled unequivocally. 'I know who it is,' he said, his eyes shining. 'Tonight, I killed the monster.'

31 January

Thirty-nine days after the disappearance

Martini hadn't been released immediately.

He had had to spend another ten days in prison after Stella Honer's scoop. It had taken that long for the authorities to establish that Anna Lou Kastner's kidnapper and probable murderer was a serial killer with a passion for red-headed girls, who had resumed his activities after an inexplicable interval of thirty years.

The man in the fog.

The name given him by Beatrice Leman had immediately appealed to the media, who had adopted it and focused their attention once again on the case. This turn of events had created a great stir, and the public couldn't get enough of it.

Martini had spent those ten days in a state of almost total indifference, in a bed in the infirmary. The official reason they hadn't yet freed him was his state of health. In reality – as he knew perfectly well – the authorities were hoping that the marks of the beating he had received in prison would fade before he reappeared in public. He could understand them: Levi had already threatened in front of the TV cameras to denounce the prison governor and to involve even the minister in the scandal.

When Martini was told to get his things ready because his family would be coming to fetch him, he could hardly believe it. He got up laboriously and slowly began putting everything in a big bag that lay open on the bed. He had a plaster cast on his right forearm, but it was his ribs that hurt most. They were tightly bandaged, and every now and again he found it hard to breathe and had to stop what he was doing. There was a purple bruise around his left eye that descended onto his cheek where it took on a yellow tinge. He had similar marks all over his body, but many of them were starting to fade. His upper lip was split and had required stitches. In the meantime, the cut on his left hand that went back to the day of Anna Lou's disappearance had completely healed.

About eleven, a warder told him that the governor had countersigned the order for his release issued by Prosecutor Mayer and that he was therefore free to go. Martini had to use a crutch to walk. The warder took his bag and led him along the corridors as far as the room where the prisoners met their relatives. The walk was interminable.

When the door opened, Martini saw his wife and daughter, who had been waiting impatiently for him. On their faces, their smiles of delight were immediately replaced by expressions of dismay. Attorney Levi, who was also present, had tried to warn them what to expect, but when they actually saw him it was different. Nothing could have prepared them for that. It wasn't so much seeing him with the crutch and that livid mask-like face that extinguished their enthusiasm as the immediate awareness they had of being confronted with a man who was different from the one they had known. A man who had lost more than twenty kilos, his face hollowed out, the skin drooping under his chin despite his efforts to hide it by growing a bristly little beard. But above all, a man of forty-three who looked like an old man.

Martini continued limping towards them, trying to put on his best smile. At last, Clea and Monica broke free of the shock and ran to him. The three of them embraced for a long time, and wept silently. As they sank their heads on his chest, he kissed both his women on the backs of their necks and stroked their hair. 'It's over,' he said. It's over, he told himself – because he didn't yet believe it.

Then Clea lifted her eyes to his, and it was as if they were recognising each other after so long apart. Martini knew the meaning of that look. She was begging forgiveness for leaving him on his own, for not being beside him at the worst time of his life, above all for doubting him. Martini returned her look with a nod of his head, and it was sufficient to make it clear to both of them that all had been forgiven.

'Let's go home,' he said.

They got in Levi's Mercedes. The lawyer sat in front, next to the driver, and the Martini family in the back. They had used a side exit to avoid the reporters who had gathered in front of the prison. But when the car with its blackened windows got to the street where their house was, they encountered another assembly of microphones and TV cameras. There was also a small crowd of onlookers.

Martini saw on Clea's and Monica's faces the fear that the

siege was beginning again, preventing them from carrying on with their lives. But Levi turned towards the back seat and reassured them, 'It's going to be different. Look.'

And indeed, as soon as the crowd saw that the car was turning into the drive of their house, they started applauding. Some even let out cheers of encouragement.

Levi was the first to get out. He opened the back door to reveal the Martini family, at last reunited and happy, for the benefit of the photographers and cameramen. Clea was the second person to get out of the car, followed by Monica and finally the teacher. As the applause and cheers grew in volume, they seemed in a daze. They hadn't expected this.

Martini looked around. While the flashes went off, briefly lighting up his careworn face, he recognised many of his neighbours. They were crying his name and waving. The Odevises were there, too, all of them, and the head of the family, who not so long ago had slandered him on television, was now trying to attract his attention and bid him welcome. Martini didn't stop to think about the hypocrisy of it all. Preferring to show that he didn't bear any grudges, he raised his arm to thank those present.

Once they were inside the house, Martini went straight to the sofa. He was tired, his legs hurt and he needed to sit down. Monica gave him a hand, supporting him on one side. She helped him to sit, then lifted his feet onto a pouffe and took off his shoes. It was a gesture of great tenderness such as he would never have expected from his daughter. 'Would you like me to bring you something? A cup of tea, a sandwich?'

He stroked her cheek. 'Thanks, darling, I'm fine like this.'

Clea, in the meantime, was hyperactive. 'I'll make lunch right away. You will eat with us, won't you, Signor Levi?'

'Of course,' Levi replied, knowing he couldn't refuse the invitation. As Clea headed for the kitchen, he turned to his client. 'After we eat, the two of us have some important things to talk about.'

Martini already knew what his lawyer was going to say, the speech he would make. 'Of course,' he replied.

For days now, he had been stuck in this damned hotel room in Avechot. He'd had to unpack his bags and remain 'at the disposal of the authorities'. The formula chosen by Mayer was perfect: it meant everything and nothing. They didn't have enough to charge him yet, because the investigation into his conduct was still in progress, but at the same time he couldn't leave because the prosecutor might still need to question him. Vogel wasn't afraid things would move quickly. The idea that he had falsified the evidence that had led to Martini's arrest was only a hypothesis, and one that was hard to prove. The official version was vague, talking only of 'accidental contamination' of the evidence. But when it was put together with the Derg case, the episode was bound to put an end to his career.

As he walked about the room, moving from the bathroom to the bed and back to the bathroom, it occurred to him that they probably wouldn't dismiss him. They would just make sure he resigned, to soften the effect of the scandal that was now engulfing even the higher echelons of the police. He would leave quietly, for what would be described as 'personal reasons'. In this sense, the man in the fog was helping him. Right now, the attention of the media and public opinion was on the monster, relegating everything else into the background. That was why Vogel had to be clever and negotiate the conditions of his own exit from the scene.

But that wasn't enough for him.

He couldn't swallow the fact that they were getting rid of him like this. For years, he had solved cases that had earned him headlines in the newspapers, and for years, his chiefs had taken advantage of his successes. They had posed beside him at conclusive press conferences, taking part of the credit and using it to advance their own careers. The bastards! Now that he needed them to save his arse, where were they?

The main reason he was so angry was the press conference that Mayer – a woman who used to claim she didn't like to appear on television – had called and which had been broadcast on all the networks the previous evening.

'From this moment on, the investigation is being resumed with increased vigour,' she had said. 'We have a new lead, and we will also do justice to the six girls who disappeared before Anna Lou.' It was an idle promise: she must have known that, after thirty years, it would be almost impossible.

And when someone had asked if the police would now be pursuing the man in the fog, it was Officer Borghi – that ingrate – who had replied. 'You journalists like coming up with these sensational names to excite the public's imagination. I prefer to think that he has a face and an identity and isn't simply a monster. That's the only way we'll catch him.' The boy had adapted quickly, Vogel thought. Maybe he'd underestimated him. But he still needed his mother to blow his nose, he'd never be able to stand the pressure.

What truly infuriated him was the aura of sanctity in which Martini was now wrapped. The transition from 'monster' to 'victim of the system' had been almost immediate. Part of it was the fact that the media had a lot to apologise for: they could well be sued for libel. Those reporters who had been lynching

Martini for weeks had now come after Vogel. That was why, although he was forced to remain in Avechot, he couldn't move from this damned hotel room. The hordes waiting for him outside wanted nothing better than to crucify him.

But he wouldn't go quietly with his head bowed. He had thought of a way out that was more honourable and, above all, advantageous for him. If he had to go, then he would get what he could out of it. Money would at least partly soothe his frustration and massage the wound to his ego. Yes, that was the right idea.

He just had to recover a certain object.

After lunch, he had said he felt very tired. So he had apologised to Clea, Monica and Levi and gone up to the bedroom to rest. He had slept for almost five hours, and when he woke he hoped that the lawyer had gone. He wasn't yet ready to listen to the speech Levi was dying to make. But when he went down to the living room, he was still there. It had been dark for a while outside, and Levi was sitting on the sofa next to Clea. They were holding steaming cups of tea in their hands and chatting. When they saw him at the top of the stairs, his wife stood up and went to help him. She walked him to the armchair.

'I was sure you were going to sleep until tomorrow morning,' Levi said, displaying his usual smile.

'You never give up, do you?' Martini replied, having guessed his game.

'It's my job.'

'All right, then tell me what you have to and let's have done with it.'

'I'd like the whole of your family to be present, if possible.'

'Why?'

'Because I know it's going to be hard to make you see reason, and I need all the support I can get.'

Martini snorted. But Clea took his hand. 'I'll go and call Monica,' she said.

Soon, they were all gathered in the living room.

'All right,' Levi began. 'Now that all the interested parties are here, I can tell you that you're an idiot.'

Martini laughed in surprise. 'Don't you think I've already been insulted enough?'

'Well, let's put it this way: it's definitely the insult that most corresponds to reality.'

'Why's that? Come on, let's hear it.'

Levi crossed his legs and put the cup of tea down on the coffee table. 'Those people owe you a debt,' he said, pointing outside. 'They were about to ruin your life and, from what I can see, they almost succeeded.'

'What should I do?'

'Sue the prison for damages, for a start. And the Ministry. And then ask for a huge amount of compensation for how the police investigation against you was conducted.'

'I got justice in the end, didn't I?'

But Levi wouldn't listen to him. 'And that's not all,' he went on. 'The media are just as responsible for what happened as the police. They put you on trial. Worse still, they passed sentence on you without giving you the chance to defend yourself. They also have to pay.'

'But how?' Martini asked, sceptically. 'They'll plead the freedom of the press and get away with it.'

'But they have to save face with the public, or they'll lose credibility – and ratings. And besides, people want to hear

your version, to celebrate your regained freedom with you . . .
Even to adulate you, if necessary.'

'Should I ask to go on TV to rehabilitate my image?'

Levi shook his head. 'No. You should be paid for that, that's
the only way you'll really be compensated.'

'I should sell interviews to the highest bidder – is that what
you're saying?' Martini's tone was horrified. 'As I told Stella
Honer once, I'm not going to make money from the Kastners'
tragedy.'

'This isn't about making money from the Kastners' tragedy,'
Levi retorted. 'It's about making money from your tragedy.'

'It's the same thing. I just want to forget this business. And
to be forgotten.'

Levi turned to look at Clea and Monica, who up until now
had remained silent.

'I know you're a good man,' Clea said gently to her husband.
'And I understand your reasons. But those bastards hurt you.'
She uttered these last words with unexpected anger.

Martini turned to Monica. 'Do you also agree?'

The girl nodded, eyes full of tears.

Levi picked up the briefcase he had next to him and took
out some sheets of paper. 'This is a contract from a publish-
ing company. They're suggesting you write a book about your
story.'

'A book?' Martini said, surprised.

Levi smiled. 'You're still a literature teacher, aren't you? It
shouldn't take long. And when the book comes out, there'll
be invitations to appear on TV, interviews in the press and
online. I'm sure you'll find that easier to accept when you have
a book to promote.'

Martini shook his head, amused. 'You've painted me into

a corner,' he said. Then he looked once again at his wife and daughter and sighed. 'All right, but it mustn't last ad infinitum. I want to finish with all this as soon as possible, all right?'

At eleven in the evening, Borghi was still sitting at his desk in the operations room. All the others had already left, and the desk lamp was the only light in the big empty gym. He was studying the media reports on the six girls who had gone missing before Anna Lou Kastner. Their profiles were so similar, the idea that they were dealing with a serial killer was all too plausible. The killer had returned after thirty years to strike again, and this time he had deliberately drawn attention to himself – what else was the point of shooting that video? – as if to take credit for his crimes.

But why?

It was this very point that Borghi couldn't explain. Why let so many years go by? Of course, it was quite possible that he had struck again in the meantime, somewhere else, or that something beyond his control had prevented him from doing so. For instance, he might have served a long sentence for another crime and had resumed his activities on his release. But he had changed his modus operandi. In the first six cases, he had protected his own anonymity, in the seventh he had sought attention. True, thirty years earlier the media hadn't been so prepared to give maniacs the limelight, but all the same it struck Borghi as strange.

That afternoon, he had been back to see Beatrice Leman. The woman who for so long had preserved the documentation on the case in the hope that someone would knock on her door and ask her about it had greeted him with unusual coldness. The first few times, Borghi had felt that she genuinely wanted to cooperate with the police. After this last visit, he was no longer so sure.

'I've told you all I know,' she had said curtly from the doorway, not moving her wheelchair one centimetre to let him in. 'Now leave me alone.'

It wasn't true. She was hiding something. He had already discovered that she had tried to contact Vogel several times in the days following Anna Lou Kastner's disappearance. Why? She had said she'd only wanted to ask him for an interview, and Vogel had denied having met her. But they were both telling lies. Except that Borghi understood why Vogel had lied: he wanted to avoid getting into any more trouble, for example, for conducting a parallel investigation without informing his superiors. But what reason did Leman have to lie? In addition, she had received a package a while earlier, as they had discovered during a check. This was odd, because she didn't see anyone these days and never received any mail. What had the package contained? Was it something to do with Vogel?

Before Leman had closed the door in his face that afternoon, Borghi had glanced inside the house and something had immediately caught his eye. In the ashtray next to the front door, along with the usual cigarette ends – the brand that Leman smoked endlessly – were those of another brand. Stella Honer had been there, Borghi had thought. So that was the reason Leman was keeping silent. She had sold her story. He didn't blame her. For years, she had suffered indifference and solitude. Everyone had forgotten about her and the battles she had fought through her own newspaper. Now she had an opportunity to get her own back.

As he was carefully reading through the report on the first of the missing girls, Katya Hillman, a noise echoed through the gym. Alarmed, Borghi looked up. But because of the desk lamp, he couldn't see anything. So he swivelled the lamp round to point towards the back of the room. He still couldn't figure out where the noise had come from. But he noticed a light running under the door of the changing room.

He got up and went to check.

He opened the door slowly and saw a shadowy figure doing something next to a cupboard, a torch in his hand. Borghi took out his gun. 'Stop right there,' he said calmly, aiming the weapon.

The figure froze. Then he raised both arms and started to turn.

'What are you doing?' Borghi asked as soon as he recognised him. 'You can't come in here.'

Vogel put on his falsest smile. 'I saw you on TV, you know? You're good, you've got what it takes.'

'What are you doing?' Borghi repeated.

'Don't be hard on your teacher,' Vogel said, pretending to be sullen. 'I just came to get something that belongs to me.'

'This isn't your office any more, and everything that's in this room has been sequestered for the purposes of the investigation into your conduct.'

'I know the rules, Officer Borghi. It's just that sometimes officers do favours for their colleagues.'

Vogel's mellifluous tone was starting to get on his nerves. 'Show me what you took from that cupboard.'

'It's confidential.'

'Show it to me right now,' Borghi said defiantly. He was trying to appear resolute. He still had the gun in his hands, although he was no longer pointing it.

Vogel slowly lowered his left hand and opened his coat, then with equal calm slipped his right hand into the inside pocket and took out his black notebook.

'Put it on the table,' Borghi said.

Vogel did as he was told.

'Now I must ask you to leave the building.'

Borghi didn't take his eyes off Vogel as he walked towards the exit. He was sure the special agent would want to have the last word – as indeed he did.

'We could have made a great team, you and I,' he said contemptuously. 'But maybe it's better this way. Good luck, kid.'

As soon as he had gone, Borghi lowered his weapon and sighed. Then he approached the table on which Vogel had placed the notebook. He had always been curious to know what Vogel was constantly writing down. He was fascinated by that method of working, which gave the impression that nothing escaped Vogel. But when he opened the book, he discovered that the pages were filled with obscene drawings. Explicit sex scenes, as vulgar as they were childish. He shook his head incredulously. Vogel was definitely mad.

As he walked in the deserted open space in front of the school gym, Vogel congratulated himself on the clever way he had made Borghi believe that he had gone back there to get his notebook. He didn't care what the young officer would think when he discovered the contents. What mattered much more was what he had really taken from the cupboard.

He took out his mobile phone, made a call and waited for the reply. 'Twenty-five minutes before the others,' he said. 'I'm still keeping my word.'

'What do you want?' Stella asked irritably. 'You have nothing more to sell me.'

'Are you sure?' Vogel instinctively lifted his hand to the pocket of his coat. 'I bet Beatrice Leman told you about a diary.'

Stella said nothing. Good, Vogel thought: she was interested.

'Actually she didn't tell me much,' Stella admitted cautiously.

He had guessed correctly: the two women had met. 'A pity.'

'How much do you want?' Stella asked straight out.

'We'll talk about details like that when the time is right. But I also have an added request.'

Stella laughed. 'You're no longer in a position to dictate conditions.'

'But it isn't much,' Vogel said ironically. 'I heard that after you ruined me with your scoop, the network gave you a studio show all of your own. Congratulations. Now you won't have to freeze your arse off on location as a correspondent.'

'I can't believe it. Are you asking me to invite you onto my show?'

'And I want someone else with me.'

'Who?'

'Loris Martini.'

22 February

Sixty-one days after the disappearance

He was sitting in a reclining chair in front of a mirror surrounded by brilliant white lights. He had Kleenex stuck in the collar of his shirt in order not to get it dirty. A make-up girl was applying foundation to his cheeks with a soft brush and Vogel was savouring the touch of it with his eyes closed. Behind him, the wardrobe mistress was ironing his jacket. For the occasion, he had chosen a blue woollen suit with a yellow silk handkerchief in the breast pocket, a powder-blue tie with little floral patterns and simple oval cufflinks of rose gold.

Stella Honer came into the dressing room without knocking, wearing the dark tailored suit in which she would go on air. She was followed by a distinguished-looking fifty-year-old man carrying a briefcase. 'We're ready to start,' she said. She held out her hand. 'Where's the diary?'

Vogel didn't turn, didn't even open his eyes. 'All in good time, my dear.'

'I kept my side of the bargain, now you have to keep yours.'

'I will, don't worry.'

'Oh, I'm not worried. But how do I know you're not trying to screw me?'

'Your editorial team received a page, you checked the authenticity.'

'It was only a photocopy. Now I want the rest.'

Lazily, Vogel opened his eyes, looking for Stella's reflection in the mirror. She was understandably nervous. 'But it did match Anna Lou Kastner's handwriting.'

'At least tell me what's written in that fucking diary.'

'Shameful secrets,' Vogel said, with deliberate theatricality, hoping to play on her nerves.

'Was Anna Lou having a relationship with an older man?' Stella ventured, hoping to catch a hesitation that would confirm such a dark theory.

'Whenever we speak on the phone or meet, you try to get me to reveal something. But I won't say a word until I see the little red light on the camera.'

'I have to know. I can't allow you to conduct the game just as you please. It's my show, I can't be kept completely in the dark on the topic we're talking about. Why did you want Martini to be here, too? What's he got to do with Anna Lou's diary?'

He had nothing to do with it, but Vogel had no intention of telling her that. The diary had been only the pretext to obtain a joint interview. He already knew what he would do when they went on air. He would apologise to Martini on behalf of the police and would admit his own mistake, causing great embarrassment to his chiefs – the same bastards who had abandoned him. Maybe after his apology, the teacher would publicly forgive him. Persecutor and persecuted might even be able to embrace in tears – people always appreciated such scenes of reconciliation. Anna Lou's diary would be the icing on the cake. Vogel would read the passage in which the girl wrote about Oliver and his name written on her forearm as a token of love. Who knows, maybe Stella's editorial department would be able to trace the mysterious young man while they were on air. His testimony, live by telephone, might be the high point of the show.

But Stella, who didn't know his plans, was obviously getting restless. 'I could put a stop to this thing whenever I want,' she threatened. 'No broadcast, no teacher. And I'll put all the blame on you.'

Vogel laughed. 'He accepted immediately,' he said, referring to Martini. 'I'm surprised.'

Stella smiled smugly. 'I think he did it because he can't wait to kick your arse on live television.'

'Has he laid down any conditions?'

'That's none of your business.'

Vogel raised his hands in surrender. 'Forget I said it, sorry.'

Stella turned to the man with the briefcase and motioned him to come forward. 'I want to introduce to you the lawyer who represents the interests of the network.'

'I'm sure he does,' Vogel said ironically.

The man took a form from the briefcase and placed it on the table in front of Vogel. 'I'd like you to sign a document guaranteeing that the diary is genuine and absolving us of any legal responsibility.'

'A whole lot of big words to say something extremely simple.'

'I respected my part of the bargain,' Stella growled. 'It wasn't easy to convince Martini, I can assure you.'

Vogel was pleased to hear that. It meant the teacher was still afraid of him. 'I heard he's writing a book about his story. Do you know yet what role he's reserved for you in it? Are you the crusading correspondent or the unscrupulous reporter?'

Stella walked around the chair and placed herself in front of him, so that he could look her full in the face. 'Be careful. I don't want any tricks.'

'Apparently, freedom suits famous ex-convicts. I'd be curious to know how much money Levi has tapped you people for.'

'That won't be the topic of the interview, so don't even think about bringing it up.'

The lawyer again intervened. 'To make sure that everything goes according to our agreement, the broadcast will go on air with a five-second time-lapse, to give us the possibility of cutting you off.'

Vogel pretended to be shocked. He looked at Stella. 'Don't you trust me any more?' he asked sarcastically.

'I've never trusted you,' she said, and left the dressing room.

After about ten minutes, a production assistant came in to collect Vogel and lead him to the studio. He put on his jacket and gave himself a last glance in the mirror. Go on, old man, he told himself. Show them who you are.

The assistant, equipped with headphones and clipboard, escorted Vogel along a corridor. Then she opened a fire door and they entered a large dark space. The studio reserved for Stella's show was huge. They walked along the back of the set, with the assistant constantly moving forward and every now and again saying something into the microphone placed under her headphones. 'The guest is arriving,' she announced to the control booth.

As they walked, Vogel could hear the murmur of the

audience. Stella had assured him that the spectators had been selected in a survey and that they were strictly divided between those who thought he was innocent and those who thought he was guilty, because they didn't want there to be any claque in favour of either him or Martini. Vogel had taken the reassurance on trust, because in reality he didn't care: very soon, he and the teacher would be on the same side.

They came to an area reserved for the guests, and the assistant handed him over to a technician who started arranging the radio microphone on his tie. As he got him to pass a wire under his jacket, he said, 'Even though we're not on air yet, from now on they can hear every word of yours in the control booth.'

Vogel nodded to show that he had understood. It was a ritual precaution, because guests were often overheard making comments they shouldn't. Vogel, though, was far too experienced to take that risk.

'Now, ladies and gentlemen, we'll be starting soon,' said the man who was there to warm up the studio audience. His voice was amplified. A few people clapped and there was a bit of laughter.

Despite the fact that the topic of the evening was a dead girl's diary, the audience were excited. The idea of being seen on television transformed people, Vogel thought. They wouldn't be famous, or rich, but their lives would change all the same. They would be able to boast that they had been part of the show, in however insignificant a role. Anything to appear on that damned screen.

'May we remind you not to comment out loud on what happens, and to applaud only when indicated by our assistant,' the warm-up man concluded. More applause.

As the make-up girl made a last-minute adjustment to his foundation, Vogel turned distractedly towards the gap in the set through which guests were led into the studio. It was as if the lights stopped at the edge of the set. Behind the scenes, a pleasant semi-darkness reigned.

In that border between light and darkness stood Martini.

He hadn't noticed Vogel and, with the curiosity of a child, was peering through the gap at what was going on in the studio. He was only a few metres away, close enough for Vogel to see that he had almost recovered from his ordeal. The bruises on his face had disappeared – either that or the make-up girl had done an excellent job. And the plaster had gone from his right arm. He still needed a stick to move, but he had also regained weight and no longer looked like a skeleton.

It was his general appearance, though, that had changed radically compared with the past.

His clothes were quite different. No more corduroy jackets and fustian trousers, and he had finally bid farewell to his worn old pair of Clarks. Now he was wearing a lead-grey suit, clearly made to measure. And he had chosen an elegant red tie. In Vogel's opinion, it suited him. The fact that, when it came down to it, Martini looked just like him made him feel proud. *I took you to the dark side of the light. Because even the light had one. Not everybody could see it.* Vogel had built his own fortune on that talent. He also noticed the expensive watch that Martini was wearing on his left wrist. *Your life has changed, my friend, you should thank me for having pursued you.*

It was then that the teacher made a small, almost insignificant gesture. He adjusted the cuff of his shirt, perhaps because he wasn't used to wearing cufflinks. In doing so, he pulled up

292

the sleeve of his jacket by a few centimetres, partly uncovering his forearm.

Vogel noticed a detail he found hard to make sense of at first. Something secret, something only he and Anna Lou could know. Because the girl had written about it in her diary and Vogel had read it.

So what was that circular mark doing on Martini's arm?

The little O – O for Oliver – written in biro.

23 December

The day of the disappearance

She wanted to stay at home to decorate the tree.

But on Monday at 5.15 there was the children's catechism class and she had agreed to teach the youngest group. Her brothers were too old now to be part of it, which was why they could spend the afternoon arranging coloured balls and silvery festoons on the branches. This year above all, Anna Lou was particularly keen to do that. It was partly because she suspected it would be her last chance. Her mother had already started to say strange things on the subject. Things like: 'Jesus didn't have a Christmas tree.'

When she did that, it always meant that there would be a change in their routine.

Like the fast day when the family didn't touch food for twenty-four hours, only water. And then there was the day of silence – 'the speech fast,' Maria Kastner called it. Every now and again, she would make a new rule or establish that such and such a thing had to be done in a different way. And then she would talk about it in the assembly hall and try to convince the other parents. They always agreed with her. Anna Lou liked the brotherhood, but she couldn't understand why certain kinds of behaviour were wrong. For example, she couldn't see anything wrong in wearing red in church or in drinking Coca-Cola. She couldn't remember reading anything about that in the Scriptures. And yet, as far as all the others were concerned, it seemed to be really important to act in a particular way, as if the Lord were constantly judging them and silently deciding, even from the slightest things, whether or not they were worthy of being considered his children.

Anna Lou was certain that even the thing about the Christmas tree would end up the same way. Luckily, her father had intervened, saying that 'children still need certain things'. Usually, he was submissive and would give in to his wife in the end. But for this year at least, he had held his ground. And Anna Lou was happy that at least one habit from her childhood had been saved, however briefly, from change.

'Darling, hurry up or you'll be late!' Maria yelled at her from the foot of the stairs. Anna Lou did as she was told, because her mother didn't like to keep Jesus waiting. She had already put on her grey tracksuit and trainers, all that was missing was the white down jacket. She still had to pack her satchel. She put in the catechism books, the Bible and her secret diary. It was quite a while since she had last updated the other one, she thought. Ever since she had discovered that her mother liked to search surreptitiously in her things, she had decided to keep two. Not because the other one was used for lying: she always wrote the truth in it. It was just that she avoided putting what she felt in it. Feelings were things you could only tell yourself. And besides, she wanted to protect Maria, who worried a lot about her children. She didn't want her mother to think that she was sad, but nor did she want her to think she was too happy. Because in their home, even happiness had to be rationed. If there was too much of it, it was quite likely to be the hand of the devil. 'Why else is Satan always smiling?' Maria would say. Jesus, the Virgin Mary and the Saints never smiled in the sacred images.

'Anna Lou!'

'I'm coming!' She stuffed into her ears the earphones from the MP3 player her grandmother had given her for her birthday and ran down the stairs.

On the floor below, Maria was waiting for her, leaning with one arm on the banister, the other crooked at her side, making her look like a teapot. 'What music are you listening to, darling?'

She had been expecting the question and held out one of the earphones. 'It's a nursery rhyme I found and wanted to teach the catechism class. It's about children and kittens.'

'That doesn't sound like it has much connection with the Gospel,' Maria objected.

Anna Lou smiled. 'I want them to learn the psalms by heart, but to give them practice I have to begin with simple things.'

Her mother looked at her dubiously, but there was nothing she could say to that. Instead, she moved her wrist so that the bead bracelet Anna Lou had made for her jangled. It was an affectionate gesture, meaning that they were connected. 'It's cold outside, cover up well.'

Anna Lou kissed her on the cheek and left the house.

*

When she closed the door behind her, she shivered. Her mother was right, it was freezing out. God alone knew if it would snow for Christmas. It would be wonderful if it did. She zipped up her down jacket and walked along the drive to the street, then along the pavement in the direction of the church. She would have liked to make confession. Ever since she had broken with Priscilla because of Mattia, she had felt a little guilty. She had even erased Priscilla's number from her mobile. She knew she ought to make it up with her friend, but she still couldn't get over how she had treated that poor boy. Deep down, what had he done that was so bad? She had realised that he might have a crush on her. She hadn't encouraged him, but nor could she ignore him. Priscilla didn't understand: as far as she was concerned, boys had only one thing on their minds. She would have liked to tell her about Oliver, and about what she felt even though she barely knew him, but she wasn't sure Priscilla would understand. Maybe she would even laugh at such childish feelings. But Anna Lou needed him. She needed him so that she could daydream. That was why she had written his initial on her arm. She didn't want to lose something that, when it came down to it, was hers, and hers alone.

As soon as she turned the corner at the end of the block, she slowed down.

A car was parked at the kerb. At first, she didn't understand what she was seeing. Why was that man holding an animal cage? And why was he looking around? What was he looking for? Then the man turned and she thought she recognised him. She had seen him in school, he was a teacher. But not of her class. His name was . . . Martini. That's right. He taught literature.

'Hi.' He had seen her, too, and was greeting her with a smile. 'Have you by any chance seen a stray cat around here?'

'What kind of cat?' Anna Lou asked, keeping her distance.

'About this big.' He mimed the size. 'Ginger and brown, with mottled fur.'

'Yes, I have seen him. He's been wandering around here for days.' She had even given him something to eat and put one of her bracelets round his neck. But she didn't want to give him a name yet because she was afraid his owner would appear at any moment and claim him. He looked too well cared for to be just a stray.

'Will you help me to look for him?'

'Oh, but I have to go. I have a meeting in church.'

'Please,' the man insisted. 'He's my daughter's cat, she's desperate.'

She would have liked to tell him that, outside the house, her mother didn't think she should talk to people who weren't in the brotherhood. It wasn't very convenient, although unlike all the other things she wasn't allowed to do, Anna Lou did think this prohibition was sensible. But the man had a daughter, maybe a little girl who'd been crying for days because she had lost her best friend. So she decided she could trust him. 'What's the name of the cat?'

'Derg,' he replied immediately.

What a strange name, she thought. But she went closer all the same.

'Thank you so much for helping. What's your name?'

'Anna Lou.'

'Well, Anna Lou, I'll try calling him, and while I do that, you hold the cage.' The man held the cage out to her. 'As soon as he appears, I'll force him to come towards you and you catch him in this.'

Anna Lou wasn't quite sure how it worked. 'He looked docile to me. Maybe it's easier to catch him with your bare hands.'

'Derg hates travelling in a car and, if I don't put him in the cage, I don't know how I'd get him home.'

So Anna Lou took the cage from the man and turned. 'The other time, I saw him in the neighbours' garden,' she said, pointing to the place. The last thing she saw was a hand covering her mouth with a handkerchief. She didn't scream, because she didn't know what was happening. The sudden constriction of her nasal passages instinctively forced her to take a deep breath. The air was bitter, it smelled of medicine. Her eyes glazed over, and she couldn't do anything about it.

'I want to be honest with you . . . At least about this.'

Where is the man's voice coming from? Do I know him? It seems to be coming from a long way away. And what's that little light? It looks like a gas lamp, the kind you use when you go camping. Daddy has one like that in his garage.

'I know you're wondering where you are and what's happening. Let's begin with the first question. We're in an old abandoned hotel. The second question's a bit more complicated . . .'

I don't have my clothes on. Why? First I was sitting, now I'm lying down. It's uncomfortable here. Where's up and where's down? I don't know. I feel as if I'm looking into a crystal. And who's the shadow dancing around me?

'The cat's name isn't Derg. Actually, the cat's dead. His body's in my four-by-four. Believe me, I don't want to scare you, but it's only right that you should know. I had to kill him because I don't want anybody to find him. They'll find his hair and his DNA when they search my car. Because they have to suspect me right up until the end, otherwise my plan will never work out . . . Anyway, as I was saying: Derg isn't the name of a cat, it's the name of a person. And when I discovered his story a few months ago, I realised how lucky he'd been. Of course, he had to pay a price for his luck. He had a stroke, but when you think about it, he also got a new life . . . And that's how I got the idea.'

The shadow has stopped, fortunately. He's putting the track-suit top back on me. Maybe he thinks I'm cold. I am.

'I always tell my students: the first rule of a good novelist is to copy. That's how I realised I had to find someone who would teach me how to do something I'd never have thought of doing. How to kill. I spent whole afternoons in the library looking on the internet for the lesson I needed. And then one day, I found it . . . It was on a website set up by a journalist named Beatrice Leman. I don't think anyone had visited it for ages. But that was where I found what I'd been looking for. Thirty years ago, in Avechot and the surrounding area, six girls your age went missing. Not all at the same time, but at more or less regular intervals. They were special, because they all had red hair and freckles – just like you. Nobody had been terribly concerned about what had happened to them, but this Leman woman believed that they had all been kidnapped by the same person. She had identified a monster and had even given him a name: the man in the fog. It was perfect. I would just have to copy what the police call the modus operandi, and then what I was preparing to do would be blamed on him – even after all those years. In fact, if everything goes as it should, he'll be my alibi, the thing that gets me out of prison . . . '

Now he's putting on my tracksuit bottoms. I can feel them sliding up my legs. They tickle a bit. I don't know if it's pleasant.

'As I was saying, they have to suspect me. So I'll scatter clues. Actually, I already started, with Mattia. He was the one who led me to you. Because, I have to say, it wasn't easy to find a girl with red hair and freckles. Then one day, while the class was in the gym for physical education, I was wandering about between the desks, busy preparing a lesson on the Romantic poets that I was due to give next period. As I walked to the desk where Mattia had been sitting, I noticed the camcorder. He'd left it behind, so I switched it on and discovered the girl who was the main character in his videos . . . *You* . . . So all I had to do was follow him around – he was following you, I followed him. That's how I found out that you like cats. I made sure my car appeared in his videos, because I wanted Mattia to notice me. I hope the police see them and come looking for me. When I tell them I was alone in the mountains today, and especially when they see the cut on the palm of my hand, they'll start to suspect me. I have a knife with me, and I suppose it'll be quite painful when I cut myself, but don't worry: you won't have to watch . . . '

That's the noise the zip of my jacket makes when I pull it up. But I'm not the one doing it. It's the shadow who's talking to me. And now he's putting my shoes back on my feet. And lacing them up.

'I'm hoping they'll send a particular police officer here. His name's Vogel and he's good at putting together a case. He convinces everybody that he's right – he certainly managed it with Signor Derg, for instance. He'll ruin my life, I know that. But I have to lose everything, otherwise it'll all have been pointless. Everybody will have to suspect me, even my own family. Yesterday, your friend Priscilla left me her telephone number. I think I'll call her or send her a text, then she'll go on television and make everyone think I was trying to groom her. And then I really will be the monster everybody needs . . .'

It smells damp in here. Even though I'm dressed, I'm still cold. I feel drunk, like when I was six and I drank my grandmother's currant liqueur in secret. By now, my brothers must have finished the Christmas tree. It's going to be beautiful, I know.

'Apart from his instinct, all that Vogel will have on me will be a lot of circumstantial evidence. No actual proof. I'll have to get him to the point where he thinks he'll only be able to arrest me by forcing the truth a little. I'll show him my injured hand – I have to make sure it doesn't heal. When we meet, I'll leave a bloodstain behind. I know he'll be tempted to use it straight away, but he'll wait until he needs it. Then when they find your satchel in a ditch, I'm convinced he'll do the same thing he did with Derg – he'll twist the truth for his own ends . . . But for that to happen, the mechanism I've set in motion has to function like clockwork. Everything in its own good time . . .'

Whatever mistake I've made – I beg you – I can't stand it any more. Forgive me. Let me go home.

'I'll go to prison. It'll be hard to be away from my family. I might even be scared I'll never get out again, but I'll just have to hold on. In the meantime, on the outside, the mechanism will continue turning all by itself . . . You know, when I was a child I was good at organising treasure hunts. I loved to create questions and riddles and scatter clues. That's why I'll send something of yours to Leman, but add Vogel's name on the package. I found a diary in your satchel, I chose it to arouse his curiosity . . . A little while ago, I filmed a video message – you didn't even notice. I already know where I'm going to bury it. But I'll also send a copy to the media . . . For everything to be perfect, Vogel must fall. It's only when he's in the dust that I'll be able to rise . . . And then the story of the man in the fog will come out again. Most likely, he died sometime in the last thirty years. But he'll come back to life and they'll look for him because they want you to have justice. While I'll be free.'

The fog's already here, I can see it. It's all around me. It's cold and light.

'Now comes the most difficult question. You must be wondering why I'm doing all this.'

No, no . . . I don't think I want to know.

'It's because I love my family. I want them to have everything they deserve. And I don't want to risk losing my wife again. I know you don't have a clue what I'm talking about, but *the thing* was a terrible time for us. I felt inadequate: a humble secondary school teacher . . . But soon, Clea and Monica will be proud of me. Because I won't sell out immediately, I'll hold back. I'll show them what an honest man I am. But, let's admit the truth, every man has his price, it's useless to deny it.'

I also love my family. And they love me. Why can't you understand that?

'Well, there you are, that's all. I'm sorry to involve you, but it's just like in novels: the villain *makes* the story, readers wouldn't be interested in stories where the only characters are the good guys. But your role isn't a minor one. And, who knows, maybe one day someone really will find the man in the fog, and then six girls everyone has forgotten will have justice. And it'll all be thanks to you, Anna Lou . . .'

Why are you telling me this story? I'm not interested, I don't like it. I want my mummy, I want my daddy, I want my brothers. I want to see them one more time, I beg you – just once. I have to say goodbye to them, even though I don't want to. I'll miss them.

'Now you'll have to forgive me, but I see that the effect of the ether is wearing off. I'll be quick, you'll hardly feel a thing.'

There's something pricking my arm. I open my eyes a little, I can do that now. He's sticking a needle in my skin and looking at the O that I've dedicated to Oliver. He's wondering what it is. It's a secret.

'Goodbye, Anna Lou, you're so beautiful.'

I'm cold. Mummy, where are you? Mummy . . .

23 February

Sixty-two days after the disappearance

The night everything changed for ever, the fog seemed to have finally seeped in through the window, filling the room like a subtle chill.

When Vogel had finished his story, he paused for a long time. 'Did you know that hate isn't the prime motive for murder? Borghi tried to tell me that, but I didn't listen to him. If I had, maybe I'd have understood everything earlier . . . The prime motive for murder is money.'

'No, I didn't know that,' Flores admitted.

'The whole mechanism turned on a simple, even banal idea . . . Nobody was ever to find Anna Lou's body. That was the whole trick. Without a body, there was no proof. That's why he got away with it.'

'What about the initial on his arm? Why run the risk of being discovered? I don't understand.'

'On average, a murderer makes twenty mistakes. More than

half of those are unwitting. Most are the result of inexperience or carelessness. But there's a type of mistake that's due to the murderer's particular character, one we can call "voluntary". It's like a signature. Unconsciously, every murderer wants to take credit for his work.' He now quoted Martini. '"The devil's most foolish sin is vanity." When it comes down to it, where's the fun in being the devil if nobody knows you are?'

Flores was starting to understand. 'After the show, you followed Martini to Avechot and killed him.'

Vogel put his hands together in his lap. 'You'll never find him. He also ended up in the fog.'

At this point, Flores lifted the receiver of the telephone on his desk and dialled a number. 'Yes, it's me. You can come in now.' He hung up.

They waited in silence. Then the door of the office opened. Two uniformed officers entered the room and took up position on either side of Vogel.

'An angler who always catches the same fish.' Vogel laughed at the thought. 'It's really been a pleasure talking to you, Dr Flores.'

It was almost six in the morning when he got back home. Dawn would rise soon, but for now it was still dark and everything was silent. In the little house with the protruding roof, the heating had been on for a while, and along with the heat there was a kind of torpor that felt good. Sophia was fast asleep in the bedroom upstairs. Flores thought of joining her, of slipping into bed beside her and trying to get at least a little rest. But then he changed his mind. He was no longer sure that he would manage to get to sleep. Not after a night such as he'd just had. So, without making any noise, he went down into the basement.

This was where he had his taxidermy workshop, where he stuffed his *Oncorhynchus mykiss*. The room was small, with just one narrow window. Flores raised his hand and pulled a rope. A small light came on above his head and swayed slightly, making the shadows of objects dance along with it. There in front of him was his old wooden work bench with all his equipment. The flasks of ammonia and formaldehyde to arrest the process of decomposition. The transparent paints to bring out the natural colours. The pure alcohol spray. The jar with the paintbrushes and the aqua regia. The little knives arranged tidily on a grille. The box of pins. The bottle brushes and the hollow-tipped scoop. The Borax powder and the salicylic acid. The heat lamp.

Flores was nearing retirement and this would soon become his new den. He also kept a lot of his fishing equipment here, and he would move into it the old junk he had in his office. It would be sad to say goodbye to a lifetime's work, but he could already imagine himself in this place, protected from stress and anxiety, devoting himself patiently to his hobby. Every now and again, he would bring his grandchildren down here to show them what their grandad did. He wouldn't be at all upset to transmit his own passion to them. Down here, he would lose all sense of time and around mid-morning would recognise Sophia's steps on the stairs as she brought him a tray with a sandwich and a glass of cold tea. Yes, it would be a nice way to spend his old age.

Flores put both his hands on the table and relaxed his shoulders. He took a deep breath. Then he got down on his knees. Under the bench there was a neat pile of boxes, in which he kept his fishing bait. Every Christmas or birthday, his nearest and dearest would give him a new one, because they knew that these were the only kinds of gifts he liked to receive. Some were actually very expensive. But near the bottom there was also an old metal case with a padlock. Flores took it out and placed it on the bench. The key to open it was one he always kept with him, although it was mixed up with the others in the bunch: the keys to his house, the car and the office. He found it, slipped it into the lock and opened the lid.

The six locks of red hair were still there.

They reminded him of a period in his life which, all things considered, had been happy. He was married to Sophia and two of their three children had already been born. Nobody had ever found out what he sometimes did instead of going fishing. They saw him come back home as usual, never imagining that the joy on his face was due to something quite different.

The angler who for the last thirty years had always caught the same fish – a rainbow trout – had previously devoted himself to capturing the same kind of girl. One with red hair and freckles.

And now everyone was wondering what had happened to the man in the fog. He would have liked to be able to tell them that every now and again he was still tempted to leave the house and set off in search of prey, but that after the heart attack that had almost killed him at the age of only thirty-two, he had made a solemn promise.

No more girls with red hair and freckles.

Over the years, people had forgotten all about him. But now, because of Loris Martini, the man in the fog was once again in their thoughts. They'll never trace me, he told himself. Vogel's timely act the previous night had sorted things out. Once again, they'll think the monster is dead.

Flores stood there for a little while longer, looking at the metal case. Maybe he should get rid of it. Not because he was afraid those locks of hair might be evidence to nail him. No, it was because it often occurred to him that if he had another heart attack, a fatal one this time, his family – the people he loved most in the world – would find his secret collection. And they probably wouldn't understand, might change their ideas about him. He didn't want them to discover that side of him. He wanted to be loved.

But once again, he decided he wouldn't destroy the contents of the case, because certain affections were difficult to forget. And when it came down to it, those six girls lost in the fog were his, they belonged to him. He had been taking care of them for thirty years, in the secrecy of his own mind. So he closed the lid and snapped the padlock shut. Then he put everything back under the work bench. Through the window filtered a weak ray of sunlight.

The night everything changed for ever was over.

Acknowledgements

Stefano Mauri, publisher – *friend*. And together with him, all my publishers around the world.

Fabrizio Cocco, my pillar. Giuseppe Strazzeri, Raffaella Roncato, Elena Pavanetto, Giuseppe Somenzi, Graziella Cerutti, Alessia Ugolotti, Tommaso Gobbi. For having supported me all the way in this challenge.

Cristina Foschini, who with her gentleness saves my life.

Andrew Nurnberg, Sarah Nundy, Giulia Bernabè and all those who work so passionately in the London agency.

Tiffany Gassouk, Anais Bakobza, Ailah Ahmed.

Alessandro Usai and Maurizio Totti.

Gianni Antonangeli.

Michele, Ottavio and Vito, my best friends. Achille.

Antonio and Fiettina, my parents.

Chiara, my sister.

To my extended family. Without you I wouldn't be here.

Have you read them all?

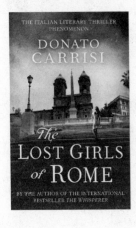

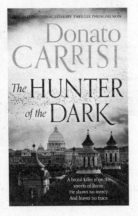